River of Sorrow

'Devils in Grey'

AND

Chicago Dolls

'Four Women. Four Targets.
One Deadly Pact'

Walt Oxer

First published in the United Kingdom in 2025 by
The Cloister House Press

Paperback ISBN 978-1-913460-92-1
eBook ISBN 978-1-913460-93-8

In Memory of

Jimmy LaFave
1955–2017
'Like Rainbows Jimmy'

Special thank you to…
Birgit Gurtier for the cover design.

River of Sorrow

'Devils in Grey'

CONTENTS

Chapter 1
LEAVING

Joe Dupree sat looking out of his study window, watching the usual fast-flowing River Lee on its entrance into Cork harbour, his mind carrying deep thoughts of the Irish situation, of a famine that was tearing the country apart, with its graveyards filling every hour of every day. Its people were dying of starvation. The year was 1857 and the Cork Examiner had finally reported the true story, the aftermath of its vanishing race. Two million dead or exiled, half a million who were illegally and violently evicted from their homes by the British army. Joe had seen the downtrodden families make their escape by crossing the big pond over to the New World, North America. It was hard to imagine just what the potato blight had done. Its crippling deadly effect had turned a man into a mouse.

Food that could have fed 18 million people was taken by British troops, leading to a devastating famine. By the time it ended, the population had dropped by 2.5 million, leaving just 6.5 million people in Ireland—far too late to save over a million lives. Queen Victoria bore much of the blame, as she allowed English landlords to use her troops to evict Irish tenants who were unable to meet rent demands during the crisis.

This violent action would leave the distressed troubled people with only one possibility: North America. Joe did not need to think twice, having already decided on taking his wife and daughter across the Atlantic Ocean to a new life. Besides, had not gold been found in California in '49, opening the American west? Rail tracks were being put down east to west. The opportunities were endless.

His father, a shipping exporter, had recently left behind a copy of *The New York Times* that he had brought back from a recent business trip to America. On reading it Joe found a job advertisement for law officers. The article offered posts in Austin, Texas. He was interested. He would need to talk with his wife, Colette, and his daughter, Janine. They would decide on the Dupree family future.

***

His French father, Lucas, had met, fallen deeply in love with and married his mother, Bridget Riley, a Galway girl. Bridget had walked one day into the offices of the Cock and Sham shipping exporters in the hope of filling their opening for an accounts manager. Lucas had at once fallen for this beautiful Irish girl; it was love at first sight, especially with her qualification from Queens University College, Cork. His son was born on the 16th of November 1826 under the shadow of the Shehy Mountains. He studied at his mother's university and gained honours in law, hoping to somehow quell the unrest and turmoil of the British ruination of his people.

It was whilst on this most painful quest that, in 1846, he met the beautiful Colette Armer, a representative of his father's French shipping import and export company. It did not take long for Cupid to draw back his bow and let his love arrow fly into the hearts of the two, driving them into a non-stop passionate affair with marriage not surprisingly the eventual outcome. Their beautiful most adorable baby daughter Janine was soon to appear.

Sadly, with times getting harder to survive, and with his father Lucas refusing to ship much-needed Irish food stocks out of the country, it was time to stop for the day in what had been a long-established partnership with the British government. His refusal, along with that of many others, would finally put an end to the starving of the Irish people. The British gave in by allowing families to be fed. The none-too-pleased merchants were feeling the heat of war approaching, with no way of stopping it; blood would be shed.

Joe's thoughts were to seek a new life in the new world that lay across the great pond. He was not going to allow his family's newfound happiness to be washed away down the gutters of Cork city streets and into the waters of an already heavy mix that entered the River Lee. His father along with his mother were also on the verge of vacating the green island and retiring back to his native homeland, France. So it was that after a family meeting Joe and the family decided to leave Ireland for the New World.

Lucas and Bridget would sell their share of the Cork and Sham and spend their last years back in Paris. They would see to it that Joe had the financial support to take him through the first years of what unknown episodes lay ahead.

***

Joe had asked Colette to go along, taking Janine to live with his father whilst he settled in Austin, after which he would send for them. But Colette would have none of it. She told him they would all go as a family together or not at all. Six months later Joe received confirmation that the law officer's job was his. He was to become part of the newly formed Texas Rangers, his first step on the ladder of obtaining knowledge of American law.

He knew that there had to be different procedures that would not apply to British law, there would be many different variations that he would need to learn afresh. His dream of an office with a brass plaque saying. 'Joe Dupree, Lawyer' would take time but he would get there.

The day finally arrived for the voyage across the Atlantic with the ship destined for New Orleans, North America. The ship *Elizabeth* would carry the Duprees into New Orleans. The year was 1858. With a passenger list of nearly 300 emigrants, Joe secured a suitable and comfortable berth, thanks to his father's influence as a friend of the captain, Patrick James O'Connor. It was a special day with it being Janine Dupree's birthday; she was a beautiful ten-year-old fiery Irish colleen.

Colette had baked a special cake for her much adored daughter. The sun was out when the ship upped anchor and moved slowly through the harbour on its way through the Celtic Sea on a westerly course to the Atlantic Ocean. It was a journey that would take its 300 or so emigrants' hopes towards a new life in America, and so away from the horrific years of depression starvation and what would bring to its poor an ultimate death.

That day was when the Duprees met up with Tom McBane, an Irish police officer who hailed from Kilkenny. Tom, who stood at around six feet in height, with a solid, muscle-bound athletic body, was in his late forties. Joe had asked Tom, 'Why the journey?' Surely the Kilkenny police would have little difficulty in surviving.

Tom had answered by saying that when you lose friends, good honest people, when you can no longer help, when the police can no longer function or control the extermination of its people, then the time has come to say enough is enough.

The truth was that Tom had bent over backwards trying to help his depressed community and had seen the attitudes of Kilkenny's police department fall into disarray by looking after their own and neglecting the rest.

The voyage would take a minimum of two months, giving time to hear of the tragic stories that had befallen Ireland. His newfound friend, Tom McBane, had noticed two Kilkenny brothers, Brendan and Peter Kelly, managing to somehow sneak aboard. The two had recently been found 'not guilty' of the murder of an eighty-five-year-old farmer and his wife, a murder that Tom had investigated to the point of expecting a 'guilty' verdict. Tom remembered the grins and the wink the two had given him on receiving their not guilty verdict, had felt the burning anger, when on their passing out of court, Brendan whispered, 'Better luck next time, McBane.'

It was well into the first month of the voyage when the disruptions began, with passengers being robbed of their only possessions. Those robbed had told Captain O'Connor that the crimes had been committed by two masked men in the after-midnight hours. It was when an attempt to rob Colette misfired, foiled by her screams and the scratching of one of the robbers, that it was time to act, especially on seeing the fresh scratch lines running down the cheek of Peter Kelly.

Tom produced from his kitbag two shillelaghs and, handing one to Joe, said, 'Let us send these two killers overboard, for there is no room for this kind of people in the new world. Believe me, Joe, we would be doing America a favour. The Kelly brothers are well overdue.'

And so, the McBane/Dupree plan was executed with the Kellys no more, clubbed and sent to the bottom of the deep Atlantic Ocean.

***

It was a bright sunny morning when the cargo vessel docked in New Orleans and the four new friends found an easy entrance into America. Joe was helped by his father's letter to a long-time Irish-American importer exporter, a very respected man who had been shipping cotton over to Lucas Dupree's company for well over 20 years. Tom, too, had a similar introductory letter of recommendation from his Kilkenny Chief Constable.

It was after meeting up with a Lieutenant Harvey in an Orleans eatery that Tom learned of a ticket to Austin. They were told of a merchant who was looking for a well-trusted man to drive a covered Conestoga wagon of hardware to a buyer in Austin, Texas. The merchant's regular driver had fallen ill, and the train was due to pull out on the following morning. With the train having a final total of 23 wagons, the Lieutenant felt sure it would finish the journey, with the experienced Bull Ferguson its wagon-master.

Joe shrugged on hearing of this opportunity and said, 'So let us find this merchant.'

Lieutenant Harvey replied, 'He's over in La Pepite d'Or, a gambling house down Bayou Road, goes by the name of Amos Critch. You're the first people I've told.' He laughed. 'So, it's the early bird that's gonna get the worm.'

Tom winked at the young Lieutenant. 'Let's hope we're the only bird.'

Two hours later Tom found himself driving a large wagon up to the train's other rigs and buggies. He took a close look at the male entourage, their age and ability to hold off a Comanche attack. The strength of the train's defence looked good, especially after Joe had informed him that there would be a detachment of troops going with them on their way to Fort Davis. More so knowing that the Major commanding Fort Davis would be bringing his wife on the train.

The very next day the wagons began to roll out of New Orleans. Colette gave a sigh on leaving what looked to be a lively vibrant French-speaking city. She told Joe that one day she would like to return. He nodded, saying, 'Yes,' after the hate of the Irish had dispersed from its mostly black inhabitants. He did not mention his viewing of the poor Irish immigrants being roughly and brutally handled, being forcefully escorted back to the departing sea vessels. For these poor souls carried shattered dreams and a God that had forsaken them.

Chapter 2
NEW ORLEANS

Tom having stationed the large, covered wagon of merchant Amos Critch in line, it was time to position, to rest up for the night and make ready for the break of dawn and the cry from wagon-master and frontier veteran Bull Ferguson raising his gun in the air and firing his pistol. Beds had been made up for the two ladies, with Joe and Tom opting for a pillow-blanket nest under the wagon that was filled with tools. It was a full moon and star-spangled night, and the two friends found themselves being invited to join four others, who were taking the journey, around a blazing log fire. The men, brothers, came from Galway, Joe's mother's birthplace. They had left the destitute homeland in search of prosperity. It certainly was a night of reminiscing, what with the Galway boys, the Ryans, having each a story to tell. Their laughter and merriment took away thoughts of the unreal situation that had hit the Shamrock Isle.

Their singing of the old Irish sea shanties brought wagon master Bull Ferguson and his son Sean out of their beds to join the party. Bull, once an immigrant Dubliner, once a merchant sailor having sailed a Dublin to Boston clipper, had entered

America, liked what he saw and decided to stay. That was all of twelve years past in 1848.

Bull had fought the Indian Cayuse war after an outbreak of measles had brought death to half the Indians. This resulted in the taking of the mission and the deaths of 13 settlers which included shaman Marcus Whitman, physician and religious leader, along with his wife. It was called the Whitman massacre and one of its unfortunate victims was Bull's wife, Irene.

The Irish sat by that fire, each with the hope that these wars were finally ending. It was a remark made by Bull that brought them back to reality. Bull, having seen a wagon train of seven large savannahs from Florida leaving on a coastal route to Galveston, told them, 'I spoke with their man in charge of that train, offering to tie up with our train. But sadly, he declined my offer. I say sadly, because I fear for their lives. The Karankawa are still active, small groups of some 40 or so warriors. Still violating, killing, picking off the easy take.'

Bull pointed at the slow, heavily loaded train, then he shook his head before finishing with, 'That train will be to the Karankawa one easy take.'

Joe asked, 'But Galveston, Bull, would that be part of our planned route?'

Bull shrugged. 'All but 50 miles. We would make Houston before heading on to Austin.' He smiled. 'Houston is about 50 miles north of Galveston. They'd have had our support for all but four or five days.'

Tom sighed. 'Let's hope and pray they won't need it.'

Bull shook his head. 'Yeah, let's hope.'

'Wagons roll,' came the dawn cry, the waking call from Bull to get the wagon train moving.

Tom took the reins of their Conestoga's two black horses, taking the eager Joe and the girls and himself into their unknown future.

It was the previous night's party that made Tom decide that

Joe's Austin opportunity was something he himself had been looking for. Was not he a policeman? He would go with Joe to the newly found Office of the Texas Rangers and offer his services.

This news delighted Joe and the ladies, for Joe knew that he was letting himself into the unknown. A job that required you to carry a gun, furthermore, knowing how to use one. He could only learn from Tom, a very experienced law officer. Somehow Joe's thoughts and those of Colette gave them a feeling of a safer introduction into providing law in the new world.

For already the unified North was having trouble with the confederate South on various issues, the owning of slaves being just one of many. So far Texas had not been involved, they stood alone, being an independent state that had already fought the Mexican wars. These actions made the Rio Grande river the American border cut-off point.

Killing and the taking of the law into any individual's hands, escalating an unstoppable rise, had to be crushed. One ongoing fight for justice. A battle to subdue the Comanche, the invading evil that was festering in the lone star state. Joe along with Tom had sat and listened to Bull Ferguson's views of an unstable situation that was developing all over the four points of the compass. North America was at the edge of an avalanche and law had to prevail.

He himself was having thoughts of moving to the railways, sensing that the future no longer rode on wheels but ran on steel tracks.

Chapter 3
MASSACRE

Bull Ferguson was a man who would take no risk when it came down to the safety of his train. This was why Joe asked him about the unrest and wars with the Indian nation, as he had found two Comanche braves wearing the Union blue were travelling with the detachment of soldiers making for Fort Davis.

Bull told them that any hostile Indian attack would not be from the also marauding Comanche. They had been moved to Oklahoma and the bad guys were now the Karankawa and not the blue-coated Comanche Indians. These were expert army scouts who knew every blade of grass on the once-owned vast prairie land of Texas. It had been their home, their hunting ground.

This hatred cascaded like a river's waterfall all through the Indian nations. How could they ever forgive the white eyes for stealing their land? Many of their wise braves had finally come to realise that their fight was a losing one. Had not the great spirit deserted them; they could see the power coming from the never-ending invading settlers.

The news had been coming into Bull's wagon train of a

massacre that had taken place around Pine Creek, a train stopping place to fill up the water barrels.

The scouts had viewed black smoke coming from an area around the creek which was burning with 26 dead settlers, men women, and children, including its wagon-master. Scalped, with their bodies put on a pier and burnt.

Bull, along with half the troops, did the burying of these poor souls. Around the late-night camp, the stories of the atrocities had been told away from the women and children.

Tom asked Bull if this was the work of the Karankawa. A Comanche scout gave him the answer that they usually took the burnt carcasses to eat later. That Bull's train was approaching would have stopped the feast.

His very words made Joe, who was eating, throw his beef joint to the wagon train's travelling hounds. His cry of 'Bastards,' could be heard throughout the train's gathered nighttime defensive circle. It had been nearly all night before the two friends heard the morning call of, 'Wagons roll,' coming from the mouth of Bull Ferguson.

**

It had taken over 40 days before the train rolled down the streets of Austin with no further events, although the duty sergeant of the troopers assured them that the massacre of Pine Creek would not be forgotten and the Karankawa would pay for their evil deed. Everything in Austin was happening so quickly. The merchant's buyer awaited his delivery of hardware, hoping and praying that the incoming news of the massacre at Pine Creek had not involved the Amos Critch wagon.

Tom had his application for a job with the Rangers accepted with a surprising result, that he was to take over the Austin office with the title of Captain. Tom would be in charge of over ten men, with Joe being one of them. Six would be on permanent duty around the clock and a cover team of four men would be led by his deputy, Jonjo Kane. When the last commander had retired and moved to Houston the job had fallen to Jonjo, but he had declined the promotion and wished only to be regarded as part-time.

The governor's office, on seeing Tom's application, had informed the governor of the Irish ex-policeman's qualifications and the acting governor's aide on these matters, who just happened to be of Irish heritage with the name of James Paul O'Brian, had welcomed Tom with open arms. But it was Tom's experience, his knowledge of policing in what had been one of the world's exploding trouble spots, Ireland, that had given him the nod. Was not North America having a similar problem with the North and South straining at the leash with the slave situation? O'Brian knew that a resulting conflict, a civil war was looming, and blood would flow. Governor Sam Houston was hoping that Texas would not swim in a river of blood. They would need to send men and horses to fight for the confederacy.

Chapter 4

TEXAN ISSUES

Texas was a state unprepared, a confused government in an unstable programme that was finding it hard to bring justice in a land where the gun was judge, jury, and executioner, where fear called for sleepless nights. A government that had no control over an escalating crisis. The army forts had been built and rebuilt north, south, east, and west in the hope of trying to bring peace; the aim was to keep law and order.

The Texas Rangers' main aim was to control the city and its outlying communities, leaving a weak military union army already deep in ongoing battles over the River Grande border crossings of the Mexican raiding cattle thieves, along with the young braves that had, against their elders' warnings, taken to fighting a war that they could never win.

It was so easy to blame any violent sadistic act onto one of these invading gangs. Any good solid branch of an arm-stretching oak was fast littering the open prairie. Bodies were hanged without trial. If you did not belong you were trespassing. If you were trespassing, then you were a thief, a killer, a horse thief, a cattle thief, sure as hell to feel the noose around your neck. Your age did not matter, as Tom McBane and his rangers would discover on their brotherhoods chase. Young braves some 14 years old ... men estimated in their eighties ... hanged.

This of course would confuse anyone without knowledge of just how the west was and just how easy it was to put the noose around some innocent's neck.

One thing that Joe was pleased about was that the rangers would be looking after Texas. None more so than Colette and Janine, who were relieved.

***

Through Lucas, Joe's father, he was allowed to buy the vacated home of retiring officer Captain Gordon Henry Boot. The home was a detached log cabin with three bedrooms and a large accompanying barn with a stable, lying some four miles north of Austin on the road to the picturesque Mount Bonnett and the passing Colorado River. A lonely part of a green-pastured Eagles Valley, it was once occupied by the Mohaves. A most beautiful part of the river, where eagles could be seen flying over the foothills of Bonnett.

Janine was given the privilege of choosing the name of their homestead and called it Parisian Dream. The spare room was offered to Tom, who graciously declined, as for the time being he had bought a room over on Main Street. That looked to be ideal for him to organise his office.

Of the years leading up to 1861 and after, the Austin Rangers having been engaged in many Indian wars, mostly Comanche and the Karankawa tribes of young braves leaving their reservations, faced the new storm, that of Civil War coming in from the north. President Abraham Lincoln invaded Galveston harbour, and the war had begun. It would not end until 1865. It would take over 620,000 soldiers to their graves, some 360,222 Union soldiers and 258,000 confederate soldiers, although there were many other undetermined civilian deaths. It was the end for a defeated south and Richmond, Virginia, the southern capital, was burning.

Chapter 5
RICHMOND

The night sky was all aglow with yellow, blue, orange with great almighty fireballs. Richmond was burning, its people, along with its president Jeffery Davis, making their way in a confused panicked escape on a heading that would take them south and hopefully safely away from the incoming Union Army.

Men, women and children formed a mass evacuation of the southern capital. Women were stumbling blindly through the scorching fire, choking on smoke that was bellowing down Main Street, dragging their screaming children, clutching onto whatever valuables they had packed into the heavy carpet bags. What could not be carried and household treasures lay cast off on the street's thoroughfare.

Terrified boys and girls of all ages struggled with small heavy loaded bags, the city's menfolk old and young race in all directions, crazed figures carrying kerosene lit torches, hurling them into any buildings not fired. Their cries, the shouting of many voices gave warning of the approaching army of the Union. All around the cries of its citizens could be heard screaming, 'The federals, they're here, leave them nothing … burn, burn, burn.'

Every available means of transport was being loaded, from mule to horse, buckboard to savannah wagons, whilst the city drunks were being chased from the saloons and hotels with their stolen bottles of whisky. Many received a shotgun blast, bringing them down wounded or dead; they lay in the dirt. Jewellery shop windows, their security bars bent, their windows smashed as the looters ran wild. The finest hotels; the Columbia, the American, spitting great balls of flames from their windows. The arsonists danced with their torches held high, the fire sticks bobbing up and down like-some giant fireflies in the night.

There was a great roar and whoosh as the roof of the great tobacco house the Shockley blew off a heavy cloud of choking smoke. The banks of Richmond, were now aflame with their contents already loaded into a black bullion wagon with officials and security guards riding out on a southern route, with a display of shotguns waving in all directions.

The following morning dawn brought an eeriness to the city. Through the dense black and grey mixed smoke of the still-burning buildings a blanket of mist coming from the James River hung over Main Street, where a group of federal officers walked, slowly inspecting the ravaged, burnt-out city; with them was their President, Abraham Lincoln.

Crackling sounds could still be heard through the smouldering fires. Dogs were heard barking as they sniffed the dead, searching for their masters, whilst over by the James River the Danville and Petersburg rail depot no longer stood, its rail bridge hanging down, sinking into the water below. Alongside it the great Hayall Mill had been destroyed. The arsonists had kept the best for last in the blowing up of the Confederate Arsenal and the burning of the Ironclad Patrick Henry along with all other vessels that had moored in the river.

The President and his entourage stopped for a moment to look down onto the boardwalk where a young boy in his early teens sat, his arms wrapped around a much younger girl. The girl was sobbing while the boy held her head away from the body of a middle-aged woman, lying in a cross-like lifeless pose. The woman's tortured face was burnt, her blank eyes stared. One faithful friend, a hound, lay by her side, gently nudging, pawing, licking her body. Lincoln ordered an officer to see to the children's care. The sound of the burning, the girl's heavy sobs and the distant sounds of hound dogs howling made for one bizarre morning.

***

Meanwhile, in a wildflower meadow alongside the Appomattax River, an early morning blanket of mist floated over the littered grassland that once held the armies of the north and south engaged in battle.

Now cannons stood silent, looking over the bodies of the fallen northern-uniformed blue and the diverse-costumed southern grey. The dead and the dying, the wounded lay in the mud. Moans could be heard coming from the badly wounded, their dying cries echoing all over the field. Those that had any chance at all of surviving were being helped by able comrades from the battlefield … both armies having no fight left in them, allowing each this period of ceasefire.

Black crows perched on branches, their eyes blinking. Their cawing mixed with the cries of the dying. They shuffled and flitted, flying nearer to each mournful sound. Two which settled on one cannon looked down on a dying young soldier.

A stiff breeze was blowing over the aftermath. With one last desperate action a young confederate soldier tried to pocket a letter. His eyes closing, his grip slackening, the envelope flew from his hand, stolen by the breeze. It floated across the meadow, momentarily sticking to a large tree trunk, displaying the words written on the letter: "To my dearest love, Charlotte". A burnt blood-stained hole stained the letter.

Not too far away a white Union flag flew from a pole in front of the courthouse of Appomattox. Beneath lay the discarded flag of the south. The Stainless Banner lay in a burnt, torn, crumpled state. Inside around a large desk stood General Ulysses Grant with officers of the Union Army. They looked down on the sad face of General Robert E Lee, sitting with a pen and document before him. The Union officers smiled and nodded to each other, shaking hands as Lee signed the document of the southern surrender.

***

Passing through a large wood in Louisiana trod a disengaged, frightened and confused-looking section of the Southern Army of some thirty men. Their heading south, their progress slow as they plodded, some with difficulty, down a woodland trail. Many hopped on crutches made from tree branches; painfully they stumbled along. Those most able to walk, having made straps hooked over their shoulders, dragged the gravely wounded on made-up stretchers.

They constantly stopped, listening, looking behind. The silence was broken only by the wounded's moans or by some disturbed partridge powering out from the undergrowth. Fear could be seen on each face. Still, they struggled onwards, their feet dragging like a snare drum's brushing rhythm.

Chapter 6
EL DORADO

Around a campfire in a forest clearing, west of El Dorado, Louisiana, with dusk rapidly approaching, sat eight Union soldiers. On one tunic was the flash of the troop's commanding officer, thirty-year-old Lieutenant Tobias Devlin, while alongside this young clean-shaven officer sat one giant of a man, much older and showing a bearded weathered face, carrying the stripes of a sergeant. Ernest Wallace. They were drinking coffee, with the young officer thinking of home, and his wife Elizabeth and his two-year-old son, Arnold. How he wished the damned war was over. The reasons for fighting his fellow American brothers he could never understand. The horror seen he could never forget.

He looked at his experienced sergeant, whom he had come to rely on in the planning and sorting out of their many confrontations with the enemy, the boys in grey. He had found Wallace to be an unmarried man with no thoughts of going home. Wallace was a born soldier was married to the army.

Devlin estimated him to be nearing his sixtieth year and thought that he would find it too hard to change a life. Wallace, he knew, had fought in the Rouge River Indian wars but had never spoken of his past or of Native American lives that he must have taken. He had never shown any reaction either for or against the taking down of his fellow southern brothers. Wallace was a man who followed orders to the letter.

A look of hatred showed in the eyes of his sergeant, who was now gazing over at the rebel prisoners.

Six men in grey sat across from them, some ten yards away. Six Confederate prisoners who were bound, hands tied together with their backs around the circumference of a large oak tree.

One who sat bound, grinding his teeth, wore the grey tunic of major. He struggled, snarling, giving one hateful look at the bluecoats. He looked to his left, at his corporal who shrugged, shaking his head. His men sat wearing the face of defeat. Attempting to break their bindings, they both spat over at the gathered bluecoats.

Suddenly there was a disturbance. A young Union soldier came dancing and dashing from out of the bracken, waving his rifle above his head. The men by the fire quickly rose and went for their pistols. The Sergeant stood and screamed, shouting angrily out at the soldier.

'Davis! You trying to get yourself killed, boy? You idiot. Don't you ever come into camp like that again, you hear me?' Shaking his head, putting up a finger, tapping his brow, he turned to the Lieutenant.

'Brain dead, that boy.'

Davis in excitement, cried, 'I bring news, Sergeant, good news!' Gasping, he turned to the others. 'The war's over. Lee, he has gone and signed a surrender, up in Virginny. We can go home. It is over.'

Wallace shrugged. 'Over? What yer talking about, boy? War's over? How? Who told you that?'

Davis lay down his rifle. From his tunic he pulled out a ribbon-tied scroll. He handed the scroll to Wallace. 'Courier, he gave me that, Sergeant,' pointing to the document. 'He handed me that, Sarg. He told me.' Nods to them all. 'Dun' told me it is over, Lee, he surrendered.'

Holding a hand up, he shook his head. 'He also said that the President, Lincoln, he is dead, shot. Murdered in Washington.'

The prisoners were all smiles, they nudged each other. The Major grinned, winking to his corporal, who slowly spat.

Wallace opened it and read. He shook his head and shrugged, before handing it over to Devlin, who, along with the others, had risen. Wallace slowly nodded. 'Boy's right, sir, damn God-forsaken war's over. Finished a month ago, ninth of April.'

Devlin looked, read. He too began to nod, shaking his head. 'So, here we are, been a-running around this fucking hell hole, scrambling in and out of God knows what ...' looked over to the prisoners, 'for what, sweet Jesus. Why only a week ago, I lost seven men getting them bastards tied. Only a week ago, seven men!' He spat into the fire. 'Not knowing that the war's been over since early April, for God's sake.'

Wallace said, 'I tell yer, if that ain't bad luck, Lieutenant,' he gently patted Devlin's shoulder, 'then what the fuck is.' He smiled, spreading out his arms. 'But it's all over now. Surely calls for some celebration, don't ya think, Lieutenant?'

Devlin nodded and smiled. 'Get out that corn gut-rot, Wallace. Yes, the war's truly over.' He sat back down. With a fist, he punched the air. 'Yes, and we won the fucker!'

The men, too, sat, looking into the fire. They stared at the licking flames. Devlin stretched out a leg and with a boot heel pushed a detached log back onto the fire. He looked up to the heavens, clapping his hands.

'It is over, we are going home, boys! Home away from this land of shite. We're coming home – Philadelphia!'

By the oak, the Major in grey spat. His corporal grinned, nodded and he too spat.

Davis took out his harmonica from his shirt pocket and began to vamp on a lively jig.

One soldier jumped up and began to dance; the rest, still sitting, clapped and stamped their feet. The Sergeant leaned over, putting a hand on the Lieutenant's shoulder. Giving a backwards nod he asked, 'What about those bastards tied up back there? What we gonna do, leave the fuckers tied up?'

Devlin smiled. 'Cut them loose, Sergeant. Ain't they had enough of our northern hospitality?'

Wallace with a serious look, whispered, 'Cut them loose. Yeah, sure Lieutenant. Seems—'

Devlin interrupted, stabbing his finger. 'Yeah, but with no rations, they leave as caught. They can eat fucking grass.' He looked over at a long string line of horses, nodded and smiled at Wallace. 'Their horses we keep, they leave on foot.'

Wallace, turning, looked back at the Greys, shouting at them, 'Yeah, hear that? Yeh set of miserable bastards. War's over. You lost. You southern Irish freebooters can return to your low life cargo humping. Yeah, back to yer trench digging. Get a nice black master. Now would not that be nice?'

Wallace turned back to the men and pointed at Privates Andrews and Stokes. He shouted, stabbing a finger over at the prisoners, 'Andrews, you and Stokes get those rebels untied. They're free to go home.'

Andrews just could not believe what he heard. He strode up to Wallace, with his hands up and open and his mouth agape. He stared into the face of his sergeant before asking if he was hearing his sergeant right. 'Yeh letting them go, Sarg? Yeh cannot be serious. Why, they are part of the Louisiana Tiger brigade, they fought this war for dollars, sergeant.' He turned to Stokes and shrugged, shaking his head. 'Fucking freebooters, paid help, Irish dockers, fucking shit shovelers.' He scuffed the dirt with a boot and spat.

Stokes nodded, smiling at the sergeant. 'Yeah Sarg, I'm in agreement with Andrews.' He scratched his beard. 'You sure about this, Sarg? If the boot was on the other foot,' he nodded over at the prisoners, 'why, that set of bastards would have gunned us, butchered us. They take no prisoners.' Nodding at Andrews, 'They're evil, Sarg, born evil,' jabbing a finger, 'I fucking well feel it. I tell you, Sarg.' Again, he shook his head. 'It's a huge mistake to set those bastards free.'

The Sergeant whispered, away from the Lieutenant's hearing, and pulling the two men to him, with his eyes blazing and with a slight grinding of his teeth, said, 'Don't you pair of shits think I don't know that? Lieutenant's decision, not mine. So let us get the fuck on with it, cut them loose.' He snarled, 'Ask me, I'm happy to see the back arse of them, besides. Those six Irish Texans, they have a long fucking walk ahead of them.'

Wallace stood watching with a pistol as the rebels were cut free. Their Major rubbed his wrists, giving a loathing glance at Andrews and Stokes. He then gave a sickening grin and began leading his men out. He nudged his corporal and winked. The Corporal slowly acknowledged him, nodding.

Wallace walked up to the Major, waving his gun. Face to face, smiling, he said, 'If I'd had my way, you would have been tied to nature. You're so fucking lucky that we got a generous officer in charge, the Lieutenant having a soft heart.'

He spat at the Major's feet, put a finger to the air, twirled it, then pointed to a section of the woodland and snarled, 'Texas is that way. Be careful how you fucking well go.' He winked. 'Paddy, me boy.'

***

The much-awaited news that the war was over was being wired to all corners of the United States, even to a quiet homestead in Austin County. Taylorville was a picturesque place that sat in the heart of Eagles Nest Valley. It was late morning when the forty-year-old ranger, Joe Dupree, came out onto the wicker-fenced veranda.

The forty-year-old, athletic, handsome six-footer walked over to the balustrade, looking at the child's swing hanging from a nearby willow. Where was his beautiful fifteen-year-old daughter? Janine was reading a book.

Pushing back her long flaming red hair she looked over at him and smiled. 'Good morning, mister sleepy head.'

'Good morning, sweetheart. What's the book you're reading?'

She smiled. 'Oh, it's good, Papa, *David Copperfield*, it's by Charles Dickens. He's English.'

'Sounds interesting. Let me read it when you have finished, baby. Er, where is your ma?'

Janine pointed over to a large barn. 'Ma, she's gone to see if the chickens have laid.'

Joe looked over to the barn where his wife Colette was coming out, carrying a basket. Joe smiled as she approached. At thirty-five she could still make Joe's heart go faster with her long black hair, shining like glass, and a body that still held its shape. Colette approached and spoke, with a slight French accent.

'Oh, I see the master has risen.'

'Oh, and a good morning to you too.'

'Well, it is noon, Joe. Are you still taking us into town? You promised.'

'Would I ever let my two most precious possessions in all the world down? Let's get ready, I will hitch up the buggy.' He shouted over to Janine, 'Come sweetheart, let's leave David Copperfield a while, Daddy's taking you to town. You can visit Chrissy, see all the new dresses in from France, while I go to see Uncle Tom.'

Collette put up a finger at him. 'Now Joe, you said things were quite … Didn't you say Tom would call if you were needed?'

She brushed past him, making for the cabin's door. Stopping and turning to him she shrugged. 'Sometimes I wonder if we'd have been better living in town.'

Joe laughed before waving with a smile, with arms outstretched and giving a floating spin, twirling his body. 'What! Give up Eagle's Nest valley? This panoramic paradise? No way, baby doll. I am in Tom's for words, not work.'

Two hours later and Collette was driving the buggy into Austin, humming a French ditty, Janine alongside, in time to the melody. Joe rode alongside, waving a hand, conducting the humming coming from Collette.

Chapter 7

DEVILS IN GREY

In that woodland clearing just west of El Dorado night had closed in on Lieutenant Devlin and his troop, who sat slightly intoxicated around the crackling fire, laughing and joking. Soon they were well boozed up. There was a large scattering of empty corn liquor jugs at their feet. Over between the oak and a line of three white tents their muskets, powder and shot were stacked, like some Indian tee-pee frame. The young private, Davis, took a mouth organ from his tunic. He began to play it, the tune "John Browns Body," while the men softly hummed and sang.

Unseen alongside the tents the recently released confederate corporal crawled towards the stacked arms and silently passed them back to waiting hands. The muskets, powder and shot soon disappeared, and the snakelike figure of the corporal went crawling silently back into the safety of the wood; moments later, coming out of the wood, the six confederates approached the well-oiled boys in blue.

They each held a loaded musket, pointed at the Union soldiers. Davis stopped blowing his mouth organ. With a look of fright and with his mouth agape he pointed, his finger trembling, at the approaching rebels. Wallace looked, following his gaze. On seeing the forthcoming danger, he swayed as he struggled to rise. Fumbling, he made for his side arm.

Wallace began snarling, shouting, 'What the? Why … why? You ungrateful bastards, we set you free, we—'

A crescendo of shots rang out. The Sergeant fell over with hole in his head. Devlin, with his men, confused, staggered and stumbled, each falling to the rebel onslaught. The rebels were quick in taking the pistols from the already slain and began to fire into any sign of Yankee life.

Soon all the blues were lying dead. A mouth organ lay in the dirt, with a bullet hole through its casing. It was its owner, Davis, who lay with a bullet hole under his nose.

The Major motioned for the pistol that his corporal was holding. The Corporal handed it over to him. The Major then pointed and fired into the already lifeless body of Wallace. He bellowed out sickening laughter, saying, 'Should have had your way, boy. You are not so lucky, cause Jack ain't so fucking generous. You ain't going home; you got it oh so wrong.'

He resumed pointing the pistol down at Wallace, emptying the gun. 'You lost, boy.' The rebels began to strip the bodies of the dead. When taking off their boots, the Major gave a nod towards the Lieutenant's shiny pair. 'They'll fit me.'

Turning to his corporal, Sneeze Eliot, he ordered him, 'See to them horses, get our pistols any ammo, maps. They will be stored in them tents.'

He nodded towards three large tents that sat with a horse line. A string of unsaddled horses was tied with a makeshift saddle rail running off. 'They have our horses, find mine, my saddle.'

The Corporal smiled. 'We got a few horses too many, Major, must be a good dozen on string over there.'

'Then we take them all. Well, we are fucking horse thieves, ain't we? That's good money for us.'

'But they've probably got cavalry markings, Major.'

'So, who is to say if we happen on a situation – we are just returning some strays.' He winked. 'For a price.' He smiled, punched his corporal on the shoulder. 'But I tell you this, some fucking northern squatters, they will be a thinking they can move their fucking arses onto Southern soil. Just fucking let 'em. Yeah. We need to start a business. Yeah, shit shovelling.'

He pointed at the body of Andrews, grinning. 'Ain't that what that fucker called us? Shit shovellers?'

'Those very words, Jack.'

The Major in anger fired his pistol into Andrews. Laughing hysterically, he then took the corporal's pistol and emptied it into the body of Andrews.

'The only shit pile we will be a-shovelling will be coming in from the north. We'll be putting it underground, a good six feet under. This war ain't fucking over, not by a long, long way. Why, it's just restarted.' The fire crackled, bursting into flames it spat.

Chapter 8

SONNINGSEN'S

It was a hot midday on the spread of a lonely homestead on Five Finger Gorge, North Austin, Texas.

Lief Sonningsen stood looking out at a fast-approaching dust cloud. He heard his cabin door opening. He turned, to see a young boy of fifteen. The boy carried a shotgun. With a troubled look he handed it over.

Robbie Sonningsen was Lief's son. With tears welling up, he said, 'I'm frightened, Pa. Who is it?'

Leif forced a smile, gently rubbing the boy's hair. 'You go back inside, Robbie. Lock and bar the door. Look after Ma and the girls.'

'You come too, Pa. Please Pa.'

Lief sighed. 'Could be Bill Peters and his boys. Yeah, didn't he say he would check in? Can't be Comanche. They like the nightfall.'

The cloud was getting closer with a sound of thundering hoof beats. He shook Robbie by the shoulders. 'Just do as I ask, son. Lock up tight.'

He watched as the boy raced back into the cabin. He broke and checked the shotgun, snapped it back and cradled it across his arms. The sound of the door latch bar going into place was followed by the sound of the windows being shuttered up.

The hoof beats stopped. He turned as the dust cloud slowly dispersed. A line of six horses was revealed with six masked riders in Confederate uniform. His eyes looked to each in turn, then finally settled on one big man who wore the uniform of a major.

Lief was sweating. 'I thought the war was over, Major. Yeah, well over a year now.'

The Major leant on his saddle haunch, growling through his mask. He pointed to the cabin's door. 'How many behind that door of yours?'

Lief stammered, 'J-just the wife, m-my son, he's fifteen, er, my two daughters. Th-they are just – one is ten, one twelve.'

A small thin man, wearing a corporal's stripes, Sneeze, with penetrating ice-blue eyes, peered at him. His voice croaked, 'Well, ain't yeh gonna invite us in? We need some fine home cooking.' He rubbed his stomach. 'A little whiskey would not go amiss. Get some of this dust out of my guzzler.' He winked. 'Oh, and some sweet female entertainment. What say you, friend?'

He turned in his saddle, waving a hand to five grinning companions, some of whom were mockingly rubbing stomachs. One, with a pleading look, clasped his hands together in prayer.

'The Major and us boys, well, we've been a riding since sunup...old bones need to rest a while.'

Lief gave a shake of his head, lifting the shotgun. 'Not gonna happen, mister.' He began to address the mounted line-up, pointing over to the spread's water trough. 'I'd like you to water your horses and leave my spread. So, if—'

The six drew their pistols; each began firing a volley into Lief's body. The shotgun fell from his hands. His body staggered backwards, with the force taking him back to the cabin door. He slowly slid down to the floor, his body twitching; it gave out a kick, then was still. From inside a female scream could be heard.

The Major looked at his corporal and grinned. Nodding to the corporal he pointed at the cabin door and snarled, 'Let's get in there.'

His corporal was quick to dismount and he strode up to the cabin door. He kicked and dragged the body of Lief to one side. Smiling, he uttered, 'Excuse me, friend.'

With his clenched fist he began hammering at the door. 'You inside, open up, open up now!' he shouted. 'You've got one fucking minute. If you do not open, we burn. Yeh hear? Burn your house down. One minute.' After the sound of the latch being lifted the door slowly opened.

The men dismounted with pistols drawn. They followed their on-waving corporal through the door. There followed a loud scream; a shot was fired. The corporal reappeared, stepping out with his pistol smoking. The Major, having dismounted, looked at the smoking pistol and pointed to it.

The Corporal shrugged, smiled. 'The boy, the kid, was armed with a shotgun. Brave boy, but a little foolish,' nodding down at the still body of Leif, 'just like his father.'

Two hours later the six sat mounted, tossing bottles of Swedish vodka around to each other. There was a shuffling sound. They drew their pistols, turning to a sound that was coming from the cabin's door. They began to laugh at the sight of the middle-aged woman, her face bloodied, eyes blackened and with multiple bruising to her half-naked body. The woman, in pain, was slowly crawling out on her hands and knees. She looked up at them and spat, 'You evil murderous bastards. My son, daughters. I'm gonna kill you all.' She looked over at the body of Lief. Crawling over to him, she hugged him, stroking his hair and kissing him. 'My man. You fucking evil bastards.'

Her eyes flashed onto the shotgun that was lying next to him. She picked it up and, pulling back the hammer, she lifted it …

There was a repeating sound of pistols firing. She moaned as the lead missiles entered every part of her body. The guns of the six fired at will; the shooters laughing hysterically as each round finds its target.

Moments later the horses were turned, with five of the six riding out. The Corporal stayed, mounted, with two lit storm lanterns in his hands.

He nudged his horse forward, stopping it just short of the cabin's open door, where pools of liquid kerosene lay shimmering, reflections caught in the sunset's final hour.

He yelled before tossing the lanterns into the kerosene. His face showed an evil sick smile as he watched the cabin burst into flames. Turning his horse, he rode off, whooping and yelling, towards the waiting others.

Carried on the breeze was the sound of a roaring fire of hysterical laughter that was coming from the departing killers.

Chapter 9
AUSTIN

One week later, gathered inside the large office and jail house were five members of the Texas Rangers. Three sat around a large desk looking at a large rolled-out map of Texas.

Walt Mitchell, a 37-year-old, was stroking his long-drooped moustache; with hair long and already going grey, he stretched out his lean six feet and gazed at his brother Jesse, whose finger was pointing down at the map. Jesse Mitchell, at 19, was the youngest ranger present. A shaven, baby-faced young man. His height fell a few inches short of Walt's, but he carried a leaner frame.

Jesse moved his finger along the map and stopped, pointing at the town of San Angelo. He jabbed his finger on it. Turning to his brother and giving Walt a questioning look, he said, 'There. I'm thinking they'd go there.'

Across the desk sat the bulky frame of 60-year-old ranger Drew Adams. He smiled through his heavy full beard at Jesse. He began to shake his head, pull down on his braces.

'No. No. No...' He then pulled a stub of a pencil out of his breast pocket and with it drew a circle around the area of

Uvalde. 'Uvalde, more like … they'd be a hitting around there. San Angelo, no.'

He winked at Walt. 'I've a gold piece that says Uvalde. You wanna cover it, Jesse?'

Jesse shrugged, giving a shake of his head.

Suddenly there was a cry of pain. They all looked over at a pot-bellied stove where ranger Ike Grimsdale was dancing around, screaming and blowing on his hand. He stamped a foot and raced over to a large wash basin and jug. Picking up the jug he began to pour into the bowl, but the jug was empty.

Ike snarled, 'Fuck that damn coffee pot, gone burnt my hand. Took the skin off my fingers.' He tipped the empty jug over. 'What's the fucking use of having a wash bowl and jug with no water for Christ's sake.'

Ike, a small middle-aged man of some 50 years with a slight paunch, looked over at the tall figure of one clean-shaven six-foot Joe Dupree. The athletic-looking forty-year-old ranger Joe was shaking his head, smiling.

'Why, that there pot's been a brewing on that stove all morning, Ike. Now one would not be a-thinking it to be cold now, would one?'

Ike snarled, 'Arrrrh, arrrh.'

Drew nudged Walt; winking, he shouted over to Ike, 'Now just you bring that sore and poorly hand over to me, Ike. Let me piss on it. Best cure there is for them stinging fingers of yours.'

They all laughed at Ike who was scowling, before angrily replying, 'Yeah, well how's about me pissing in that silly suggestive gob of yours. Yeah, you on my fingers, me into your mouth.'

They all burst into laughter.

Outside on Main Street it was a wild morning with a near-hurricane wind blowing great balls of tumbleweed in all directions. Two hounds barking madly were giving chase after them.

The street was deserted, the buildings with all doors shut tight, windows shuttered. Anything that was not secured was being tossed around like confetti, grit from the road swirled and peppered the buildings' timbers.

Directly across from the rangers' office the door of the telegraph office opened and the tall six-foot figure of Captain Tom McBane appeared.

He gripped the boardwalk's uprights. looking over the street at his office, where five saddled horses were tied. The horses were showing distress. They neighed and scuffed their feet, shuffling together against the storm.

Tom waited. The wind eased off slightly, giving him the chance to race across the street and make his office.

He ran, with coat tails flying above his head, his hat flying, dancing around on his neck. He crossed and looked up at the office sign that was banging wildly on its chains.

"THE AUSTIN OFFICE OF LAW"

He listened to the sounds of laughter coming from inside. He grimaced, taking a minute or two to listen before entering.

Inside Drew was pleading, 'Give us a cup of that nice coffee, Ike.'

With Ike looking daggers at Drew, Walt jumped up, winked at Drew and walked over to the stove.

'Coffee, yeh say, Drew? Er, let me do the honours. Don't think Grimmy's in a fit pouring state right now. You just be a resting that hand, Ike. Sure looks like you are in pain there.'

Ike growled, 'Fuck the lot of yer.'

Drew smiled.

'Say Walt, make sure that there coffee is brewed to perfection. I like it strong as a beaver's teeth, black as treacle. Yeh see, Ike, well he sure can brew up a fine... Yes sir, nobody brews like Ike. One thing for sure, it is fucking hot.'

They all, all that is bar Ike, were in tears with laughing.

They turned, looking at Ike's scowling face. They sniggered before bursting into laughter. Walt gloved up his hand and lifted the pot's lid.

'Just a wondering if it's been on the go long enough. I am a-thinking we should ask our expert here.' Walt, with eyes blinking, 'Er, what says you, Ike?'

Ike stood, making fists and grinding his teeth. He snarled and pointed a finger at them.

'I hope it chokes yeh, poisons yeh all, yeh set of bastards, that you are.'

The laughter stopped. The office door blew open and Tom entered, turning quickly to slam the door shut. He shook his head.

'Glad to hear laughter now. Seems to me, yeh be having a fun time.'

He motioned for Drew to leave his chair. Drew moved. Tom sat down.

'Yeh won't be a-laughing when you hear what I've got to tell yeh.'

He put his hand into his breast pocket and produced a paper, waving it at them. Joe walked over, putting a hand on Tom's shoulder. He bent over Tom's ear and whispered, 'Must say I'm not liking that there look, yeh be wearing.'

Tom leaned back into his chair, and sighed. He pointed at a wanted poster that was pinned up on a wallboard.

$20,000 DOLLARS REWARD. WANTED DEAD OR ALIVE.

FOR NUMEROUS ACTS OF ROBBERY, RAPE,
AND MURDER.

SIX EX. CONFEDERATE ARMY DESPERADOS.KNOWN
ONLY AS THE BROTHERHOOD.

THESE MEN ARE EXTREMELY DANGEROUS,
VIOLENT KILLERS. SIGHTINGS TO YOUR LAW
ENFORCEMENT OFFICE.

He went on to tell them, 'That bunch of evil killers,' shook his head several times, with Joe encouraging him to continue.

'Go on, Tom. What is it, yeh for telling us now?'

Tom leaned forward and began to slowly give out a deep sigh. 'They, the bastards, they were here. North of Austin, Five Finger Gorge.'

The rangers looked at each other in surprise. Drew gasped. 'Five Finger – ain't that where Lief and his family live? Surely not there, Tom?'

'Yeah, here on our patch.' He rubbed his face. 'Paid Lief a visit out on Five Finger… We fucking missed them. We fucking missed them, boys.'

Walt put a hand to his brow, muttering, 'Oh my God, sweet Jesus.'

Tom in anger skimmed his hat across the office. He stood and kicked out at his desk. Sadly he went on to say with difficulty, 'They murdered Lief, Hannah… and the kids. Burnt them down to the fucking ground.'

He went to the poster and thumped it hard with his fists. The men looked from him to each other. A momentary silence. Tom shuddered.

'Bill Peters and some of his boys, they came across what was left of the Sonningsen home. Smouldering embers.' He cried out, 'Lief, Hanna, the kids, they were all inside. Bill, he told me, what was fucking left of em. They'd been shot to pieces.' His eyes closed, holding back the tears. 'Bill put them under the ground.'

Joe whispered, 'Lief, Hanna, young Robbie, Chrissy, Joanna. Jesus Christ, Tom!'

They all looked at one another. Jesse was opening and closing his hands, making fists.

Drew walked over and looked out of the office window. He was in tears when he told them, 'I fucking loved that family.' He slammed down a fist.

'You know where we can find the bastards, Tom?'

'Bill estimates they'd be a good four days ahead of us.' He threw down a wire.

'Governor says they've been seen some twenty miles north of Uvalde. He says this comes from a good source.'

Drew nodded, giving a wink to Jesse, whilst Walt was quickly up on his feet, stabbing a finger at the map that lay spread out on Tom's desk.

'Now ain't that man over there got knowledge…'

Tom, with a bemused look, spread out his arms.

Walt nodded at Drew, clapped a hand. 'The six… You're saying Uvalde, Tom?'

'Sure, looks like its Uvalde, Walt.'

Walt, looking over at Drew, nodded. 'Drew he said they'd be Uvalde way, Tom.'

Joe put up a hand, saying, 'Now just a minute here, Tom. Yeh not be a saying that we're off on a chase to Uvalde, are you?' Joe held out his hand in a asking gesture. 'Tom?'

Chapter 10
FREDERICKSBURG

At the majestic Plantation House, owned by Mathew and Clarissa Cassidy, the six desperados assembled out on the front porch and lawn area. Four were eating and throwing peaches at each other whilst staggering, intoxicated. Each cradled a fine bottle of wine, putting it up to their lips and guzzling it down.

One fell over; he laughed at his own efforts to rise. The others gathered around and began to urinate over him. Still, he laughed.

On the porch Jack sat in a rocker with his pants around his ankles. Straddled across his lap, a middle-aged lady was held in a tight grip, his hands kneading her naked breasts. Her skirt hung like some open umbrella over the thrusting movement coming from the whooping major, who was bouncing her like some rodeo bull rider. The woman was crying in pain, sobbing. She looked over at the figure of a man, who was helpless, tied, standing, to one of the uprights, his frilled shirt hanging torn on his chest. Her eyes closed. She mumbled, a gasping screaming sound, and sobbed, 'Mathew, Matheeeeew. Tell him to stop, pl-e-a-se.'

Tears ran down his cheeks, unashamed, he sobbed his heart out and told her, 'I love you, Clarrisa, but we are undone by the devil's spawn. I'm afraid that our Lord does not dwell in their evil hearts.'

Meanwhile, dancing around, puffing on a large torpedo Havana, was the mocking figure of the corporal. He began to puff repeatedly on the cigar. He smiled at its glowing end, before prodding it into the man's left eye. The man cried out, the corporal sniggered, giggling childlike as he stabbed the man's body.

Out on the lawn the men stopped to view the acts of their two officers. They begin to clap and roar, stamping their feet in time with the major's rocking-chair rape, waving, urging him on. The corporal grinned, going face to face with the man Mathew, waving the cigar at eye level, making stabbing movements. He snarled angrily, 'Where is the fucking money? Where the fuck you hid it?'

He span on his heel, pointing at the woman.

'Best you tell me now, then we can leave. Leave yeh to yer peaches, to yer woman over there, while yeh still got yourself a good eye in yer head.'

He nodded over his shoulder. 'See my boys back there? Well, they all a-waiting for their turn to ride your woman. They never had an aristocratic blue-blooded lady before. Oh, then it's my turn.' He looked at his fingernails, grinning.

'I Hope my major – that he doesn't take all day,' he snarled. 'So, what's it to be, Peach Plantation Cassidy – do we ride our horses out of here or ride your woman?'

Cassidy slowly lifted his head, his one good eye meeting the corporal's gaze, and said, 'Go to hell, yeh evil lying little bastard.'

He spat into the face of the corporal, who snarled, eyes blazing, 'Now you just should not have done that.' He stuck the cigar into Cassidy's other eye. Cassidy howled.

***

Sometime later on the plantation house front lawn the six sat mounted. The house was on fire. The Cassidys stood on two separate stools, their hands bound behind their backs.

Around their necks a noose stretched up and over the branches of a cherry tree in blossom.

The major rode forward to where the woman stood. Taking out his pistol he shot the legs off the stool. She dropped, her legs kicking out momentarily before she hung still.

He laughed hysterically, nodding to the corporal, who moved his horse forward to Cassidy. He began to shout, 'Well now Mister Cassidy, how sad, your woman she just hung herself. But then you did not see. How could you, being blind and all. Well now, this dirty little lying bastard going to fucking well hang you.'

He pulled out his gun. Cassidy shouted a reply, 'Yeah, blinded but I ain't deaf, so you can go to hell, yeh lying piece of shit.'

With that, Cassidy jumped up high off the stool, kicking it over. His body jolted down hard, twitching then before hanging still. The corporal snarled and began firing, emptying his gun into the body of the lifeless Cassidy.

The Major gave an overhand wave, shouting out, 'Enough, let us ride.'

Chapter 11

THE CHASE

In the Austin Rangers' law office Captain Tom McBane raised his eyebrows, looked over at the faces of his men, shrugged his shoulders. Ike was looking at the map on the desk. He turned to the others, saying, 'Way I am seeing it, well would not it be better for rangers out of San Antonio to take this on?'

Tom with a deep sigh spread out his arms.

'OK. You do not have to go, but just let me say this.' Tom put a finger up to his brow. 'Just think for a minute. How many more Sonningsens are they going to continue to take. How many boys?' He looked at his men.

There followed a brief silence before Joe interrupted by giving a sharp hand clap. He walked over to the map and looked down at it, nodding.

'Tom's right, saying that. What's our strength, Tom?'

'It'd just be us, Joe. Six against six. Look boys, I know San Antonio is right for this job, but right now they're up to their neck with problems. They've one big one battling with Comancheros crossing over the Grande, robbing, killing taking the beef. The Comanche too, they got young bucks, breaking from the reservation, marauding. Governor says they have hell. That is why he is wanting us to help.'

Ike asked, 'You sure on Uvalde, Tom? Seems a long way to go if he is wrong.'

Tom picked up the map, walked over to the wall board and pinned it up. He turned to them, and with a pencil started to point to the map. He moved it, going up the length of the Sabine River, before going on to say, 'They've hit more than a dozen farms up the Sabine, and that's what we know of.'

In a zig zag movement Tom drew the pencil across the map. Criss-crossing the state he headed Southwest, Abilene.

'You can put your finger on all areas of this map, and those bastards have been there at one time or another. 'Liefs become one more family that's been added to their list.' Tom looked at each man in turn. With each man giving him an assuring nod, he looked to the office clock on the wall; he pulled out his own timepiece and checked it. 'OK we ride first hour after noon. My time's saying we are on ten-five. Let us get after these bastards.' Shaking his head he put up a fist. 'Let us not give them anymore time. Walt, you and Jesse see to them horses, best you get them out of that storm, fed and watered.' Looking at each in turn, he added, 'Say any goodbyes to yer kin, explain. Tell them we've no idea on how long this job's gonna take.'

Drew buttoned up his long coat and made for the door. Passing Tom, he said, 'First after noon. I am ready now.' He shrugged. 'Ain't no one to give any kiss or cuddle to, never been lucky enough. Be over in the Crazy Dog, just whistle when you're ready. See to my horse, Walt.'

Walt shrugged. 'Seems I will be in that Crazy Dog with yeh, old timer. Soon as we have finished the horses.' He sighed, with his head hanging down. 'Like Drew, ain't no one to give any kisses to.' Put up a finger. 'Come to think of it, can't doggone well remember when I did have a kiss 'n cuddle. Yes sir, now that must have been a long, long time ago.'

Walt smiled, showing his missing two front teeth. Jesse put a gentle hand on his brother's shoulder. Turning from him, he winked at the others. 'Wouldn't that be in yeh school days brother, er when that Lucy Clarke kissed out them teeth of yours?'

They all burst out into laughter as Walt chased Jesse out of the office, with Joe shouting after them, 'Leave my horse, Walt.' He shrugged at Tom and Ike.

'Well, it is certainly kiss, kiss time for Joe Dupree. I could not face a long journey without some kisses from my wife and daughter now.' Looked at them both. 'Well, could I?'

Tom, nodding, said, 'Just you watch out on that storm out there, Joe. Takes a good half hour getting to your spread. Go easy.'

Joe winked at Ike. 'Now yeh wouldn't be trying to put a man off getting his kiss kiss, would you, Tom McBane?'

'Don't yeh dare insult me, Joe Dupree, with that kinda talk.' Smiling, he told Joe, 'In fact, give them two fine ladies an extra kiss, kiss from Tom McBane.'

Two hours later Tom and his five rangers were saddled and ready to move out of Austin. All had said whatever goodbyes had to be said. Meanwhile the wind had dropped slightly. The sky had turned black, with the promise of a thunderstorm on its way.

***

Meanwhile, on a lonesome ranch east of Uvalde, Tor Nilsen stood with his younger sister, Inger, looking out from a chicken coop at the six riders approaching the homestead. Tor, a strongly built sixteen-year-old nudged his thirteen-year-old sister anxiously. 'Pa's in the barn. Let's warn him.'

They left the coop, their bodies crouched, and carefully headed into the large red-painted Dutch barn. There they saw their father, Henrik, busy mucking out in the stable section of the large enclosure. The forty-five-year-old Norwegian stopped his filling of a large barrow and turned to meet his children's entry. He smiled, asking, 'You come to give me a hand?'

Tor rapidly shook his head, his sister gasping, 'We got visitors, Pa, six riders ... men.'

Henrik put the pitchfork aside and went to the doors. He looked out at the six confederates who sat mounted outside the cabin. Henrik, with a concerned expression on his face, asked, 'They see you come in here?'

Tor answered with a shrug, 'I don't know, Pa, maybe, I ain't sure, Pa.' Inger added, 'We were careful, Pa.'

'Best I go find out what they're about then.' He took his hat off a hook and donned it. 'You two stay here, till I call yeh.'

He left the barn, closing the door on leaving. The two youngsters dashed to a cobwebbed window, Tor rubbing it clear. They looked through, watching their father striding up to the riders. Henrik looked at the mounted six, surprised after seeing the officer a major in confederate grey with a corporal showing the stripes on one weather-worn tunic. He engaged the major by asking him how he might help, only to find a non-reply to his question.

The corporal snarled, answering for his commanding officer, 'My major,' waving to the men, 'we're all fucking hungry and be wanting a dinner for six, accompanied by some,' he spat, 'fine liquor, get these balls of prairie dust out of our airways.' With that said the corporal tapped on his pistol holster and nodded towards the door. Henrik held out his arms, saying, 'You can see that I am unarmed. I carry no weapon.'

The Norwegian, being no fool, could see a problem forthcoming, and was thinking of the best way to rid his spread of these evil-looking desperadoes. He looked towards the barn, with thoughts of his children's safety, then back to the homestead with his wife Unni and baby Stig, mother-in-law Marrianne, and another problem arriving on the horizon with his father-in-law Arne coming home after some fence repairs.

He shrugged before telling the corporal that he could supply the six with eggs and bacon, along with bread.

The major turned to him and growled, 'We sit inside at your table along with your Scandinavian family. You're Swedish, I take it? We like to have a nice woman cook for us. You got a nice Swedish gal in there?' He pointed to the cabin.

Henrik said, 'We are Norwegian. Yes, I have my wife and baby and her mother inside, and,' he pointed to Arne who was taking his mount into the barn, 'my father-in-law.' He sighed. 'I am thinking it's best that you take my offer of the supplies. I can add a couple of casks of corn liquor.'

The major looked at his men, saying, 'Is this fucking man deaf? Did he not hear me say that we will dine at his table?' Henrik interrupted, saying that he had not the room to accommodate them all. With that the major pulled out his pistol, putting a hole in Henrik's head. Arne, hearing gunfire, rushed out of the barn only to be met by a hail of bullets. He fell with the children, Tor and Inge, racing away on a heading looking for safety.

**

Two hours later the half-naked dead bodies of Unni Nilsen and her mother Marrianne lay face down in the dirt. The bullet-ridden body of her father, Arne, lay submerged in the yard's water trough, whilst, bunched together, sitting in a macabre line on the floor, with their backs against the cabin's wall, baby Stig was lying across the arms of Henrik, with the children, infant Olav, Tor and Inge alongside. All were dead.

Outside the open cabin door, a pack of hungry hounds stood gazing at the outgoing riders. They began to tear and drag the bodies across the yard.

**

Four days later, on the eastern outskirts of Uvalde, Tom and his party came to a fork in a dirt road in front a bullet-riddled signpost with its finger indicators shot off. It was Drew who dismounted and matched up the broken off fingers. He nodded before pointing.to the road going left.

'Yeh, left it is, Tom. Post here ain't been moved, she's pointing left.'

Joe pointed to a farm track that was cutting off the main. 'That road goes to that farm over there. I'm thinking we could get to water these horses, Tom,' he slapped down the shoulder of his mount, 'mine being a little done in.'

They all looked over at the buildings standing some two hundred yards away. Their horses began to shuffle and neigh. They scuffed their hooves at the sound of dogs barking. Tom gave a shrug. 'Yeah, Joe's right, the horses, we have been pushing them hard. Walt, you ride up ahead and speak with the owners, see if we can trough em a while. We do not want to scare the people by riding in heavy-handed.'

Walt, nodding, took his mount forward and went ahead up towards the buildings. Tom shouted after him, 'See what them fucking dogs are about.'

Tom let Walt get well in front before asking his men to follow. They went ahead at a slow walking pace, the dogs' barking getting louder.

Walt entered the gateway that led to a larger than normal cabin. To its rear a large barn with hay loft. The yard was covered with bundles of scattered rags. A pack of dogs were growling, snarling and barking, tearing into the rags. They stopped at Walt's approach, and began to growl in a more ferocious manner. His horse reared up with Walt struggling to hold on. He took out his pistol and began firing at them, killing two; the others raced away in all directions. Walt moved on, looking down at the small bundle of rags.

The rags were covered in blood, with hundreds of flies feeding. Sticking out from it were the torn remains of a child's arm. Walt began to cough; he then vomited from his saddle.

Spinning his horse away, he yelled out and began frantically waving his arms towards the others.

With the sound of Walt's gun blasting the rangers were already alert; with guns drawn, they galloped at speed up to him. Walt, putting his bandana up over his nose and mouth, pointed down at the bundle. He screamed, 'Arrrh, arrrh.' Shaking his head, he rode out after the hounds, firing his pistol madly at will. Soon all the hounds lay dead. Joe looked down at the bundle. He quickly pulled up his bandana and masked his face, turning to Tom and jabbing his finger down at the bundle. 'Jesus Christ! Tom, there's a, a, child in there. A baby for God's sake!'

Tom shook his head in disbelief. Drew walked his horse around the yard, and shouted, 'Yard's full of bodies, Tom. I have counted eight. Looks like them dogs have had quite a feed. Bodies dragged all over the yard.'

Ike gasped, 'Eight?'

'Yeah eight. I have four adults, four children,' pointing to the blood-soaked rags. 'One, a half-eaten baby.'

Tom said, 'The fucking evil bastards.' Turning to Ike, 'Ike, you go look in that house. Jesse, take that barn over there.'

Joe interrupted, 'I will get me some shovels, Tom. We need to bury what's left of these poor souls. Get these fucking flies off em.' He shouted over to Jesse, 'Jesse, shovels, see if there are any in that barn.' Jesse waved an okay, with Tom nodding.

'Yeah, you do that, Joe. Drew and I, we better get them covered, ready for the ground.' Tom shouted over to Ike, 'Take a look around Ike, see if we can put a name to this family.'

One hour later, the rangers walked their horses slowly past the large heap of freshly dug soil. They looked down over the grave. A simple cross marked it. A bunch of wildflowers sat inside an old pail. Painted on the cross piece was a name.

NILSEN FAMILY R.I.P.

Tom and Joe both crossed themselves before turning away. The men then, shaking their reins, kicked and galloped their horses. In silence, the procession rode down the road pointing to Uvalde.

Chapter 12

ULVALDE

Half a day later the rangers came onto a deserted Uvalde Main Street. They slowly walked their horses. Tom pulled his rifle from its sheath and his men in unison followed suit.

Joe whispered, 'I don't like it Tom. Where is everybody?'

Tom shrugged. 'Yeah, it sure is ghostly.'

He waved for Walt and Jesse to dismount, saying, 'You boys take the boardwalks either side. Check those windows, doors, let's see if we can find some living soul. Joe, take their reins.' He looked at Drew. 'Drew, you and Ike scout around the back. We do not want a surprise party.'

Drew indicated Ike to go left and he took the right-side of the buildings.

'Keep them eyes of yours peeled,' Tom went on. He waved with a finger at Joe. 'Joe, you take right uppers, leave me to scout left.' He gave a shrug. 'Where the fuck are the people?'

Joe answered, 'If they are not a hiding from us, then they're gone.'

Tom nodded. 'Or dead.'

Jesse peered through a barber's shop widow. Tried the door,

it was unlocked. With his rifle he pushed it open and entered. The shop was in disarray. A large broken glass mirror covered the floor area. Flies crawled over a large blood-soaked sheet that covered the barber's chair. Coming out from underneath were legs with slippers. Jesse stood back and gently pulled off the sheet, revealing the body of a large man with his throat cut. The figure was tied to the chair. With an onslaught of flies, Jesse staggered back out of the door.

Back out on Main Street he shouted over to Tom, 'I got a man with his throat cut in here, Tom.'

Tom gave a deep sigh. 'Cover him up, Jesse, then shut the damn door.' Turning to Joe, he said, 'Looks like Jesse found us the barber.'

'Means they've hit this town, Tom. Sweet Jesus, how many more?'

Tom waved Joe to move on.

Walt, looking into the open door of a haberdashery store, shouted, 'Store's half-full of suits, shirts, with nobody in 'em. Looks to me like our friends have had their pick, Tom. Few empty rails and shelves in there. No sign of life.'

He shook his head and walked on. There was a sudden movement underfoot. Walt lifted his rifle. Two hounds raced out of their den from under the boards and across the street into an open door of a provision store. Above hung the sign, PETE DANSENS ALL YOUR NEEDS STORE.

Jesse, closing the barber shop door, span around at the sound, with rifle raised. He laughed, downing his rifle, as the two dogs flew past.

'Yeah, just get yeh selves in, doggies, help yeh selves, ain't nobody gonna stop yeh none.'

The hounds came back out and cowered at the door, barking. They turned and re-entered the store.

Joe looked on down the street. He saw a figure that was hanging and swinging freely. He looked at Tom, then raced his mount towards it, dragging Walt's and Jesse's horses behind him. He arrived at the figure of a bullet-riddled man. The man hung by the neck from a cross beam. Joe looked up at the sign attached to his neck, which hung down over his chest. SHERIFF WANTED APPLY WITHIN.

Tom arrived, with Walt and Jesse racing after him.

Joe sighed. 'Jesus Christ, Tom!' He looked at Tom, pointing at the man. 'This can only be the sheriff?'

Tom nodded. 'Yeh that there's what's left of an old friend of mine, Hank Stone.'

'Yeh knew him, Tom?'

Tom sighed. 'Yeh, I knew Hank, old ranger friend of mine from out Galveston way. He was a good man. One could not help but like him, Joe. Met him just after you and I moved into our jobs in Austin.'

Tom turned to Walt and Jesse. 'Let's get the poor man down from there, boys.'

Walt and Jesse gripped Hank's legs, disturbing a swarm of blow flies. Tom rode his mount forward. Pulling out a knife, he cut down Hank Stone. He nodded to Walt. 'You and Jesse, get him indoors, off the street and into his office. Get him covered.'

Blow flies were everywhere. Walt and Jesse masked up and began to carry Hank's body into the office.

Joe snarled, 'These killers, they have cleared this town, Tom.'

They hear Jesse's coughing coming from the office. Jesse spoke, shaking his head. 'There are two more bodies inside, Tom. Look to be his deputies.'

Tom and Joe dismounted and followed Jesse back into the office, where Walt was rolling Hank's body in a carpet. He looked up as Tom and Joe entered. He nodded over at the jail cell. 'Two bodies lying in the holding cell, Tom.'

Tom walked over a floor that was covered with broken glass. He looked at Joe and pointed at a wall gun display cabinet. The doors had been torn down and were hanging off, the rifle holding chain cut. The cabinet hanging empty made Tom say, 'They've added to their armoury, Joe.'

'Pistols too, Tom.'

Joe viewed the whole office area. 'No gun belts, shells… they've taken it all. He walked over to the cells, looked in and down onto two half-naked bodies. They lay across each other in a macabre position. They had been brutally abused and violated. He shook his head sadly. 'Why the fuck they have to do this?'

'Why? wish I could answer that for you, Joe. I want these bastards dead, that is what I want.'

Drew and Ike entered the office, pistols drawn. Ike, looking at the carnage, exclaimed, 'What the fuck!'

Drew, drawing in a deep breath, said, 'Back's all clear Tom, nothing, but we've got more of this across the street, down some.'

Tom said, 'What?' He waved a hand over the lying dead. 'Not more of this, for Christ's sake?'

'Afraid so, Tom, it's down the street, Mayor's office. Bright green building.' Tom strode out of the office, with Joe, Drew and Ike following.

Back out on the street and Drew moved forward to Tom and pointed.

'There, Tom, the bright green building.'

The rangers walked their horses. They scanned the buildings with their pistols drawn. They arrived at a green-painted building. It displayed a large banner above the entrance. The banner read, VOTE FOR FRANK GREENWAYS. KEEPING THE PLAINS OPEN. FRANK WILL CUT THE WIRE.

They all looked down on the horrific sight of a large naked man. His body hung unceremoniously over a hitching rail, his backside branded, cut with three xxx marks. On his bald head was a crown of barbed wire. The wire had been pressed deep into the head. Hundreds of flies were ravenously feeding on his bullet-riddled, blood-stained, whiplashed body.

Tom closed his eyes briefly. 'Get him off the street, boys.'

He nodded towards the open door of an office. 'Best take him into that office, for Christ's sake! Take that fucking crown off him.'

Joe said, 'If you'd be asking me, Tom, this fucking carnage ain't over yet. Jesus Tom, we ain't but half ways down Main Street.'

He cupped his hands to his mouth and shouted out, 'If you are hiding, then come on out. Show yourselves. We are here to help, Rangers out of Austin.'

With their eyes scanning, they gazed down a silent street. Drew whispered, 'It's sure spooky.'

Joe smiled. 'No need to whisper, Drew. Ain't nobody to hear you.'

Suddenly there was a break in the silence. The sound of a door opening. Tom held up his hand to Jesse and Walt, who were coming out of the mayor's office.

'Shhhhhhhussssh.'

They stood in silence, alert, looking down the street.

Jesse said, 'There, there, Tom, a door. The wire office.'

Walt, 'Yeah, I see it, next to the bank. It's just… it's opening.'

They all looked at the telegram office door. An elderly man's voice bellowed out, 'Rangers, yeh say?'

Joe looked at Tom, who beckoned at Joe to reply.

'Yeah, that's right, all the way from Austin. It's okay for you to come out.'

There followed a silence, with it seeming the voice wanted a little more surety before coming out.

Tom was still urging Joe, with a waving underhand motion. 'Like I am saying, we are here to help. We need to know what has happened here, so do not be afraid. You can come on out.'

The door opened fully and from it stepped a slimly built, white-haired, well-dressed bespectacled man with a cane. He walked with a slight limp out onto the boardwalk. He stood before them in striped pressed trousers, wearing a matching waistcoat.

'Six of 'em, all wearing Confederate grey. Had their heads covered with hoods, flour bags with cut outs for eyes and mouth.' He sighed. 'I couldn't get no wire away. They must'a cut it before entering town.'

Tom interrupted, 'Yeah, we did see that, old timer, they cut it just short of a farm. About a half day east of here. They took the lives of a family of nine there. We put 'em in the ground.'

The old man grimaced, giving a deep sigh. 'Yeah, that would be the Nilsen family. They moved here only last spring. Out of Canada... Norwegians. They were good hard-working people. Like I said, they spared me, why, one of them knew me. He called me Howie. My name's Howard, Howard Jackson.'

The Rangers slowly walked forward and stopped on reaching Howard. Tom offered his hand, smiling.

'Pleased to meet you, Howard Jackson. I'm Tom, Tom McBane.'

Howard nodded, taking and shaking Tom's hand, saying, 'But Austin you say? Seems a long way to come.'

Joe offered Howard a hand. 'Joe Dupree. True enough. We're two hundred miles or so from home, chasing those murderous bastards. It's been a long trail we have been following.' He sighed. 'Sadly, we're too late to have helped out here. Way things are going these killers ain't finished till we catch them.'

Howard nodded. 'Yeh, yer two days too late, but what happened here, it has been near on a week. Town's empty, there's just Smokey Turner with his son Amos and me here now.'

Tom, 'Smokey, Howard?'

'Oh, Smokey, he looks to the graves on Cemetery Hill. Be up there now putting Pete Dansen and his family down in the ground. Amos be with him, he's nineteen, strong lad. Built like a barn door. I'd help if only I could, this leg of mine...'

He tapped a leg with his cane. 'Got this in sixty-three, blast from a Yankee gun boat. Mississippi.'

Shake of his head, smiled. 'Was an old man then ,sixty-one, at that age you're just too old for a soldiering life anymore.'

He looked at Drew. 'About your age, I'd say.'

Drew smiled and nodded.

Howard pointed over at the bank. 'Well now you're here, yeah like you says, a little too late. Best you go look in there. Not a pretty sight. They took all that shined, cleaned out the safe. Whatever it held, it's all gone, along with Mary Beth.'

Joe said, 'After viewing your barber, sheriff, and mayor... There ain't nothing gonna shock us, Howard.'

Howard nodded. 'Yeah, we left them for last. Should have covered them.'

Tom winked. 'We done and seen to that, Howard.'

Howard put up a thumb. 'Oh Smokey, he'd a got to it eventually, but what with the church... the women and children... the old folks.'

Ike, turning, looked all around. 'Church, Howard? I'm seeing no church, women, children, old folks?'

Howard turned to Ike. Shook his head. 'You won't see it.' He pointed over at Cemetery Hill. 'Was up there.' Sighed. 'Was, till them bastards burnt it to the ground.'

Looked up at the sky, turned to Joe. 'Some people, mostly women and children, took sanctuary in there.' Howard took out a rag and wiped his eyes, blew his nose. 'Some. Those that did not were shot. The mothers and girls violated before being murdered.'

'This I learnt from Smokey, who luckily happened to leave with his son Amos, Pastor Higgins having asked the two to somehow get help. To see if it were at all possible to fix the wire cut, so's I could get some message out to San Antonio.'

'The church was full of the old people of Uvalde, its many families, men, women, children, their faces showing fear, their children screaming, crying. Smokey told me that Pastor Higgins had gently held out a hand, in a soothing movement, some up and down waving motion. He kissed his Bible.'

'From his dark grey smock, he produced a key. With a reassuring look, he hushed for silence. He then spoke out to them, saying that he was about to lock them in the Lord's house, that he would confront this evil that had befallen Uvalde.'

'Smokey and Amos came to the back door of my office and told me of the uneasy situation that they felt was about to begin. With this the three of us hid in the upper loft of the wire office. We could see and hear all of the brave approach of Pastor Higgins to the evil confederate Major.' Howard wiped his eyes with his kerchief.

'We watched the Pastor walk down the hill, holding his open Bible and loudly reciting from it to the hysterically laughing six, well-soaked with their heavy consumption of liquor, the people who had been hiding from this evil having appeared, coming out from the safety of their hideaways to join up with their Pastor. The six began firing indiscriminately, cutting the unfortunate believers down. The bodies of the dead were scattered up and down Main Street. Still proudly showing no fear, head held high, Higgins walked towards the killers, looking down into the Lord's book. We heard him now shouting out loud from its inner scriptures.'

'His voice was strong, he spoke with a fiery venom. He read from Jeremiah 44:29. "And this shall be a sign unto you, saith the lord." He pointed a stabbing finger at the bemused-looking Major, before continuing, "I will punish you in this place, that Ye may know that my words shall surely stand against you for evil."

'He paused on seeing the figure of the Corporal dragging a young half-naked Mary Beth towards a standing buckboard. Still stabbing his finger at the Major, standing with hands on hips, the Pastor snarled at him, "Thou shall take thy evil from this place or feel the wrath of God."

'He continued to recite from the holy book as he finally came face to face with the Major, who suddenly reacted by getting down on one knee and motioning his men to follow suit, the Corporal grinning and dragging the girl down with him. The Major showed a look of sadness to the reciting Pastor.'

'Higgins nodded, saying, "It is time for you to leave us now. Best you continue your journey. You must ask our Lord for forgiveness, for you have painted so much evil here."

'The Major jumped to his feet and saluted Higgins, before going into a bout of hysterical laughter. He pulled out his pistol and shot Higgins in the head. The others all rose and they joined in firing into the pastor's lifeless body. The evil officer then pointed to the church, saying, "Let's finish here."

'He then turned to two of his men, snarling, "Crazy, you and Duke go fetch the kerosene. The Lord's house wants warming."

'The two desperados then raced off to a nearby ironmonger's store, where they went in and reappeared, each carrying two large cans of kerosene. They rushed to the waiting four who were grinning, nodding their approval. The Major smiled. "Let's do this, Crazy. Let's warm this fucking house of God.'"

'The two then were four, each with a can of kerosene. They began to pour the liquid all around the church. The Major lit a bandanna and threw it onto the fuel. The church went up in flames. Horrific cries could be heard, screams of pain coming out of the flaming building.'

Howard sobbed, weakly muttering, 'That bastard Major was throwing up his arms at the screams coming from the burning congregation, laughing hysterically.'

A moment's silence fell. Howard looked at all the stunned faces.

'I tell you, I will never forget those screams. I, I…'

Joe put his hands on Howard's shoulders, gently squeezing them. 'They burnt a church, along with women and children?'

Howard wiped his eyes. 'Yes, sir, the old, too. They were in there.'

He turned to Tom and said with a pleading voice, 'You, you... gotta get those bastards, Captain... show no mercy.'

Tom slowly nodded. 'That's one sure thing I can promise you here and now, Howard Jackson.'

Tom, in his anger, kicked out and scuffed the dirt with his boot. Looked at his men.

'Once they are caught, and Howard, we will catch these bastards, they'll get no fucking mercy. It is at times like this that it's time to forget about being a sheriff.' Tom turned, looking over at the bank, and pulled his bandanna up over his nose, as Howard nodded.

'Well, sir, that is sure good to hear, because I do not think I will ever forget these last few days,' giving a deep sigh, 'never.' He nodded towards the bank, saying, 'I will not go in there with yeh, what you have seen already and what is in there. Well, Smokey, Amos and I will clean up after you leave.'

He walked slowly away, then turned. 'I'll sort out some supplies for you. Those killers done took a load.'

Tom nodded, saying, 'We need to pay, Howard. Let me give you some dollars.'

Howard shrugged. 'No need for that, Captain. Pete Dansen, his family... they will not be needing it They... they have all gone now.'

Joe interrupted to ask, 'Horses, Howard, we're needing fresh mounts.'

Howard nodded. 'You got them, they took fresh, along with a buckboard loaded – Mary Beth tied in the back – left their horses in the corral.'

He pointed down the street. 'That's over in the smithy, Jake Carter's place. They be well fed and watered. Maybe they be a thinking to return for them, who knows?' Deep sigh. 'We buried Jake yesterday.'

Tom patted Howard's shoulder. 'Thanks, Howard, but first we'd best take a look-see into that bank.'

Howard, waving his cane, slowly limped off in the direction of Pete Dansen's store.

Tom turned and motioned for them to follow him into the bank, turning to Walt and Jesse, telling them, 'Walt, you and Jesse see to the horses. I am thinking we rest ours. They can be collected on our way home. I am sure Howard will see to their keeping.'

Ike muttered under his breath, 'That's if we ever get to going home.'

Tom turned on him. 'Yeah, Ike, let's just see that we fucking do. You go follow Howard, give him a hand with them supplies. Drew, you're with Joe and me… the bank.'

Tom strode quickly for the bank with Joe and Drew at his heels. They entered to yet another sight of horrific murder, with three bodies lying in death's pose on the bank's floor, all shot to pieces. Tom looked down on a young man's blood-soaked attire. He was lying dressed in suit and tie, that had been pulled tight around his neck.

Flies in their hundreds were feasting on it. Drew pulled hard down on a window curtain, walked over and, throwing it over the body, said, 'Poor kid. Bank's teller, I would say.'

Joe stood over a man with no face, having taken a close shotgun blast to it, and dressed in an elderly fashion. Looking at his feet Joe saw that his boots were missing. He shook his head on seeing that a pair of old worn-out boots were lying beside him. Joe spat, 'Bastards took his boots.'

Tom sighed. 'Pull him over by the boy, Joe. Cover 'em both,' and waving his hat, brushing away at a feasting army of flies, added, 'Keep these damn flies off 'em.'

Another body, that of an elderly woman, lay blasted against

the wall. She showed one bullet hole that had entered her brow, the upper torso being riddled. Drew pulled off another drape and covered her.

Joe looked towards a back-office door with a brass plate which read, MELVIN BINCH, MANAGER. He pushed it open and went in.

He looked at the back wall of a large office. A large safe with its door open. The safe was empty. The floor of the office was littered with documents. A desk and swivel chair dominated the centre of the room. Sprawled out in in the chair was the body of a middle-aged man, his throat cut, covered in flies. He sat in a blood-soaked shirt and waistcoat with a pocket torn and hanging off. Tom, following him in, nodded at the body. 'That must be Mel Binch.'

'Yeah, they've taken all his money and his watch and chain.'

'They took his daughter too. Sixteen years old. Jesus! Let us cover him.' He shouted out, 'Drew, we got one in here. We need a cover.'

Joe, rubbing his face, shrugged, saying, 'We gotta make up on this time gap, Tom. We gotta fucking stop this shit now.'

'That'll mean us sleeping in the saddle, Joe.' Tom waved. 'Let's get out of this hell hole.'

Drew entered and looked at Mel Binch. He sighed before throwing a drape over him. Tom motioned for them to leave. Stopping for a moment, he looked down at all the covered bodies. He shook his head, before kicking the old, discarded boots into a corner. 'Bastards.'

Moments later the three Rangers found themselves taking deep breaths of fresh air back out on Main Street. Tom looked up to see Walt and Jesse approaching with the horses all saddled.

Walt said, 'We've saddled up their six, Tom. But my brother Jesse and I, well we thought to string ours along with us. They be all fed up and watered.' Jesse nodded. 'Yeah, Tom, with only

Howard and Smokey and his son, they'd be safer coming with us, especially if the killers return. We would then have an advantage. They would be looking for fresh, and there would be none.'

Tom gave him a thumbs up sign. 'Good thinking, Jesse, we're going to go with that.'

It was then that they heard the sound of a buckboard approaching. Ike was driving, with Howard sitting alongside. Ike reined in. 'Supplies all loaded, Tom.' Smiling, he nodded at Howard. 'We put a good two to three weeks on board.'

Tom walked forward to help Howard down. Howard nodded before reaching under the buggy's seat. He brought out a pile of shotgun shells and handed them to Tom.

'Thought yeh could put me a few Uvalde shells into those bastards, Captain.' Then, sadly, 'Hope that young Mary Beth's still with us.'

'You can be sure we'll be out there doing our damnedest to see to that, Howard. But we're wasting time.' He gripped Howard's hand and shaking it, said, 'Been a pleasure knowing you, Howard Jackson. I just wish we'd met in a better time my friend.'

Howard was overcome when all the Rangers began shaking his hand. Moments later, Howard stood on the street, waving his cane at the departing Rangers. Tom turned in his saddle and, looking back, saluted him.

Chapter 13

BANDERA

The desperados had camped in an old, discarded logging area with plans to hit the cattle station of Bandera and clear its bank of its holdings. The Major had decided on a night attack, with orders to leave no witnesses. The Corporal was to go in with Crazy and case the town, finding its weaknesses along with the easiest escape route. The two knew that the Major would be wanting to leave no room for error.

It was at the closing of nightfall, and the body of Mary Beth having previously been disposed of after being raped many times, that the Major told his Corporal to bring him fresh meat and to be sure of it being fresh and young. His words were, 'No old sow, no skinny bitch, but then again not a fat cow.'

It was just after midday when the two spies rode into Bandera, down a street filled with cattle being driven by drovers into keeping pens. It certainly looked as though there was money in town, meaning a safe full of dollars in what looked to be one detached stone bank with one security guard. The Corporal turned to Crazy and whispered, 'Best we tell the Major to give it another day. Sure to be more in that bank safe after the selling of the beef.'

Crazy smiled and winked, saying, 'I can't see any problems, but then again, we have the woman to snatch. Need a loner, one that won't be missed... maybe one of them saloon hussies, what you think?'

'Are you fucking serious? You wanting to give the Major the shagging pox, why I now know how you come to get Crazy for a name, best you think again, brother.'

Three hours later and the two desperadoes returned to camp with the figure of a young teenage girl slung over the Corporal's horse. One last-minute snatch had been made as the girl had been walking her dog on the lakeside of Bandera. The only witness, the dog, left dead.

The two dismounted and smiled when presenting their prize capture to the Major, whose eyes had lit up. He licked his lips at what would be a most pleasant night to look forward to. He was hoping that they had brought back with them a virgin.

But first the main task, the bank, and their report of its possibilities, both for and against.

It was the Corporal who opened with what they had seen and their agreed thoughts on a safe execution of the Major's planned robbery.

The bank it seemed, in fact they were sure, was all under control of its owner, a well-known villain of deception and most feared, a cattle baron by the name of Jefferson Finch. Finch was known to hold one of biggest herds of beef in the whole of Texas, along with Sweetwater's Pat Murphy. More so since after the war's ending, when he had created for himself a huge order book with the new United States military. This ensured no opposition on beef. Not that he had not got competition. The Irish-held grasslands north of San Angelo held by the Murphys were his only other rival. It was simply that anyone daring to move against him in his neighbourhood were quickly eliminated.

Finch was the law, with his fingers into just about everything involving money making. He supplied all the Army's forts and was known to be exporting beef on routes into other states, even going over the international borders of Mexico and Canada. He was indeed one of the only two players who controlled the import and export of beef.

The concerned Corporal, shaking his head, finished by saying, 'It's not going to be easy, Major. This man Finch has a small but powerful army we have to contend with.' He sighed. 'Ain't gonna be easy.'

The Major snarled at his corporal. Turning to his men he began to shout, the captive girl shuddering at the violent tone coming from this horror of a man. 'Okay, the plan changes, we take this self-made El President by the bollocks. He will feel my wrath; he will beg for his miserable life. You want to see how power looks when it has no support? Allow me to show you. Go out and bring the bastard to me. I promise you this, my brothers. He will crawl to open his safe.'

***

The Rangers had made suitable time by changing the horses that Walt and Jesse had contrived as the only available method of ever catching up with the killers. They were on a trail that was on a heading to Fredericksburg when they came across two county linesmen who were repairing a broken section of the run from Fredericksburg into Uvalde. They had heard that there had been trouble down the roads at a peach plantation, where a fire had burnt down the owner's mansion house, and that the owners, the Cassidys, had been murdered. They had left the house and its victims untouched and were about to inform a nearby fort but since the Rangers had arrived, they would leave them the job.

Joe said, 'After closing the time gap, we hit another hold up. When is it all going to end with these sadists?'

A brief time later and they were viewing yet another horrific scene, the peach plantation and the shot-riddled bodies of the hanging Cassidys as well as the smouldering remains of what had been the house which had been burnt to the ground.

Drew, touching the embers, remarked, 'I'd say we are about two days behind these bastards. It is like Joe said, we are gaining only to be put back by having to put these people to rest. We could do with a Smokey and Amos following us.'

Tom nodded. 'So, let's get to it, boys. The sooner we catch up the more lives saved.'

Joe questioned, 'Where the hell's their workforce?'

Walt answered, 'If they've any sense they would have run for their lives, no way would they want to be involved with this shit.'

A grave was hurriedly prepared before the Cassidys were put to rest.

The Rangers, showing a strong determination to get on with their job of catching and executing these sadistic killers, took no time to linger and took a southwestern heading, thanks to Drew's expert tracking, which was going by the heavy wheel and hoof tracks that he had followed for quite some time.

***

After one long afternoon of sexual pleasure the Major had finally arrived at a decision. They would make the snatch of Jefferson Finch and his family. Finch, then threatened with their deaths, would be made to empty his entire deposits, cash gold and silver, that were being held in that bank of his before handing them over to the robbers. Of course, the Major adding, there were to be no witnesses to the event.

It was just after midnight when the killers stole silently onto the Finch estate. They waited patiently for the bunkhouse lights to be extinguished. The Major had ordered Crazy and Duke to pour a run of kerosene around the bunkhouse of the sleeping drovers, forming a ring of fire that would entomb the twenty-three sleeping residents; the estate's work force and bodyguards to the sleeping Finch family. There was only one other alarm warning left for the desperadoes to deal with, that being the two large killer hounds that were housed by the mansion house door. These two obstructing hounds were to be poisoned a good hour before the snatch.

Then his lordship Jefferson Finch would be taken into town and what followed was to be the bank withdrawal. The inner two guards would open to his command before their assassination.

Come dawn all was to be completed. The Major smiled, thinking, 'Oh so easy.'

He had never planned such a successful operation like this before and was completely taken aback by just how easily the actual situation developed. The fires on the Finch estate burned long into the night. Screams bellowed in desperation; cries of the dying engulfed in a ring of fire. Hysterical laughter came from the desperadoes' enjoyment in seeing the house and bunkhouse go up in roaring flames, with escape impossible if not from the fire, then from the waiting shotguns.

A man with his power forever diminished walked the killers into the opened door of his bank. His guards were completely in shock at the shotguns being pointed at them, whilst the safe door was opened, and the bags of booty given into the eager hands of the masked gang of thieves.

Coming from behind, the throats of all three, the two guards and Finch, were cut.

The Major's eyes gleamed as he looked at the several bags of gold coins, with bags initialled with the marking US Army Bullion.

He clapped his hands, saying, 'Let us ride, we skirt Uvalde and make for Eagle Pass. Over the Grande and into Mexico. We have friends waiting. We have money to burn. This town Bandera,' he pretended to wipe tears from his eyes, 'Why it's so poor.' The killers all laughed.

Chapter 14
THE RIO GRANDE

A further two days of tracking brought the Rangers to a bullet-riddled signpost showing the direction that would take them into the cattle town of Bandera. As they closed in on the town Tom and his team ran into a column of troopers who informed them of the Finch estate massacre, that included the robbery and abduction of 14-year-old Tina Santorio. The troop was one of two columns that had been dispatched from Fort Lancaster. in addition, Fort Bliss, which was situated in El Paso, had been informed that the army's bullion had been taken out of the Bandera Finch bank.

The troop's acting officer, one Lieutenant Parker, gave his opinion that the killers could well be on their way to crossing the Rio Grande and the safe arms of Mexico, Santa Negras their heading, known as the town of a thousand killers. Just where they would cross one could only guess. Tom told Parker that they had one of the best trackers in Texas with them: Drew Adams. The Lieutenant wished the Rangers good hunting, ending by saying, 'Be careful, Captain McBane, these boys you chase are deadly.'

***

On an open road some five miles south of Eagle Pass the Rangers finally arrived on the banks of the Rio Grande. Drew pointed at the tracks that were showing the killers' entry, crossing the river at its lowest point.

Drew turned to Tom and spoke. 'It looks like they crossed the Grande here, Tom. Looks like we've lost 'em.'

Jesse said, 'Can't we cross? We ain't that far behind.'

Drew smiled. 'No way, Jesse. They look to be on a heading for Santa Negras, eh, Tom?'

Tom sighed. 'No man in his right mind would contemplate going there. It is a town of a thousand killers. A refuge for all that is evil.'

Joe said, 'Six against a thousand. Then it has got to be a no.'

Ike, smiling, winked at Joe, saying, 'Yeah, but there ain't gonna be a thousand coming back now, will there?'

Tom, nodding, said, 'Ike may have something there. Yeah, we could wait. Jesus knows we have come this far, a few more days ain't gonna hurt us none. Would not seem right for us to give up now.' He pointed to an area that he thought would give them most concealment. They gazed over at a jagged rock formation that was almost hidden by a clump of willows. 'Over by them rocks, those willows. They would be a perfect ambush point. Walt, the horses, take them back aways to graze.'

They looked over at a rocky ridge with covering willows. The trees hung down, with branches stretching into the river.

'We got supplies, boys. I would say we could last out a week or more.'

Joe said, 'Seems that's settled then. I'm thinking we are due a break, Tom. I'd hate to go back to Austin leaving those killers loose.'

Tom slowly nodded. Jesse, scratching his chin, looked at them all. Jesse enquired of Tom, 'What if they don't return?'

Tom gave a deep sigh. 'Then there ain't nothing we can do, Jesse. But I am a thinking that lady luck, well, she is due... due to come on out and shine on us.'

***

Five days later.

The Rangers lay in the enclosed rock formation that overlooked the Rio Grande, with their horses grazing unsaddled a good distance away. Walt sat on watch with a clear view of a cloud of dust that suddenly appeared, coming from the Mexican side, on the river's far bank. Waterfowl scattered, taking flight. The sound of a gunshot and a falling bird brought the Rangers into position, crawling to their prearranged ambush positions and taking aim, waiting for the four riders in grey to come into range of their rifles. The horses in their unease stopped grazing and stood with ears pricked. Tom smiled. 'Just a little closer.'

Joe whispered, 'There's only four of them, Tom. Where's the other two?'

Tom nodded. 'Four, with one pack horse trailing.'

Tom looked through a pocket scope.

'They're wearing the grey – they're our killers, boys. We take them mid water. Blow them out of their fucking saddles. We empty on em.' Drew ground his teeth. 'For Lief, Howard. No mercy!'

The killers, unaware, were now mid-stream. They were smoking, drinking, laughing as they passed the liquor bottle to eager grabbing hands. The leading rider was putting the bottle up to his mouth when Tom ordered his men to fire. Their aim was true; the lead rider, the one called Duke, took a bullet that broke the bottle of rye and entered his head. He fell backwards into the river.

The others were then hit, they too falling from their mounts into the Grande river. Their confused horses splashed madly as they raced out in panic up the bank. Passing the Rangers they raced over to the open grassland, mixing with the Rangers' mounts. The Rangers looked down on four dead killers, floating down the river. A white flour bag with eye holes was caught in the reeds.

***

Meanwhile two desperadoes, Major Jack Stark and his loyal Corporal Sneeze Eliot, were settling down on the farm of Harry Stark, Jack's late father's brother. Uncle Harry, though, was none too pleased to see the sudden appearance of his nephew, knowing extremely well that any wrong act or word would set the psychopathic killer's mind off and he would be liable to do any insane thing. Even kill him.

Jack Stark was a clone of his evil brother, Frank, a man to be feared, a man who hated everything of authority. Like his father, Frank, he despised obeying the law.

Had not the army caught and hung his rebellious evil father for a multitude of rape robberies and murder?

Brother Harry had at one time been forced by the elder brother to take part in these evil acts, but that was back then, when the gun was the only law. Long before the army and the Rangers came into existence, the peacekeepers.

The three sat around the cabin's whiskey-loaded table, Jack's present to his only living relative, Uncle Harry. The whiskey had come from the Cassidys' peach farm. Harry would look after the army gold bullion, melting it down and obliterating the government stamp.

It was the voice of Sneeze that was pointing a finger at Harry and saying to Jack, 'Fuck, Jack, we aren't leaving the gold with him, are we? Because if you are then we need to pre-weigh it, cannot say I would trust a one-time fucking robber with our booty.'

Jack snarled, 'You just be careful what you say, Sneezy boy. Harry is a Stark, the blood that flows through those veins, my father's blood, my blood. Not only that, even with him being older than in his heyday, I would also still take him to outdraw you. Best you keep that hole in your fucking face shut.'

Sneeze gave a grunt and nodded a sort of apology to Uncle Harry. Jack had been born in El Paso in the upstairs room of a gambling house, 'The Lucky Strike'. His mother, a famed call girl named Sally Craven, had died at his birth. And it was Uncle Harry who had brought him to the fold, his father Frank having no time for his son. The boy was forever cutting up young animals, born with a love of killing. At the early age of fourteen years, he killed his first man, the local baker's son, George Mason, a nineteen-year-old who had caught Jack breaking in and stealing bread. Jack had to somehow disappear and became a ship's cabin attendant on the paddle boat the *Golden Goose*, a gambler's river retreat that ran the Mississippi. There he would learn his craft of stealing and was known to have murdered quite a few drunken money carriers, by clubbing and throwing his victims into a watery grave. Again, he was seen to be in the act of a murderous intention and had to scarper back into Texas, to seek his father out in the hope of joining up with his band of killers. It was his Uncle Harry who informed him of his father's trial and death by hanging at Fort Bliss. Still, he joined his father's gang of merciless killers, eventually becoming their leader. That was until his fall, the taking of a sixteen-year-old Houston girl and a sentence of ten years imposed on him. Soon the word was out that Jack was not happy, and he ordered his gang of marauding cretinous servants to get him out.

The way the escape was planned was for his men to capture the prison warden's wife and so bring about his release. This they did, bringing them one perfect exchange, an exchange that included the release of his cell mate, Sneeze Eliot, a white-haired half-caste, half Mexican and half European, with staring ice-cold blue eyes. A true oddball who was not far behind Jack in his lengthy list of killings. A slimy weasel of a man who stood just five feet six and carried as sick a mind as Stark. Jack had reached the age of twenty-five with an ever-increasing total that stood at thirty-four sometimes sadistic killings, murders in the first degree. One cattle man's loss of twenty or so long horns that had been taken across the Rio Grande into Mexico did however cause the capture of several of his gang and their following execution by hanging. Bob Parker had organised the victorious posse that had secured the gangs. Jack swore to make Parker pay. But first things first, he was now down to five gang members who, along with himself, were on the run, running away from a 30-man chase. Jack found himself left with two options, either stay in Santa Negra safe on the Mexican side of the Rio Grande or join the confederate army.

Robert E Lee was desperately asking for men. Men who he hoped would drive the blue-coated infidels out of the south. Lincoln was already taking Yankee gunboats into Galveston. Jack chose the army of Lee. A choice that would take his remaining five into doing what they were best known for – killing without mercy. It was not being able to stand the orders coming from confederate army major Percival Howard that decided Jack to take charge, by having Howard killed; a bullet from his gun would silence the unsuspecting Major. It was in a battle in the heart of the Louisiana woods against the Union, led by Lieutenant Devlin, that Jack Stark got the opportunity to play out his murderous action. He mercilessly shot the major in the head, with Sneeze Eliot seeing to Howard's loyal corporal. The confederate confusion led to Devlin gaining a victory after the loss of several of his troop.

Jack now wore the major's coat, Sneeze donning the slain corporal's jacket. He had smiled on seeing the soldiers in blue putting their dead along with the rebels into a grave. Captured and released and following a campfire massacre the six desperadoes were left to commit their evil deeds.

***

The next morning brought relief to Harry Stark as he gazed at his nephew's departure with that snake of a partner Eliot. They looked to be heading east, maybe Austin. No matter; someone somewhere was going to die.

Chapter 15

HOMEWARD

One hour later on an eastern trail that would take the Rangers back to their base in Austin, the men found themselves riding with a string of horses and a supply wagon holding the killers' saddles and weapons. Sadly, they had no Mary Beth to take into Uvalde and a waiting Howard Jackson.

Drew, who had been scouting ahead of the main party, returned, telling them that he had come across two horse tracks, showing that two of the killers had never crossed. He added that they were on a heading east. He snarled, saying, 'Bastards never crossed, they turned back east, we missed them.'

Tom spat. 'I'm sure we'll be hearing from them again. Those two won't stop. Let's get these horses into Uvalde and give Howard the bad news. No Mary Beth, for fuck's sake!'

***

Later, the Rangers gave Howard the upsetting news of the probable death of Mary Beth Binch; she had not been with the four dead. What remained, and the only hope left for her, was that she was still with the missing two.

Howard's evil Major and Corporal were the ones un-accounted for after a close examination of the four desperadoes' bodies. But the lawmen thought that a miracle would need to happen for any hope of Mary Beth surviving. Of course, there was always the off chance of her being left in Santa Negras. If so, then she would be better off dead.

Drew, who had returned to his tracking, was finding that the tracks left by the killers were fading out, becoming lost in muddy ground due to a period of heavy rain. Soon they had disappeared completely.

***

Eight days later, and with night falling from an already black sky, the two desperadoes found themselves travelling a road some ten miles east of Austin. Thunder was banging its roar, its warning, following the many forks of lightning that speared across the panoramic landscape. The never-ending sheets of heavy rain bounced off the riders oilskin capes and leggings and they rode with bandanna-covered faces and hats firmly tied down. It was through this blanket of rain that the yellow glow of a storm lantern showed in a lonely homestead window.

The riders approached with eyes peering over their bandannas. The Major, Jack Stark, a large six-foot hulk of a man, pointed to the light. His accompanying Corporal, Sneeze Eliot, nodded. They entered a track leading up to the house, coming to a large cabin with front veranda and all-around balustrade. The cabin sat back looking onto a muddy, soaked flower garden. The whole was surrounded by white-painted wicker fencing. They reined in beside a small gate entrance. Jack motioned for Sneeze to dismount. Sneeze, nodding, jumped down from his horse. He turned, catching Jack's reins being thrown to him. Then Jack got down from his mount. Sneeze scurried to the gate and opened it. He bowed, moving one arm in an underhand action, like some matador's held cape.

Jack pulled down his bandanna mask, from a face of heavy stubble. He smiled. Nodding, he then raised a gloved finger over to a barn. He whispered, 'Get these horses out of this shit, over to that barn. See if there is fresh.' He grabbed Sneeze by the shoulder. 'Take care.' He then put his finger up to his eyes and twirled it. He pointed to the cabin.

'We make sure that whatever is in there is all we have. Take a good look around. We want no surprise party quickly visiting us.'

Sneeze nodded. With the horses trailing behind him, he slipped and slid in a rush to the barn, one hand tightly gripping the reins and his other pulling out a pistol from its sheath. The lightning forked, the thunder rolled. Jack, pulling out his pistol, slowly and silently moved through the gate and onto the veranda. He carefully moved up to the window that was showing a shaft of light. He could hear music. A piano was playing; the young female voice of Janine Dupree singing a French ballad.

At the window he peered in, to see her sitting at a small grand piano. Janine was playing and singing. In a rocking chair sitting opposite, swaying, and humming in time to the music, was Colette. Her long coal-black hair hung over one shoulder. Her hands were busy sewing. She was working on a patchwork quilt.

Jack's eyes flashed and he licked his lips. Turning, he looked to see Sneeze, who was creeping towards him. His boots, caked with mud, caused him to slip on the veranda's wet floor. Sneeze snarled, 'Shit!' Jack put a finger to his lips. 'Sshhhhhuuushhh.' Sneeze pulled down his mask from a shallow clean face, with cold ice-blue eyes. He smiled, whispering, 'All clear, Jack.' He jabbed a finger at the cabin. 'We've what is in there, fresh mounts in the barn. Er, so what we got, brother?'

Peering under the arm of Jack, he looked through the gap in the curtain. Jack bent down to his ear.

'The woman, she's mine. You got the girl. I know how you've a liking for a tight pussy.'

Sneeze rubbed his hands, grinning. Jack pulled down on his shoulder. They backed off, away from the window, and crept to the door. Jack grinned, pointing up at a sign that hung over the door frame. He nudged Sneeze, who was scratching his chin, and Sneeze asked in a whisper, 'What's it say, Jack?'

The sign reads PARISIAN DREAM. WELCOME.

Sneeze again whispered, 'What's it saying?'

Jack smiled and whispered, 'Ain't yeh ever done any fucking school? It is la-de-dar French shit.' He winked looking face to face. 'Why, it is a-saying, welcome to fun night. Come on in to dip yeh dicks.'

Sneeze grinned and winked back. 'Oh well, you and me brother. we most certainly gonna dip our fucking dicks.'

Jack with a silent motion lifted the latch and pushed. It was locked. He shook his head and backed off a few paces. Waving his pistol he motioned for Sneeze to stand back.

Sneeze bowed and with his hat did the matador's cape swoop. Jack charged the door. His body weight hit with force, causing the door to cave in.

The women screamed as the door gave way, its lock flying across the floor. Jack crashed into Janine, who flew off her piano stool, running into Colette's arms. Colette reacted by hurling her embroidery at him. She looked at a shotgun that was leaning by a cupboard. Dragging her terrified daughter she made for the gun. She froze on hearing the voice of Sneeze, looking back over her shoulder to see Sneeze standing at the open door with his pistol pointing at them.

Sneeze, giving a wicked smile, spoke. 'Oh, no, no, no, lady, I would not do what you are thinking.' He gave a shake of his head. 'It would be a most foolish act on your part. Why?' he pouted. 'You may very well ask why because, dear lady, I would be inclined to blow your fucking brains out.'

He pointed over to Jack who sat grinning and kicking off his boots. Pulling off his oilskin cape and undercoat he sat on the piano stool and took off his leggings and pants. Removing his waistcoat and shirt he faced them in long johns.

'Er, like I was a-saying you would be a-missing one long night of love making. As you can see my brother is ready, he's raring to go.'

The two men laughed hysterically. Sneeze continued, 'Me blowing you away, well, we'd be having to give it all to little missy.'

He waved his pistol at Janine, who was cowering behind Colette's back.

'She'd be a having all the fun. I lie not to you in saying what a fucking fun night you would be a missing, dick-dipping nonstop.'

Colette grabbed Janine and hugged her closer. With fiery breath and in a French accent she snarled, 'Get out of my home now, yeh hear me! You pair of retarded scumbags.' Her eyes blazed. 'Do you know who I am, whose home you have dared to enter, who my daughter is? Well, do you, yeh two pieces of slime? Yeh vile pigs!'

The two looked at each other. They pointed at Janine. They shrugged their shoulders with a mystified look on their faces.

'Oh well it's plain to see you don't. My husband is a Ranger, a Ranger, do your cloth ears hear me?'

There was a silence that was only broken when the girl began to sob uncontrollably. The two men acted out a show of fear. Sneeze began to bite his nails. Jack went over to him, hugging him. Then they had another bout of hysterical laughter. Jack pointed at a now frightened Colette. He shouted at her, 'Get that nice French arse of yours into that fucking bedroom now!' He spat, rubbing his hands in expectation. 'You dirty no good French whore.' He scratched between his legs. 'My balls are full, they need to empty. You'd best not give me any French pox.'

Colette, with fists flying, went for Jack, with Janine screaming and clinging on for dear life. 'No Mamma, no.'

Jack struck out and Colette fell to the floor. Turning to Sneeze he shouted, 'Get that little missy out of here, out of my way. I'm gonna ram this Parisian bitch.'

Sneeze rushed in and violently pulled Janine away from her mother. The girl was gasping, sobbing, 'Mamma, Mamma, Ma—' Sneeze slapped and shook her. He snarled, 'Shut the fuck up. You be a good girl. Yeh you be nice for daddy. You ain't ever gonna have a night like this, little missy.'

Janine began to kick out at Sneeze. 'Let go of me, you horrible little man, you pig, you dirty pig!'

Sneeze slapped her hard. Her eyes swimming, she looked over at her mother, who was being dragged by the hair out of the parlour. Colette cried out, 'Please, please... I beg you... let my daughter go... please.'

She held out a hand, blood flowing from her nose and mouth. 'Don't you touch her! You, you bastard!'

Jack kicked her. She cried out. Janine screamed. Sneeze shook her. 'Shut the fuck up or you'll get the same as Mamma.'

He stared at her. 'Don't you go fighting me, I'm your lover boy.' He pouted. 'My dick's at attention. It's wanting you, little missy,' shaking her and snarling, 'Your bed, where's your bed?'

Janine, with a look of fear, glanced over at a door. Sneeze, smiling, picked up the storm lantern and walked to the door, dragging the sobbing girl behind him. He kicked the door open and entered the room. The parlour fell into darkness.

In the dark, cries of women in pain could be heard, and as the lightning flashed, heavy rain could be seen pouring in through the open door. The parlour lit up briefly, showing the piano keys stripped and lying like scattered dominoes on the parlour floor. Thunder roared.

***

One hour later and lightning struck. Sneeze walked into the parlour. He wore an oilskin cape over his long johns with boots and hat. He pulled the frightened Janine towards the cabin's open doorway. The girl wore only a night slip and walked barefoot. She slipped and knocked over a glass dish that smashed when it hit the floor. Whilst down on her knees she palmed a small sharp glass spear, before being violently lifted to her feet. Sneeze pushed her through the cabin door out into the heavy downpour.

Sneeze walked her off the veranda, pushing her forward onto the mud-soaked garden. Lightning flashed and thunder rolled.

Sneeze snarled angrily, 'Well, where the fuck is it?'

Janine indicated with an outstretched arm to the back of the cabin. Sneeze reluctantly walked through the mud to the side of the cabin. He saw a slim wooden detached box. 'Is that it?'

She nodded.

'Well, git on in there. Do not be a-taking all night. I am fucking cold, soaked to the fucking skin out here. Yeah, and do not be trying to run from me cause if you do and I catch yer…'

He wagged a finger at her, then spat and rushed back under the veranda, shouting out, 'Off yer get now.'

Janine rushed to the privy and entered. Lifting her now-soaked night gown she sat on the toilet box. She began to make stabbing movements with the glass spear, tears streaming down her face.

Sneeze sat on a bench under the veranda's shelter. The rain hammered down onto the roof above him. He tried to light a cheroot but failed. Tossing it away, he pulled the oil cape over his body. From the cabin, he heard Jack roar, 'Hey, you greedy little bastard. You done with little Missy? I am finished with her ma.'

Sneeze stamped his foot and shouted back, 'Yeh I'm all done brother, she's in the privy. I'm ready for her mamma. Hope yeh ain't knocked all the give out of her?'

He heard Jack's hysterical laughter. Jack screamed back, 'Oh, don't you worry none, she ain't no give left, she's fucking dead.' He began to giggle. 'I have cut the French whore's throat. She done my face with scissors. Oh, that girl of hers, she gonna pay for that, she be getting the full fucking treatment.'

In the darkness of the toilet Janine stared. Tears began to flow on hearing the bellowing voice of Jack coming from the cabin, that her mother had been murdered.

Gripping the spear tighter she cut deep into both wrists. Blood began to spurt and pump from the wounds. The spear slid from her hand, blood falling, forming pools at her feet. Her eyes closed and she slumped forward.

Sneeze shook his head and spat before rising to his feet and stumbling on his way to the privy door. He banged a fist on the door, shouting, 'Hey missy, you all done in there? It does not take a fucking hour to have a shit. Get that arse of yours wiped and get yourself out. My brother, well he is a-waiting.'

There was only silence. He shouted once again, 'Get that arse of yours out now! You hear? My brother's a-wanting you. He is a-gonna punch that peehole of yours and…' He looked up at the sky. 'I'm getting fucking soaked out here.'

With that he pulled open the privy door. A flash of lightning lit the inside. The girl sat slumped forward, with her wrists slashed, blood pouring from the wounds. A pool lay at her feet with a glass spear floating on it.

Sneeze turned away, slamming the door shut. He scurried, stumbling, falling onto the muddy sludge. Cursing, he raced back to the cabin, shouting, 'Looks like we have hit a pair of fucking queens, brother. The girl, she done slit her wrists. She's fucking dead too.'

When he reached the cabin door Jack shouted, 'Get fucking dressed, we are out of here. Fucking hell, what we gonna do now, brother? Big bad mister Ranger, what is he gonna do to us? I am so fucking scared I could piss in my pants.'

A short silence was followed by his hysterical laughter. Sneeze, sniggering, joined in.

'We got fresh mounts in that barn, brother.'

'Good. Get dressed. Saddle up, leave ours out in the field.'

Sneezed held up a gold locket and chain and put it around his neck.

The two killers were soon out on the open road in the driving rain, stopping only briefly to take in the sign telling them it was 50 miles to San Antonio.

They followed the sign, not bothering to look back on a lonely homestead without a door, that had allowed the sheets of rain to pool on its lounge floor.

Chapter 16
HEARTBREAK

Seven days later and the Rangers found themselves back home, riding down Main Street, Austin. They carried thoughts of a job only half done, one uncomplicated mission that they knew had to be finished. Two sadistic killers still out there – this they could never allow. But some poor souls in the state of Texas they knew were suffering. Now the waiting period, the call, the wire, that they felt surely would arrive, pinpointing their continuing acts of horror.

Tom had thanked the Lord that he and his men had suffered no losses. What losses they had seen would remain with them forever. How could a man ever rid his mind of Uvalde, Bandero, the Nielsens and the Cassidys. Each with its own act of horror.

Howard Jackson and the horrific story of Pastor Higgins and the burning of his house of the Lord, then closer to home the murders of Lief Sorensen and his family.

The Rangers stopped at the horse rail outside the law office, and in unison wearily dismounted. They looked to Walt and Jesse to unsaddle, feed and water their horses. Tom stretched and yawned before telling them to hang around some, that information, fresh orders,could be awaiting them in the office. There just might be a wire, could need to talk with them. Walt looked over at Joe, who was tying his horse to the rail, rubbing his back.

'Leave mine here, Walt. If I'm not needed, then I'm home.'

Jesse nodded over to the saloon. 'We will be over in the Dog if you are a-needing us, Tom.'

Drew smiled. 'Sounds like an excellent idea, Jesse. Get some of this dust out of my airway.' He looked at Tom, who stamping his feet. Tom waved a hand at them.

'Yeah, that's fine, boys. Call yeh if needed. If I do not, then take it yer done for the day.'

Ike looked up at the sky. 'Yeah, couple a more hours it will be dark.' He rubbed his stomach. 'Yeh know, I'm starved for some good grub. Think I'll eat first.'

He walked away, waving back at them. 'Catch you boys later.'

Tom walked off, still stamping down on his feet. Joe tied his horse and followed him to the office.

Tom scowled, 'God damn feet fallen asleep on me, be old age creeping up on me, Joe.'

He put a hand on the door handle and turned to Joe. 'Let's just hear what kinda holiday Jonjo's been having. Don't think I could take anymore shit.'

Joe put a hand on Tom's shoulder. 'I will go over and check out the wire office. Could be news on the two. If not, then I am home, Tom.' He shook Tom's shoulder.

'Oh, I'm forgetting to tell yer, I wired Colette, told her I was bringing you over for dinner.' He whispered, 'It's our anniversary. Janine, well, she's making that onion soup that you like. Colette, well she be on with some fine fillet steak, Tom.' He once more shook Tom's shoulder. 'We've got dauphinois, fresh baked bread and wine from Bordeaux.'

'Jesus Christ, Joe, you're making me hungry. Better you confirm my seat at that fine table, Joe.'

Joe winked, turned and walked across the street. Tom shouted after him, 'Yeah good, Joe, er, let me know, I will hold my dinner back. Yeah, you can tell Walt to leave my horse saddled.'

Joe put up a hand up as he climbed the steps to the wire office. He opened the door and went in. A bell rang from above the door as Joe entered. Joe looked down at the figure of clerk, John McFee, who was lying back in a large leather chair with his mouth wide open, snoring. Joe smiled and with his hand held high began to ring the bell in one long continuous movement. John's eyes shot open. Muttering to himself, he looked up at Joe and began to fumble. 'My spectacles, er…'

Joe smiled. 'They're on your head, John.'

John felt for them, looking embarrassed. 'So they are, Joe. You boys just got back?'

Joe nodded. 'Has anything for Tom come in, John?'

'Wire did come in, was some congratulations thing, I gave it to Jonjo.'

'Anything on the two? Tom's asking for anything, John.'

'Sorry Joe, nothing on those two. I must have sent out a hundred wires for information on those bastards,' shaking his head. 'Got nothing back as yet, Joe.'

Joe sighed. 'Oh, they will be dishing out their evil on some poor souls. That I am certain of, we just gotta keep our ears open. Oh, Colette, my wire?' John pointed to the tray on his desk.

John shook his head. 'Still in the tray, Joe. Colette, well she ain't been in town this last week or so.' Scratched his head. 'I did speak with her friend, Chrissy Adams. She ain't seen her either. Ain't seen no head nor tail of her, Joe.'

Joe quickly span on his heel and left the office. John stood and waved a paper and gave Joe a half shout. 'Joe, you want your wire?'

Silence. There was no reply. John threw the paper back into the tray. 'Guess not.'

Back in the law office Jonjo placed a cup of coffee in front of

Tom. He was reading a wire. Suddenly the door flew open, and a grim-looking Joe came in. Jonjo said, 'Fresh coffee in the pot, Joe.'

Joe shook his head and stared out of the window. 'Thanks, but no, Jon.'

Tom smiled, waving the wire. 'We got a big thank you from the Governor, Joe. Still wants the two though.'

Joe said, 'Yeah good, Tom.'

Tom looked at Joe and threw down the wire. 'Hey, come on, man, what's going on? Why the face?'

Joe shrugged, sighing deeply. 'Could be nothing, I suppose, but John Mcfee, well, he says, Colette, she ain't been in town all week.'

Tom looked at Jonjo, who scratched his face. Tom asked, 'Would that be unusual for her not to come into town?'

Joe nodded. 'Yeah, I would say it was. It gets kinda lonely out there on my spread. She, along with Janine, they try to get in for a natter. Seems her friend Chrissy Adams, well, according to John, Chrissy ain't seen head nor tail of Colette for well over a week now. Bit worrying, yeh know.' Jonjo walked forward, putting his hand on Joe's shoulder.

'That could be down to the weather, Joe, we have been having lots of rain. It has been heavy rain. Been pouring for these past two weeks. Seems Texas has never had so much water. I do not remember as much falling, ever.'

Jonjo held up his arms and shook his head. 'They say the Pecos has flooded over.' He looked out of the window. There was a flash of lightning and a roll of thunder. 'Looks like we got more coming.'

Joe pointed at the clock. 'That clock right, Jonjo?'

Jonjo pulled out his pocket watch and nodded. 'Yeah, Joe, quarter to five. It will be dark in an hour.'

Joe gave a deep sigh, saying, 'I'm out of here, Tom. I'm praying Jonjo's right, that it's the storms.' He sighed. 'Yeah, don't think they would ride into town in heavy weather. No, I am sure about that.'

Tom stood as the lightning flashed and the thunder rolled. He banged his fist down on his desk. 'I'm coming with yeh, Joe. Let's get to the horses. Best put my skins back on.' He looked at Jonjo, shaking his head as he dressed quickly. 'Sorry, old friend, but I am asking for another day of your time. Cover for me, Jon.'

Jonjo winked. 'No problem, Tom. You and Joe better get going now, it's looking like another heavy night.'

***

The two Rangers trotted their horses down into Eagle's Valley. The lightning forked across the sky. Thunder followed. Tom shouted over the weather to Joe, 'Rain like this, it's fucking unreal.'

Joe shouted back, 'Farmers won't want it, what with the Pecos overflowing. Should be seeing my cabin now, Tom. Look for its light, over to the right.'

Tom, scanning, said, 'I'm looking, Joe. Nothing as yet.'

Joe, becoming worried, cried out, 'Something's wrong, Tom. We should be seeing something clearly at last.'

Joe kicked his horse into a gallop, racing it down a winding track. Tom followed, the lightning forks lighting up the cabin. There was no light in its window. Joe reined in at the white willow gate. Vaulting off his horse he raced up to the cabin door. It lay flat, off its hinges. He gasped, drawing his pistol. He entered. Tom reined in and dismounted. He walked up, stopped, and looked down at the door. Pulling out his pistol he too raced into the cabin.

For a moment a flash of lightning lights up the parlour. Tom enters to see the cabins disarray. The piano sits with its keys, black and white like discarded domino's covering the floor. Sheet music lying everywhere. One ear piercing cry comes out from the bedroom.

Two rats race across the floor, and out into the night. Lightening flashes Tom seeing a storm lantern, pick it up shakes it. From an inner pocket, he puts out a match. Striking it he likes up the lamp. Tom carried the light to the open bedroom door. He entered the room to see Joe down on his knees, by a bed showing the naked Colette, the bed soaked in her blood. Her throat had been cut. The body lay with most of the face missing; along with the eyes, the breasts were no more.

Joe heaved deep, uncontrollable sobs. 'Oh, my God, Colette, oh, baby.' He turned, hearing Tom entering. He cried out, 'Tom, fucking help me! Oh, Colette, see what they have fucking done, Tom. See what they have done!'

Tom picked up a discarded sheet and gently covered the body. Putting a hand on Joe's shoulder, he shook it gently, whispering, 'Come Joe, we gotta go look for Janine. We gotta find her. Let's go look. There is nothing left for you here, Joe. Collette, she has gone. Let's go look for Janine.'

Joe, his face frozen, rose stiffly to his feet. He raced past Tom and out of the bedroom. Tom, crossing himself, followed him out.

Tom brought in the lantern, its glow lighting up Janice's bedroom, to see Joe standing and holding his head in a rocking motion. Joe cried out, 'She's not here, Tom. Janine, she is not here. Oh my God, where's Janine? What have they done to her?'

Tom looked at the bed. It was empty, its sheet showing spots of blood. 'Let us go and look, Joe. Who knows, she could be hiding. Let us go and look now.' Tom turned and left the room. He walked over to the cabin door and stepped out onto the veranda. He shouted, 'Janine, come on out, baby. Uncle Tom's here. Tom's here with Daddy. If you're hiding, I know you're scared, it's Tom with Daddy. Please come on out.'

Joe rushed past him, shouting, 'The barn, Tom, she would hide away in the barn. Yeah, that is where… the barn, Tom.'

Tom, discarding the lantern, followed Joe out through the heavy mud towards the barn.

The two Rangers raced to the barn, slipping and sliding on the mud. The barn stood with its doors open wide. All was silent. Joe cried out, 'Janine, it's Daddy, baby. If you are in there, please come on out.'

There was a moment of silence, before Joe, realising that Janine would surely have answered their calls if she had been in the barn, said, 'Oh, my dear God! Where are you? Janine!'

He cautiously entered the barn with Tom close behind. He span around to see Tom with his pistol at the ready.

'My horses, they've gone. She ain't in here, Tom. They've fucking taken her. Just like Mary Beth. They have taken her, Tom! Oh, what we gonna do?'

Tom told him that his horses were out in the pen. 'We should get them in, out of this rain, Joe.'

Joe blinked, went to the door and looked out. He sighed.

'Those horses ain't mine, Tom, they ain't mine, I tell yer. They have fucking taken her. Oh, fuck, they have my daughter, Tom, Janine, she is only fifteen. Oh, sweet Jesus, help me, help me.'

Tom hugged Joe, whose eyes were full. They turned and walked out of the barn, their feet sloshing in the sloppy ground on the way back to the cabin. The wind started to pick up. The rain continued to pour. Suddenly they noticed the sound of a door banging, coming from the rear of the cabin. The Rangers stopped dead and held out their pistols.

'You take the left, Joe. I'll go right.'

Joe said anxiously, 'You, you think?'

'Let's go see, Joe, let's go look.'

Joe nodded and crept off to the cabin's left gable end. Tom went to his right. Tom came around the corner. He looked over at the privy door, which was opening and closing with the strength of the weather. Joe came round and looked at Tom, who was motioning to the door.

'Privy door, Joe. Best I shut it.'

Tom walked up to the door; as it flew open, the lightning flashes lit up the inside. The blood-soaked body of Janine lay slumped on the privy seat, her body in a half decayed state. Blow flies feasted on the remains.

Tom slammed the door shut. He slicked out onto the mud. Joe stared at him, looked at the privy. 'Tom. Tom – you okay? What's in there?'

Tom held up a hand. 'Don't yeh fucking go in there, Joe. Don't open that fucking door.'

Joe shuddered. 'Let me see Tom, I gotta see. Janine in there?' He cried out, 'Janine? Tom?'

Tom nodded his head. Joe raced past him and opened the privy door. He began to howl like a wounded coyote, crying out, 'Nooooo. Noooooo...'

***

A blazing fire engulfed the cabin. Joe and Tom stood back, watching the roaring flames. Joe turned to Tom, tears in his eyes. 'When the fire dies, I will bury them, Tom.'

He points over at a small hill that overlooks the valley. 'Over there. Up on that hill.'

Tom nodded sadly. Joe sighed deeply. 'They used to sit and picnic there. They loved watching the eagles glide over the valley.'

Tom replied, 'Yeah, I think they'd like that, Joe.'

A few hours later the two mounted Rangers were looking down onto the freshly dug grave. A sign read:

COLETTE AND JANINE DUPREE.
BELOVED WIFE AND DAUGHTER
REST IN PEACE 1867

The two crossed themselves before turning away. Tom pulled the two killers' horses as they passed the embers of the cabin where only its stack still stood.

***

Two weeks later in the office of law, Austin, Tom sat in his chair holding a mug of coffee. The door opened and Drew entered. Tom pointed at the stove. 'There's fresh coffee in the pot, Drew.'

Drew nodded as he walked over, selected a mug, picked up the pot and poured. 'Just caught Joe leaving. He was heavily loaded, Tom, I shouted but he did not stop, just gave me an over the shoulder wave.'

Tom sighed. 'Yeah. Joe – he is away for a spell. He handed me his badge. Said he was through with all the shit, the murders.'

'He's away after the two, ain't he?'

'Yeah. I told him to hang on to the badge, that he may well need to use it…'

Tom shook his head, drumming his fingers on the desk.

'Got a wire in last night, from up north, family brutally murdered.'

'You gave it to Joe?'

Tom held up a hand. 'I had to, he has been living in that wire office. Ain't we followed every fucking lead on those bastards?'

'So, Joe, he's going it alone?'

'Like a hound dog chasing a jack rabbit, he was saddled up, wearing a fierce determined look on his face. Like I say Drew, a hound dog after two jack rabbits, he was out through that door.' He sighed. 'I am just praying.'

'Praying, Tom?'

'Yeah, praying that he returns with a smile on his face.'

Chapter 17
HENDERSON

Joe had been given the wire that had been issued to all county telegraph offices throughout Texas. News had come to John McFee who had eagerly handed it over to the ever-waiting Joe.

John shook his head as he watched Joe race out and mount his horse for a ride that would take him to Henderson, over 200 miles north of Austin.

John informed Tom of Joe's departure after receiving a wire of a horrific homestead murder that had taken place up in Henderson. Tom had asked that John wire ahead to inform the law office of Joe's intended arrival and to aid him in any way they could. Tom had passed on to Drew why Joe was eager to leave and pursue what he knew had to be the work of the remaining brotherhood killers, although he knew that by the time Joe rode into Henderson the killers would be long gone.

Drew shrugged, saying 'You know something, Tom? if Joe had told me of his intentions, then I'd have gone with him.'

Tom patted Drew on the shoulder. 'Think he would a liked that, Drew, best thing he could have, a friend along with him, but knowing the man well, he would not want you to take a bullet, Drew.'

Drew shook his head and replied, 'Jesus, Tom, he has sure got to avoid those two evil bastards. He is gonna need some help.'

***

Stark and Eliot had smiled on seeing the two women hanging out the family washing. Mother and daughter, with the mother looking attractive, not more than 38 years old, the daughter a young woman in her early teens. The killers had spent some time taking in any foreseeable problems but they found none. The homestead had only a weak-looking pair of males in residence, the elder of which looked to be the woman's husband. The younger could well be his brother. They, along with two youngsters, a young boy and girl of kindergarten age, were the only opposition.

Sneeze asked Jack how he wanted to play the hit on the lonely homestead, which was situated around five miles from Henderson, with no immediate close neighbours. Stark replied that they would take out the men, and with a gun put to the two children's heads the women would ensure a most enjoyable night of food and drink followed by an hour or two of humping.

It came as no surprise to Sneeze that Jack's planned hit played out most successfully. With the young man answering a knock on the cabin door, and being shot as he opened it, the elder, who was sitting unarmed was executed where he sat, taking several bullets to the head. The women were made to serve up a meal and supply the raw whisky, with the children being locked in an outdoor storage shed.

The night was one of continuous rape with the desperadoes making several exchanges. They laughed hysterically with the children cowering, hugging each other, absolutely terrified at hearing the screams of their mother coming out of the homestead and into their dark locked prison shed.

Come sunrise and the homestead was on fire. The screams had long since died, with four bodies burning in its interior. Outside, the storage shed too was a fireball, with the children inside, while the killers were on their way to Stephenville.

***

It had taken Joe nearly two weeks to make Henderson and he was warmly welcomed by the local law officer, Bill Armstrong. He explained that he had received a wire from Tom McBane about Joe pursuing the two remaining brotherhood members and that the price for their arrest was now a cool 50,000 dollars. Bill added that this had sparked off a few well-known state bounty hunters to take up the search. Bill sighed, for there were two insane killers who could be anyone, as nobody had a clue what they looked like. Young or old, fat or thin, identification was urgently needed.

Joe told Bill of the one witness, a wire officer name of Howard Jackson down in Ulvalde.

Howard had seen the two confederate desperadoes. One was a well-built bull of a man wearing the uniform of a major. Howard estimated him to be in his forties. His companion, a corporal, was a weasel, a slimy piece of shite, a younger individual, much smaller but like his major completely insane.

Both carried sadistic tendencies that left no witnesses. Howard thought one of the brotherhood knew him, and that was why he was spared.

Bill told Joe that the murder incident at Rainbow Gorge was now more than three weeks old. He went on to say that the victims, the murdered family, were so severely burnt that they were unrecognisable.

He told Joe of the burnt-out shed that had held the two children, before finishing his report by telling Joe to plod on, that there was nothing here in Henderson to keep him. Of course, he was welcome to stay and await the next wire, because as sure as God was his judge those two devils hadn't finished. They were two mad, insane pieces of shite that had to be stopped. Bill, wagging a finger, added, 'I do mean stopped, Joe, exterminated, need I say more?' He then offered Joe a night's accommodation in his jail cell, adding with a wink that it would not be locked. Joe smiled, saying he would rest up on the offer, thus giving his horse a rest before resuming his pursuit of the killers come daybreak, thinking of heading west.

Bill told him he would see that his horse was fed and watered and would also get a good lady friend of his to cook up a meal.

Joe said, 'I got dollars, Bill.'

Bill said, 'Best you keep them, you are going to need them. I've a feeling your quest is going to take time. My treat, on the house. If I am ever down Austin way, I would expect you to put me in a cell and feed me.' They both laughed.

Bill finished by saying that Tom McBane had told him the reason for Joe's hunt for the killers, and that he had only to ask if he needed support, support of any kind, that he could organise a small posse if needed. After all these killers had committed their evil in Henderson, so they would aid Joe while in Rusk County.

'We are only a small community Joe, fewer than 900 residents, but that family, the Parkers, they were good people, Joe. Hardworking souls who had friends, were loved by many and will be sadly missed.'

Chapter 18
STEPHENVILLE

Sneeze Eliot sat in the corner of the Dirty Dog saloon after Jack had sent him in to see if there was any possibility of a woman being abducted, and brought back to their camp, by a dry rocky riverbed, where Jack eagerly waited. He easily recognised the women who were prostitutes, knowing that they would be a no for Jack. He had asked for a young virgin. On a nearby table a guy in the uniform of the union was muttering in an intoxicated manner about a shipment of gold bullion that was being brought to some out-of-town relay station.

Sneeze decided to join the soldier and learn more. He took his bottle of red-eye over and took a seat alongside the well-soaked soldier. Stephenville was a town of drovers, men that brought beef to the many scattered army forts than ran in all directions and covered the state of Texas. The beef for a total of the eight forts that were in line with state security. The Native American Comanche had been an ongoing problem. Settlers had not been allowed to settle; the buffalo were in decline, along with the red man, for his existence was threatened.

Sneeze had returned without a girl, to Jack's bitter disappointment, but the news of a gold bullion shipment had taken away any thought of a night's sexual pleasure. So it was early evening when the two desperadoes found themselves lying and viewing the relay station. Sneeze had told Jack how the soldier had giggled at him when he was asked how many would be guarding such a high-value cargo.

Slurring, the soldier replied, 'Why, you gonna rob it?'

Sneeze nudged him and gave a laugh and a wink, replying, 'Thinking about it.'

The soldier sleepily said, 'What, you gonna take down six federals and the four relay guys? Best you stick to your beef driving, cowboy.'

With that the soldier fell asleep and Sneeze left the saloon, returning to Jack Stark with his excitement about the gold that the army would take into the relay station, ready to be collected by incoming receivers, cattle barons that worked their herds on a never-ending cycle taking and supplying the army's fortifications. Stephenville was a cowboy town with less than a thousand residents, who were mostly drovers, dollar-a-day cattle herdsmen.

Sneeze giggled. 'Six guards, Jack, what yer think?'

Jack winked, smiled. 'Why we take them, squirrel, then we find us a delightful place to hide it. Then we let the search die down before we take it over to Uncle Frank.'

Sneeze spit out tobacco juice, saying, 'That uncle of yours is holding quite a lot of yellow rock of ours, Jack, hope he ain't looking to do a runner, calling on some of the old Stark gang members, because if it is like he was saying that your pa had call on twenty guns, then we have one mighty problem.'

Jack snorted. 'Frank, he'd never do that. You best keep those thoughts to yourself, squirrel. Do not let Uncle Frank hear you, that is if you are aiming to live a few more years. He gets his cut, he is happy with that. He is a Stark, never took a man down in his life.' Jack winked.

'So, how we gonna work it, Jack?'

'We ramble into that station after sundown, hide a couple of pistols near their outside privy. They will be wanting our sidearms which gives them a feeling of safety. We await the opportunity to enter that station unarmed and innocently looking for a rest-up. You are not feeling too good – we do not rush it. You need the privy, you leave, faking an illness, returning with the guns. We blow them apart and await the soldiers bringing in the booty; your drunken informer says a six-man escort. We let them dismount before we hit 'em with the Henry repeaters.'

'The four station attendants, Jack, won't they want to see them?'

'Sure, we sit their bodies at the table with a deck of cards and a bottle of rye, leaving the door open. Meanwhile I approach from behind the cabin and take 'em down, with you, my little squirrel, coming out of that privy. You wait for the safest choice before coming out. I shall be watching for your move. When you go so shall I.'

'You know , Jack Stark; you make it sound so easy.'

'Oh, it's far from easy, it has to be a sure thing, or we don't go.'

'So, you're saying, Jack, we have to gain entrance to that cabin?'

'Why that little squirrel brain of yours is beginning to think. Only other choice is if we can take 'em down with the Henry's but then they would need to be all outside. We gotta play it as it comes, as far as the army goes, well, that's the easy part.'

'I'm a hoping you're right, brother, but what if the beef suppliers send a few of their pick-up guys to take their payments?'

Jack spat. 'Then it's a no go. We cannot fill a fucking graveyard. Those barons won't send fewer than six well-armed cowboys, and if they do then we hit the weakest on their way home.'

Jack sat and watched, cursing the approaching drovers that had suddenly filled the relay station. He counted twelve gun-toting issues who looked to be well and truly into their mission of taking the pay dirt back to papa. Jack instantly gave Sneeze a nudge, saying, 'Let us get the hell out of here, we ain't got the boys with us. We ride to San Angelo and if we happen to come across a party of gold-carrying drovers, then things could change.'

It was early the following morning when the two desperadoes came across the two drovers that were driving a few strays in a southern direction.

Stark winked as he spoke to one drover. 'You stealing that beef, cowboy?'

The drover and head crewman for the Murphy ranch snarled at Jack, saying, 'I'm Andy Grant, head boy for the Murphy family. My companion here is Ben Shepard. We are taking these here strays back to the main herd that's on its way to Forts Worth, Graham and Gates.'

Jack gave a head shake and drew his pistol. Sneeze followed suit and shot Ben Shepard, putting several shells into his already lifeless body. Andy got as far as reaching his holster before Jack emptied his pistol into the Murphy head drover.

Sneeze shrugged. 'Tell me, Jack, why the cowboys? What we gonna do with the cows?'

'Why we gonna return them to the Murphys. Then my little squirrel, why, we take over the two vacancies left by Grant and Shepard. Give you and Jacky boy time to learn the cattle business before becoming ranch owners.'

Stark gave a hysterical laugh before adding, 'Oh, your brother Jack, he's got plans, Sneezy baby.'

Chapter 19

SAN ANGELO

Six months later, in Gloria's eating house, San Angelo, Tom McBane sat at a table eating breakfast. Across from him sat Pat Murphy, a fifty-year-old, well-built, six-foot red-haired fellow Irishman. Pat wore a neatly trimmed moustache and beard. He was holding aloft an empty mug, waving it across the room at a fine-looking lady. The lady, a forty-year-old, with a stunning well-kept figure, was smiling. Gloria Gains, who wore her auburn hair tied up in a bun, walked over to them holding a coffee pot.

She stopped and poured out into both mugs. Gloria winked, saying to Tom, 'This man drinks more coffee than whiskey. Now would yeh not think that unusual for a big Irish cattle ranch owner?'

Tom, leaning back, smiled. 'It's cheaper, Gloria, yeah whiskey would be far too costly for such a poor soul. A man with over four hundred head.' He picked up his mug and drank, smacking his lips. 'It's sure good coffee, girl.'

Pat pointed at his mug. 'With coffee like that Gloria I tell no lie, well it's just pure nectar. Why, must be the finest brew this side of Alabama.'

'Why, thank you, Pat Murphy, nice for a gal to be appreciated.' They laugh as the door opened, and two drovers left. It's then Joe Dupree entered un-noticed. He crept up behind Tom and spoke. 'Hope there is a cup in that pot for me, Tom McBane?'

Tom, with a look of surprise, stared at Pat. 'I know, I know that voice.' He stood and turned to see a smiling Joe, laughing.

'Oh, well I never, Joe! Where have you been keeping yourself this past year or so?' Tom turned to Gloria and Pat. 'This gentleman just happens to be my best friend, Joe Dupree.' He pointed to a chair.

'Get that arse of yours down at the table Joe, oh and meet my friends, Miss Gloria Gains, proud owner of this fine restaurant, and Mr. Pat Murphy, cattle ranch owner, out on the Sweetwater.'

Joe put out a hand to Gloria. 'Nice to meet yeh Gloria.'

Gloria on taking his hand, said, 'Any friend of Tom's is our friend, ain't that right, Pat?'

Pat held out his hand. 'Pat Murphy, a poor cattle ranch owner from out of the old country. County Mayo, Castlebar.'

Joe, smiling, took his hand. 'Joe Dupree out of County Cork. Pleased to meet yeh, Pat.'

Pat looked over at Tom, scratching his beard. 'Joe Dupree… you sure that's Irish?'

'Yeah, my mother's name was Regan, my father was French out of Auxerre. I was born in Cork.'

Pat nodding his head, looked at Tom and smiled. 'Born in Cork, I can go with that. You're Irish, Joe Dupree.'

Gloria, walking away, shouted over her shoulder, 'You want breakfast, Joe?'

'From what I've been hearing, bring it on over, Gloria, whatever.'

'One belly buster coming up, Joe.'

***

Joe mopped up the last of his breakfast. Pat looked at Tom and shook his head.

'That's one of the most horrific stories I have ever heard. Those bastards still running free… good God!'

Tom added, 'You should have seen it, Pat.'

Pat shook his head several times. 'I don't think so, Tom. There's no fucking way I'd want to come home to Maureen and find what Joe found.'

Pat turned to Joe. 'My wife, Joe, or Kathleen, my daughter. No fucking way would I want that. So sorry, Joe. You do not want any reminders coming from me.'

Joe sighed. 'Understandable, Pat. I went back to Austin to see Tom and Jonjo told me you'd moved here. He said you were working along with the army, something about a liaison with Fort Worth.'

Tom nodded. 'Right on the dollar, Joe. I'm not working along with Major Storie although he's a good man. There's a place with me, that's if… if you're thinking on a comeback, I could use a good man, Joe.'

Joe shook his head. 'Thank you, but no Tom. I have done with all that. I am still looking for retribution. Yeah, I am wanting those two.'

Pat looked at Joe; leaning back in his chair, he put up a finger. 'Why not come work for me, Joe, then if Tom hears anything at all on them evil bastards, well, you'd be free to go. From what I've been a-hearing, I just may let some of my boys ride with you.'

Joe smiled. 'You know something, Pat Murphy, I'd like to take you up on that offer. Your boys… couldn't ask them, Pat. These bastards are out of the devil's loins.' He shrugged. 'The job, yeah, I am all for it. But I know nothing about cattle, could not tell a cow from a bull.'

Pat leaned across the table and whispered to Joe. He pointed over at Gloria, who was drying dishes. 'Well, you see that fine girl over there, well, Gloria you could say, if she was cattle, well, she would be a nice cuddly cow!' He nudged Joe. 'Now a bull, well he'd be a-chasing her, bit like Tom McBane here.'

Pat put his fingers up to his head and made like horns. Pat made the sound of a cow, 'Mooooo, mooooo.' The three fell about laughing.

Gloria, with a stern look on her face and wagging a finger, shouted, 'I am watching you three. Why are you looking at me with those silly grins on your faces?' They continued their laughter. Gloria threw a towel at them.

Pat held up a hand. He nodded at Joe. 'Wouldn't want you working on the beef side, Joe.'

Joe said, with a puzzled look, 'How come, Pat… what other?'

'You'd be something like an overseer. I'd be wanting you to do the general running of the yard.' Looked at Tom, shrugged. 'He'd be seeing to supplies, bringing in the feed, repairs.'

Tom, smiling, gave a thumbs up. It had been a long day, with Tom promising Joe that he would feed any information on the killers to him. But San Antonio had not received any reports of further incidents that he could relate to their action. He told Joe they had gone to ground. A long day, with Pat taking Joe back to his ranch to begin a new life in the cattle business, with a promise not to reveal any of Joe's past horror and his search for retribution.

There he would meet up with the crew of drovers, and head man, Jack Stark, but would remain his own man, answering only to Pat. He would be in charge of handling supplies and general yard maintenance. He would get to know Cookie Warren, who would supply him with the weekly food order that would necessitate a weekly wagon ride into town. A young, able-bodied teenager, Cord Stewart, would come under his wing. He would also handle the safety of Pat's wife, Maureen and daughter, Kathleen, whilst Pat was seeing to the beef side, which would take him out of town on overland drives. Joe was already beginning to like his new nonviolent occupation.

Chapter 20

SWEETWATER

Three weeks later, out on Murphy pasture, drinking from the Sweetwater creek under a scorching hot sun, stood two horses. One, a brown and white Pinto, was drinking freely; it was saddled, with its reins hanging loose. On the saddle's horn hung a bow and quiver of arrows. By its side a magnificent coal black stallion was drinking. It was unsaddled, tied to a nearby hanging willow. Flies constantly attacked both, they nodded and shook their heads in defence.

In a kneeling position, filling a buckskin pouch, was a young Comanche brave. He suddenly jumped to his feet. The horses became disturbed, they stopped drinking, began to snort and neigh. The brave made a dash to reach the Pinto, putting a hand to the bow. He stopped, turning to see three men on horseback looking down on him.

Pat Murphy sat in the middle of the trio. His hands crossed, he leaned over on his saddle horn. To his right and left the others sat with rifles drawn across their saddles. Pat said, in a firm voice, 'My name's Pat Murphy and I own this land on which you trespass.' With an arm he motioned in all directions. 'North, East, South, and West is Murphy land. My warning signs are all around. You… you should be with your tribe over the Snake River. I do hope it is only water you're taking, and not my beef.'

The brave, spreading out his arms, spoke. 'I am One Knife, son of Little Owl. I stop only for water.' He pointed down at the skin water bag that lay on its side. 'I go to my father's camp. I take no beef.' The man to Pat's right is Jack Stark. On his face, a scar ran from one eye to his mouth. Heavy built with a six-foot frame, he pointed with his rifle at the black shiny stallion.

'That's one hell of a piece of horseflesh you've got there.' He put a finger up to his brow. 'Now where have I seen that black shine?'

They all gazed over at the horse. The rider to Pat's left, Sneeze Eliot, a half caste small slim-looking man with nearly white hair and ice blue eyes, shouted, 'Hey, Jack, I knows where we have seen him. I remembers now. Didn't we admire him up in Jed Collins yard?' Sneeze nodded to himself. 'Yes sir, he was with Jed.'

Jack smiled. 'Yeah, you got a good memory, Sneeze. Yeah, he was a-standing at Jed's.' He scratched his chin. 'Didn't he call that shine Midnight, after some Crow squaw he was a-humping?'

One Knife began to jump up and down in frustration. He started to shout, 'No, no, Midnight. Horse comes from Kentuckian trapper. Matt Price. I pay many racoons, beaver pelts, four fox skins, two black bear coats for him.' Pat nodded, and looking at his men, put up a gloved hand and wagged a finger. He turned to Jack and laughed.

'Now come on, Jack, Sneeze, we all fucking well know that Jed Collins… well, he never owned a decent horse in any of his born days. Fucking crippled miners' mules is all that is in his yard.' He pointed at the shine. 'Nothing like the class of that, never.'

Suddenly a shot rang out from the rifle of Jack Stark. One

Knife, clutching his breast, fell back into the creek. The black struggled to break free, the Pinto walked up to his outstretched body and sniffed it.

Pat spun round in his saddle, looked at the smiling face of Jack and snarled, 'Just what the fuck? Did I ask you to shoot the boy? Son of Little Owl. We will have the whole Comanche nation down on us.' He shook his head. 'You got nothing upstairs in that brain of yours. Fucking Jesus Christ, Jack.'

Jack looked around the back of Pat and, seeing Sneeze looking at him, he nodded. Sneeze dismounted, walked over to One Knife and kicked him. One Knife moaned. Jack put a second shot into the brave's head. One Knife shuddered then was still. 'Well, what do you think, Sneeze? A man shoots a fucking dirty Comanche horse stealer.' Sneeze nodded. He went over to the Pinto and removed the bow and the pouch of arrows. Stringing the bow and loading an arrow he pointed it at Pat.

Pat showed fear and alarm. 'What the fuck?' looking at Jack. 'What's he doing? Best you put that down, Sneeze. You fuck crazy or what?' They both began to laugh. Pat began to panic and went to withdraw his pistol, shouting, 'It's not funny, Jack.'

Jack nodded to Sneeze, who reacted by firing at Pat. The arrow went through his neck. Pat fell out of his saddle and rolled down the bank. From his neck spurted a fountain of blood. He began to shiver whilst Sneeze reloaded the bow and fired another arrow into Pat's heart. Pat closed his eyes for the very last time. Sneeze looked up at Jack, who was wagging a finger at him.

'Now look what you've gone and done, Eliot. What yeh got to say for yourself, boy?'

Sneeze, his mouth agape, stuttered, 'Jack, Jack yer just gotta believe me, my fingers lost all feeling, they just slipped.' There was a moment's silence before the two began to laugh hysterically. Jack dismounted, walked over and looked down on the two dead men.

'We'll lift Murphy, hang him over his horse. Leave them arrows in him. We take him in. The Indian,' he pointed to a clump of willows, 'put him under those trees, let the bobcats feed on him.'

He walked over to the black stallion; he went to stroke it. The horse reared up at him. Jack backed off. Sneeze smirked.

'Doesn't seem to like you, Jack. See the fire in that shine's eyes. Nasty.'

'Oh, but he will, Sneeze. He needs to be taught a fucking lesson on who's boss. He's mine. That Pinto you can take up to Jed Collins. Poor man's never had a decent horse in his born day. Best he has ever had is crippled miners' mules.' They both laughed as they struggled to lift Pat's body across his horse.

Sneeze walked over and untied the shine, retying him on the horn of Jack's saddle. 'Nice bit of horse flesh you've acquired there, Jack.'

Jack winked. 'Got it off some Kentucky trapper, er, name of Matt, Matt, er, Price.'

'Say Jack, yer think I should give the Pinto to the girl?'

Jack smiled, shaking his head. 'I know you, Sneeze, why that little squirrel brain of yours is thinking of humping her.' Peered at him. 'Not the right time yet, but soon, soon. I got plans, yeah, plans to change that Murphy ranch name. Gonna be Stark, hanging over that gateway.'

Sneeze shrugged. Jack pointed at the bow and quiver of arrows. 'Best keep that bow, them arrows, hidden out of sight. We may need them again.'

Later against the falling daylight, could be seen a silhouette against the skyline of Jack and Sneeze. They were riding out, pulling three horses, one carrying the body of Pat Murphy slung over it. They would arrive back at the main yard, where the evil Jack Stark would act out his plan of getting his men to mount up and give chase to a non-existent Comanche war party. He would of course keep them well clear of the west pastures, sending his men north.

***

Two months later, in the main area of the Murphy ranch yard, on what was a hot night, a lantern's yellow light spilled out of an open bunkhouse window. Through it the sound of a man's voice was heard, bellowing out, 'Damn well folded, Jesus Christ! He would only have a pair of fives.' A moment's silence is followed by belly rolling laughter. 'I'd a pair of royals. I had fucking kings.' There is more laughter and a stamping of feet.

Across from the bunkhouse sat a large white painted detached house. Standing on a rise, it overlooked a neat flower garden with a balustraded veranda. A light shone out of one downstairs window. There was the sound of a fiddle playing a jig.

In a rocking chair on the veranda sat the rocking figure of Jack Stark, with his feet up, resting on the rail. He sucked on a large cigar. In one of his shovel-like hands, he cradled a half bottle of rye whiskey. Rolling the cigar across his mouth, he lifted the bottle up to his cracked lips and drank. He began to choke; coughing, he grounded his feet. He stood and leaned over the balustrade; he vomited out onto the flower bed.

The rye bottle fell and rolled away. Jack, swaying, with spittle running from his mouth down his open shirt, began to open his pants, fumbling, and finally getting to urinate over the rail. From inside the house, the music stopped playing and the door opened. A beautiful young girl, Kathy Murphy, with long flowing red hair, walked out. She looked over at the figure of Jack pissing on the flowers. She shaded her green eyes and screamed, 'Mother, Mother, Mother!'

The drunken Stark just shook his head at her, grinning. Going full frontal at her he smirked, 'You want to play with Jack's fish pole? Come on, Missy Kathleen Murphy, I ain't gonna hurt yeh none!'

She turned and ran to the door, into the arms of her mother, who was rushing out and hugged her distressed daughter to her.

With eyes blazing she shouted at the swaying, grinning Jack Stark, 'Stark! I want you off my spread come morning! You are fired, you dirty foul piece of horse shit. Off, you hear me? Take that half caste friend of yours, Eliot, with you!' She continued, 'I do not ever want to see that face of yours again. Joe will pay you what is owed.' She spun away and, cradling Kathleen, walked back into the house. She shouted before the door shut, 'Daybreak, you hear!'

***

In the yard's main hay barn a young man was sweeping up chaff from the barn's floor. He wiped his brow, but stopped on hearing angry voices coming from outside. He heard a door being slammed, followed by silence. Putting the broom to one side he walked over to the barn door. A storm lantern stood on a barrel, putting out its light. He half opened the door and peered out. The figure of Jack Stark could be seen sitting in a rocker on the house veranda. Jack had his hat pulled down over his face. The young man shrugged before sliding through the gap and leaving the barn. The barn door creaked on being closed. The young man turned with a look up at the house. He carefully slid the latch, locking it, then walked towards the corral where horses were poking their heads through the rails. He pats and strokes them in passing. One gave off a loud neigh. On the house veranda Jack's hat fell forward from his face and down into his lap. He stirred and opened his eyes. He looked towards the corral to see the young man walking away from the horses.

He shouted, 'Stewart, Cord Stewart. That you, boy?'

The young man stopped and froze.

'You hear me, boy?'

The light in the downstairs window went out; a curtain moved. 'Yes sir. I hear you, Mister Stark.'

Jack spat. 'You done all the critters, they all fed and watered?'

'Yes, sir, Mister Stark.'

'You sure now, boy? Seems to me they be wanting something, wouldn't yeh say?'

'They all done, sir. It's the heat. Hot night, Mister Stark.'

Jack growled, 'Heat, did I hear you say heat, boy?'

Cord gave a deep sigh and kicked up the dirt. 'Yes sir.'

Jack kicked the empty rye bottle into a bed of flowers. 'Then best we cool them. You string em, take them to the creek. Yeh, let them splash a while.' There follows a moment's silence before Jack bellowed, 'You hear me, Stewart?'

Cord shouted back, 'Loud and clear, sir.' Under his breath, 'I hear you, you bastard of a man.'

Jack, smiling, opened his pants and began to piss on the flowers. 'These pretty little flowers. They sure need some watering, don't yeh think? This heat.' He half turned to the house. 'Be gone come morning, she says. Irish fucking bitch. Not a chance in hell.' He screamed out, 'Bitch, bitch, bitch!'

Cord stared; with anger showing on his face, he raced back to the barn, pulled back the latch and entered. Cord struck a match and lit the lantern. He hurried over to a corner. He pulled down on a wall board. Putting his hand behind it, he brought out a bundle, a rolled-up oil rag. He began to unwrap it. From it he took out a pistol; he checked and twirled it. Then he froze, hearing a sound coming from behind him. The voice of Joe Dupree. Cord gave a deep sigh before turning to Joe. He put the pistol behind his back, tucking it into his belt, then he pulled down his shirt, covering it.

Joe said, in a casual manner, 'Working late, Cord?' Smiled, thumbed over a shoulder.

'Heard you and Jack at it out there. I'm here to give you a hand. Something about horses to cool?' Joe walked over to a hook holding many string leads and pulled off a bundle, then turned and pointed at Cord. 'You put that pistol you're hiding, put it back from where you got it.' Shake of his head. 'That's if you wanna live. You ain't got a prayer against the likes of Stark. Drunk or sober, that man will blow you away.'

Cord hung his head; he took out the pistol and rewrapped it, before putting it back behind the board. He shoved the board back into place.

Joe nodded to him, putting one arm around Cord's shoulder. 'Let us go splash them horses.' Cord sighed as they left the barn.

A cool breeze was blowing off the creek. Joe and Cord sat on the bank with their boots off. They dangled their feet in the water. The horses splashed around in their newfound enjoyment; the black shine ate the dew-covered grass; he was munching around Cord, untied.

Joe nudged the boy, saying, 'I hope you don't mind me saying, but I've noticed that, well, yeh got something going.'

Cord blinked, looking questioningly at Joe.

Joe went on to say, 'Seems to me you have quite a bit more than a liking for Miss Kathy Murphy.'

Cord coloured up, picked up a stone and skimmed it into the creek. 'Well, I could be thinking the same in regard to you and Kathy's ma, Joe.'

Joe nodded and smiled. 'Been over a year since Pat's murder. Yeah,' he nodded, 'I guess you could say I am looking after two fine ladies. They are my friends. All Irish family.' He stamped his leg, splashing the water. 'Yeah. Something I missed doing back in 1870. Something that I ain't gonna let happen again.'

'You know, Joe, I hate that scar-faced bastard. Yeh see him Joe, pissing on Kathy's flowers?'

Joe half turned and grabbed Cord by the shoulder, shaking it. 'I am telling you now, boy. You keep a distance from him, he is out of hell's gate. That slime Eliot, him too. A snake in the grass is that one.'

He gave Cord's shoulder another shake. 'What you are doing

here, taking this shit off that man?' He smiled. 'Oh, I know why you stay. Ain't you got family?'

Cord sighed. 'At least yeh know where you are from, Joe. Ireland.' Threw another stone into the water. 'Me, I'm Scottish, I think.'

Joe said, 'You think! Don't you know?'

Cord smiled. 'I was told that my mother died after giving birth to me, that her name was Maggie. Maggie Stewart. My father, seems he went off a-chasing the gold, in those days of forty-nine.' He sighed.

'I was put into an orphanage, Gordon's, New York City, by my mother's sister. So the story goes. Hey, Joe, could be we are not too far away on blood lines?'

'What makes you say that? How come?'

'Well, for a start they both come from over the pond, Ireland, Scotland.'

Joe laughed. 'Oh no... oh no, you are not taking me there boy, just no way. No way, you hear, that you're putting Joe Dupree into a skirt.'

Cord laughed. 'Been about everywhere, Joe. So, one day I am in San Angelo doing my thing, looking for work. Find myself outside of Ward Peterson's store. There's Cookie Warren struggling to load supplies. I give him a hand.'

'Go on.'

'Yeh, I am there when these two beautiful ladies approach. Mrs Murphy, Kathy. They asked Cookie if he could use me full time. A job. Cookie, he said he was pleased with me, he said yes.'

Joe nodded, winked. 'Yeah I just bet he did.'

***

Daybreak, and one of the drovers, Abe Summers, stood looking into the horse pen at the black shine, who was digging a front hoof into the dirt and clawing it back. Abe turned to see Jack walking towards him.

Jack shouted out, 'Hope yeh gonna tell me, Abe, that you have broke that black, that I can finally get to put a saddle on his back?'

Abe gave a shake of his head then spat out tobacco juice. 'No such luck, Jack. Whole damn crew's had a go at him.' He nodded over at the black. 'Broke Bill Tyler's leg. He one crazy critter, Jack.'

'You Abe Summer, top of the fucking tree, beaten. I do not believe it.'

Abe sighed, 'I tell you, Jack, that shine, well, he is a breed of his own. Your kick, Sneeze, he came so fucking determined to break him. Swishing a rope.' Abe laughed. 'Sorry Jack, but I just gotta laugh, man. Sneeze he come back out like the devil himself was a-chasing him. I'm sure he done and shit his pants.'

Jack, scowling, shouted, 'Well, any fucking problem, I will deal with it. Nobody fucks with Jack.' Jack turned to the house and screamed, 'Nobody fucks with Jack Stark. You fucking hear me?' Jack turned back to Abe, pointing over at the cookhouse. 'Tell that arsehole Stewart to cut out on the black's feed. Yeh, his water too. We will break the fucker.' He spun on his boot heels and bellowed in the direction of the cookhouse. 'I am ready to ride. You are fucking lazy bastards if you ain't out here and in your saddles in fifteen fucking minutes.' He snarled, 'I'm in such a bad fucking mood. I'll shoot any man that's late.'

The men came racing out from both the cookhouse and bunkhouse. One was hopping with one boot on and one off, others still shoving their breakfast down their gullets. Jack looked over at the yard's entrance. Two riders were coming in. They rode up and dismounted. Jack helped a tall lean-looking rider unsaddle, before asking, 'How did the night watch go, Pete?'

Pete Russell smiled. 'Oh, kinda spooky but quiet. We had a little luck going our way, Jack.'

Jack said, 'Luck, Pete?'

'There was promise of a storm brewing over the north pasture. Few lightning flashes but they were distant. It blew over.' Pete turned to his partner, a plump Mexican. 'Yeah we were lucky, eh Crako?'

Crako nodded and grinned, showing a gold tooth in his mouth. Jack clapped his hands, saying, 'Luck, yer saying, Pete. Guess that is what being in the cattle business is all about, when Lady Luck is a smiling on yeh. That sweet-tasting wine hits your lips. Belly's full and bursting.' He ran his tongue across his mouth.

Crako smiled. 'Jack, he is right. Me now ready to burst a belly. Taste that sweet wine coffee of Cookie Warren's.' Crako rubbed his belly. They started to laugh; Jack gave a nod over towards the cookhouse. 'Go grab some grub, boys. You've earnt it.'

They both nodded, dropping their saddles by the rail. They led their horses into the pen. Pete, closing the pen's gate, turned to Jack. 'Oh, by the way, Jack, we seen a family of sod turners on the north pasture.'

Crako nodded.

'They looked to be heading west. They did not stop, just carried on through.'

Jack's eyes blazed, he snarled, 'You sure they passed, Pete?' Both men nodded. Jack turned to the drovers, who had mounted their horses. 'Yeh all fucking hear that? We got squatters on the spread.' He spat, 'Yeh all listen to me. If them fuckers stop, yer move 'em on. If they are a-digging a hole, yer fill it, yeah, with them in it.'

Pete and Crako walked away, shaking their heads. Pete whispered to Crako, 'Jesus, wish I'd never told him.' They turned and looked back at the men riding out. Jack mumbled indistinctly as he mounted up, Sneeze Eliot already in his saddle, waiting.

Chapter 21

HORSESHOE CREEK

Cord sat on the front cross board of the chuck wagon. Cookie Warren, a small, long-bearded man in his middle age, climbed up. Sitting alongside Cord, he took hold of the reins.

Cookie asked, 'We all ready?'

'Yup, ready to go, Cookie.'

Cookie shook the reins of the two pulling horses and moved the wagon towards the gate. The black shine standing in the corral began to neigh and nod his head. Cord pulled Cookie's shoulder.

'Just give me a minute, Cookie.'

He jumped down off the wagon and raced to the barn. A moment passed before he was back out with a quarter bag of oats under his arm. He went over to the pen and poured the oats into a feed trough. The black nudged him. He ran a hand down the shine's neck, gently patting it. He then raced back to the wagon.

Cookie gasped, 'How come – and don't you hold out on me boy – how come that shine's okay with you?' He spat. 'Bet you could get a saddle on his back, eh boy?' He winked. 'Am I right?'

Cord looked at him, smiling.

'Look boy, you are going behind Stark's back, feeding him. It is gonna get you killed, boy. You cross that man, he will put you six feet under.'

Cord just smiled and began to polish a shotgun. Cookie shook his head. Then Cord asked Cookie about his life, how he happened to become a cook for the Murphy family and how come he came into Texas, his accent not being one with the Texan drawl.

Cookie answered him, saying he was an east coast Bostonian, that his father had been a trapper and his mother a Red River girl. They had fallen in love before moving, along with his sister and him, north up into Dakota county, his father being a true what you might call mountain man. He had always had a loving connection with the many tribes of Native Americans, tribes like the Pawnee, Sioux, Mandan, just some of many that lived alongside the lakes, rivers, and Great Plains. So much so that his father took on the representation of these downtrodden people. All his life he had carried a deep heartfelt sadness about the invasion by the French and British settlers taking the Native American Indians' land. He had gone on to fight openly for Indian rights.

'The result was that hatred for my father caused the family to move reluctantly back into our mountain cabin and the safety of North Dakota. However a series of broken promises brought the tribes into a prolonged period of war. Still my father tried to negotiate a peaceful solution, one that would give the Indian nation an agreeable end to the conflict. As for myself I became a man of nonviolence, a simple cook, who worked the many cross country wagon trains bringing the settlers from east to west. My father found it hard having a son who helped these foreign invaders to buy up the ten-dollar land grants. I walked the road of shame, so much so that I finally found myself working the earning houses of New York in the hope of my father's forgiveness. The Warren name was a curse in the government offices. But even this cretinous group knew that my father would be on call to aid and translate, for he knew many of the Indian languages.'

Cord then asked, 'Did you get it, Cookie? Your father, did he forgive you?'

'In the end, boy; his last years when all was lost regarding the Indian Washington settlement. Most of the tribes had to accept, ending their lives on reservations, land that was unwanted by the invading settlers that were now amassing from all corners of the planet: France, Great Britain, northern and Central Europe, the likes of Germany, Norway, Sweden, some Baltic states. The Indians found themselves becoming a dying nation. It was either accept Washington's proposals or die.'

Cord shook his head. 'But the murder of Pat Murphy? The Comanche, Cookie, they are still fighting this unwinnable war.'

Cookie shrugged. 'So it seems, boy, so it seems.'

**

Maureen and Kathy still grieved enormously grief for Pat, and they needed time for their loss to heal. They thanked the Lord for having Joe and Cord around to guide and protect them. As the two youngsters sat by the creek, cooling the horses, Kathy had told Cord of her love for her birthplace, Ireland, wishing that the family had never crossed the great pond. She told him that if they had never made the crossing her father would still be alive. Having Cord was her only reason for staying in this hell.

Cord had smiled, saying, 'But ain't Ireland got its problems, Kathy, with your Catholic and Church of England not living a peaceful life? Your country having to fall in with the English crown?'

She shrugged. 'I suppose you are right, why should a country be forced to suffer; for Ireland, too, had and still was taking part in a civil war, just as there has been here in America. I could never understand the reason for one killing a brother.'

***

The chuck wagon was well on its way to the drovers' gathering point, which was situated on the north pasture. Cookie sat on the wagon with Cord still polishing the shotgun.

Cookie growled, 'Will yeh stop polishing that damn gun? You are giving me the fucking willies. Point that barrel away from my face. I am fifty years old,' he stared, nudging the boy, 'I'm wanting to see sixty.'

Cord pointed the gun away and smiled. 'Fifty, Cookie… yeh look older.'

Cookie growled, 'Oh yeh, how old?'

Cord looked Cookie up and down. 'Hmmm, let me see now. Yeah, I am thinking on seventy, seventy-five.'

Cookie took off his hat and wafted it at Cord. 'Fucking lying little toad.' He pointed to the selected spot on the side of a freshwater creek. 'Here we are, boy, Horseshoe Creek.' Cord put the gun under his seat, then jumped down off the wagon.

'Get them water pouches down to the creek an' fill em while I get us a fire going. Then I'll be a-filling that pot with some beef stew.' Cookie took out his watch and looked at it. Cord gave him a nod and laughed. Cookie looked at him, puzzled. 'So, what the fuck's funny?'

'Why, you are, Cookie. We set up, like always at Horseshoe. You look at your watch, saying, time to rustle up some grub, empty bellies to feed.'

Cookie smiled and winked. 'Now there stands a man, who knows a man, a man that takes notice.' He spat. 'And here is me a-thinking that the man had no fucking brain.' He took out his watch and winked at Cord. 'Time to rustle up some grub. We have empty bellies to feed.'

Cord pointed to a rider approaching them, Riding flat out on full gallop. 'Looks like we got company, Cookie.' Cookie looked to where Cord was pointing.

'Go fetch me that shotgun, boy, he's not one of ours.' Cord raced to the wagon and took the gun from under the seat, before rushing back to Cookie and handing over the gun.

The rider, a middle-aged man, reined in, his hat flapping down his back. He wore pants held up with braces and an open shirt. He looked at the two, saying, 'You can put the gun down, friend, I am unarmed. I carry no weapon.' He raised his hands. Cookie looked and walked around him with gun still raised.

'You're on Murphy land, mister. On this spread you're so likely to get yourself shot.' Spat. 'I ain't yer friend, sod turners ain't got no friends in cattle country.' Shake of his head. 'You're so fucking lucky that you have found me, a listening man. So you can drop your hands, I am listening.'

The rider nodded a thank you. 'Dan Tucker's the name. Just north of yeh here I have got my Savannah. It's standing with a wheel off. Holding pin snapped clean in two. Wheel itself and shaft are good.' He sighed.

'I got my wife, Mary, she is back there with my two young boys. David is ten years old, Adam is seven. My wife, well she is not too good now. My sons are too young to help their Pa.'

Cookie shook his head, pointing a finger at him.

'I know who you are, Dan Tucker. You're a no-good fucking sod turner. Squatter. Ten fucking dollar land grabber.'

Dan began shaking his head, pleading, 'Not so, sir, you're so wrong. My family and I are passing through on our ways to San Francisco to my brother's, he has got work for me there.'

He looks at Cord's now sad face then back to Cookie. 'You've just gotta believe me, I have got proof back in my wagon, a letter.'

Cookie kicked up some dirt, looked over at Cord, and said, 'Well, Dan Tucker it so happens it's your lucky day. My friend

Cord, well, together we are going to help put that wheel back on your wagon.'

Dan put his hands together, prayer fashion. 'Oh, thank you, thank you, sir.'

Cookie asked. 'You got a Jack bar, a lifting rod?'

'Yes sir, just need the manpower.'

Cookie nodded. 'That you got. How far north?'

'Two, maybe, but no more than three miles.'

'Well, what yeh waiting for, best you get back to that family of yours. They sure will be missing you. Yeah, better tell that lady of yours that Cookie's coming with some hot beef stew.'

Dan closed his eyes and mouthed a thank you. He then turned his mount and rode away. He shouted, 'North for three. I'll be waiting.'

***

Sometime later, the chuck wagon was ambling along with Cookie on the reins. Cord was standing up in his seat.

'Where are they, Cookie? Must have done all of three miles by now.'

Cookie answered, 'Keep those eyes peeled, boy. They are around here somewhere.'

Cord shouted, 'Rider approaching from off that high ridge.' He pointed. 'Looks to me like Jake Potter.'

The rider drew nearer, with Cookie nodding, 'It is Jake all right, he is in quite a bit of a hurry.' Cookie stared at the approaching rider, he spat, 'Yeh, it's Jake. What's he wanting?'

Jake reined in on the two. Cookie halted the wagon. He stared at the worried face on the middle-aged, bean pole of a man, who seemed highly frustrated and constantly peered nervously back over his shoulder. He gasped, 'What you doing here, Cookie? This ain't Horseshoe.'

Cookie, spitting out tobacco juice, answered, 'We are out on a mission, Jake. We—'

Cord interrupted, 'Yeh, looking for a family, the Tuckers. They're out here with a busted wagon wheel. We said we would help.'

Cookie asked, 'You seen 'em, Jake?'

Jake once again looked over his shoulder. 'Oh, I've seen 'em, Cookie.' He pointed at a cloud of black smoke that was rising above a distant ridge. 'What's fucking left of them. It's too fucking late. Oh my God,' jabbing a finger at the smoke cloud. 'Oh, sweet Mary mother of God, they are fucking burning the wagon. I am out of here, Cookie, I want no part of this.'

Cookie jumped from the wagon and rushed at Jake, grabbing him and pulling him down out of the saddle onto the dirt. Cookie snarled, 'Too fucking late? What the fuck's gone down, Jake?'

He kicked out at Jake cowering away. Jake went for his pistol, but stopped on seeing Cord, now standing with a shotgun pointing at him. Cookie pulled Jake's gun from the holster and aimed it at him.

'You tell me, Potter, or I swear to God, I'll blow yeh fucking brains out.'

Jake was down on his knees and started to sob, 'That family we came across, man and wife, two little boys. They were asking for help. Wheel off their wagon. We—'

'Who is 'we', Jake?'

Jake hissed, 'Jack n Sneeze, they, they...' Rubbing his face, with Cookie snarling, 'Out with-it Potter. You were saying?'

'Stark. He takes the woman into that wagon, she is a-screaming. He is raping her. Sneeze, he then follows. The kids, they are bawling their eyes out.' Jake banged his fists down into the dirt. 'The man, he is, he is, spread-eagled across the wagon wheel. The woman's screams... they stop. That Sneeze comes out of the wagon.' Jake shakes his head. 'The woman, she did not.'

'So, you did nothing to that family, Jake? Yeh did nothing and Stark, he let yeh ride away?'

'Yeh.'

'That don't sound like Stark to me, he would not let you ride.'

Jake, tears flowing, shrugged. 'Sneeze, he ordered me to go on lookout. They were fucking laughing at me.' He looked pleadingly from Cookie to Cord. 'Yeah, calling me a yellow belly because I would not join in the fun. Fucking fun they called it.' His sobbing increased. 'Sneeze violating them little boys, Cookie. Fucking fun! Then he gets out this bow, starts shooting arrows into them. The man, their father, he was going fucking crazy.' He sighed. 'That was until he got the arrows too. Stark he then done and scalp them.' Jake told the two that Stark wanted the killings to look as if they had been done by some Comanche raiding party. He pointed again at the cloud of black smoke that was bellowing up. 'Do you fucking see, Cookie? Fucking look... They've torched the wagon. Oh, sweet Jesus they are burning that family.'

Putting his hands together Jake pleaded to Cookie, 'You gotta let me go, Cookie. I am a dead man. They cannot let me live, with what I have seen them do.'

Cookie pulled the sobbing Jake to his feet. He put Jake's pistol back into its holster, saying, 'You're gonna need that, Jake. You take off now. See McBane in Angelo, tell him what you have seen. Tom McBane... he will know what to do.'

Cord nodded in agreement. 'Yeah, you do what Cookie says, Jake.' He looked at the smoke funnel. 'I would get going while you're ahead. You gotta report this, Jake, for that poor family. If anyone asks, well Cookie and I, we ain't seen yeh.'

Jake looked at Cookie. Cookie nodded. Jake remounted his horse, riding away without another word. Cookie pointed after him. 'He ain't headed for Angelo.' Gave a shake of his head. 'Potter he is headed west. Big Spring, I would say. Be trying to make Odessa, then the Grande River into Mexico.'

'That's sure one hell of a ride ain't it, with one horse?'

Cookie sighed. 'Never make it, boy. That idiot has gone west. Let us get back to Horseshoe.' He looked at the smoke. 'We got bellies to fill. If anyone asks, we ain't seen Potter. We keep our mouths shut tight. That is, if we want to see tomorrow.'

***

Later at Horseshoe, Cookie and Cord were loading up the wagon. Cookie walked to the fire and poured water over it. Cookie looked at Cord and shook his head. 'Glad that day's the fuck over.'

Cord pointed, saying, 'Not quite. There is another mouth coming in.'

They both watched as Sneeze Eliot approached, pulling a saddled horse with no rider. Cookie informed Eliot, 'You're too late for grub, Sneeze.' He pointed to the riderless horse. 'Looks like you lost a cowboy.'

Sneeze began to tie the saddled horse to the rear of the wagon. 'Yeah, Jake Potters, found his horse west of here, all on his ownsome.' Gave the two a deep sigh. 'No sign of Jake, though. Can you take the horse in, Cookie?'

Cookie said, 'Yeah, I can do that.'

Sneeze added, 'Oh, er, watch out for Comanche raiders. They have been seen a-running wild again. Looks like they got Potter.'

Sneeze turned his horse and galloped away, with Cookie and Cord watching him go. Cookie pointed after him, snarling, 'That man's caught and done Jake, boy. I'm telling yeh now if we want to see tomorrow's sun.' He stabbed a finger at Cord. 'We keep our fucking mouths shut.'

Cord asked, 'You ever known a Comanche leave a horse and saddle behind, Cookie?'

Cookie wagged his finger. 'Now what have I told you, boy? We know nothing. Keep the fuck those thoughts to yourself, because I want to live to see tomorrow.'

***

Late afternoon and Joe found himself sitting with Maureen, taking tea on the veranda of the great white house. It was then that he got to hear of Pat and Maureen's story, their introduction to America. He had often wondered how this beautiful family came to own many hundred head of cattle. And so she began her story. It was in early August, 1845, that the life of Patrick Murphy, a young owner of a small farm some 20 miles south of Dublin, was about to change. A letter marked as of some urgency had arrived from one of Ireland's most respected companies, Dublin's Hunt Nolan and associates, with a long history of services to only the absolute best of Ireland's major business companies. When it came down to issues of law and representation then Hunt and Nolan were undoubtedly the number one company, they were simply the best.

Strangely the letter was addressed to Maureen, which was quite unusual, and this gave Patrick cause for concern; thus Patrick handed the courier's wax-sealed letter over to his young and beautiful wife, Maureen, to open. Had not they struggled in these times of great famine, to hold on to what remained of the family heritage? Their love and Maureen's drive were thankfully the greatest supports that had kept Patrick from going insane.

The recent arrival of their beautiful baby girl, Kathleen, gave them both the extra strength that was needed to survive this period of deep depression. So it was with trembling hands that Maureen had opened the scrolled document that morning; she looked at it and read its contents, with Patrick eagerly grasping her hand, wishing for good news. His thoughts were mostly concerned about the farm. Was Maureen about to lose the last of the McCall family possessions? He spoke in a whisper, hugging her and kissing her brow. 'What is it, my heart? The letter, not shocking news? The farm?'

Maureen, showing a somewhat reassuring shrug, squeezed Pat's hand and lifted it to her lips. 'They don't really say, my love.

It's puzzling. They would like us to appear for a most important meeting at their Dublin house. They ask we make a three o'clock appointment on the 17th for a consultation with the renowned R.S. Collins, Solicitor General of Ireland.' She could hardly speak, her voice became barely a whisper. 'Pat, I am frightened. We are being asked to see Ireland's top man, the Solicitor General.'

Pat, having hugged his wife closer, spoke. 'Do not be afraid, my heart. I shall be with you. We face whatever this R.S. Collins wants of us together.'

She had smiled, saying, 'Whatever it is, my love, can only be of the utmost importance for the Solicitor General to summon me to Dublin.' Patrick could only nod his agreement to his wife's thoughts.

The more Maureen continued with her story, the more Joe was becoming intrigued, looking forward eagerly to its eventual ending. He took a drink from the porcelain cup and urged her to continue. 'Please do go on, Maureen. This Collins, you were saying?'

Maureen, nodding, continued, 'Oh our Solicitor General just happened to be the most perfect gentleman. We sat just having a traditional Irish tea, hot buttered scones with jam and added cream. It came as quite a shock when he told me that I had inherited a large parcel of land on the Sweetwater grasslands north of San Angelo, Texas. Land that held over a few thousand head of cattle, that I had in fact become a multi-dollar millionaire.'

'My aunt Charlotte, my mother's sister, had married into money. She was, you could say without any doubt, the driving force behind the McCall family, my grandfather having been the adventurer and, dare I say, trained Charlotte. Oh, what she wanted Charlotte got, especially after having lost his only son Sean to some incurable disease. Sean was just nineteen years old. My grandfather James was devastated, falling into suicidal tendencies till Charlotte got hold of him, bringing him away from death's grip.'

Joe spoke, saying, 'Charlotte must have been one hell of a lady, Maureen, that special kind.' He gently held her hand and gave it a reassuring squeeze.

It was then that Maureen had a feeling that only her beloved late husband Pat had given her. Butterflies, as if she was aloft, on air. She shuddered, bringing herself back to reality, carrying the thought, who was this man, Joe Dupree? A man who had suddenly appeared that day with Pat. A man to whom Pat had given the job of ranch yard supervisor, what you might call errand boy to the girls, a bodyguard. Why the sudden newfound feeling of safety, of warmth, a smothering of love, that she was getting?

Joe again reached over and patted her hand, saying. 'You okay, Maureen? You want to go on with this?'

Maureen smiled, and returning the gentle squeeze of Joe's hand, replied, 'I am good Joe. Where was I now? Ah, yes. My mother Molly had offered to help share what had become the family's need of togetherness more than ever when lightning struck twice in less than a year, with the passing of my grandmother.'

Maureen was now thinking just how easy it was to confide in Joe about her family's history, strangely like sitting with Patrick. The feelings she was getting could only be described as unreal. If truth be known she was falling in love with this man. It was his voice, sympathetic, that brought her out of this period of weightlessness, this drifting sensation.

Joe asked, 'Patrick, Maureen? Your man.' Joe slowly motioned with his palm. 'I cannot believe I had such a short time to know him.' Shrugging. 'To have Pat as a friend was a never to be forgotten moment in any man's life. Jesus only knows, I loved the man.'

Slowly nodding her head, she replied in barely a whisper, 'Patrick was the son of my father's best friend, Declan Murphy.

Patrick and I had spent our entire life together from kids to adulthood, hardly ever being more than an arm's length, a voice call away from each other.' She took a moment before going on. 'We were the perfect match, thought the same thoughts, liked the same things. We became inseparable. Marriage was our aim and we took it with open arms, much to the support coming from both families; the Murphys and the McCalls were truly happy. Never more so than when baby Kathleen arrived. She tied securely a never to be broken link.'

Joe, having nodded his understanding, said, 'Yes, I can see that you had it all, Maureen. The perfect partnership. I am so sorry for your heartbreak, your loss.'

'Yes, Joe. We had it all.' She waved a nonchalant hand over the entire ranch area. 'From the very day of our arrival, our meet-up with Andy Grant, my late aunt Charlotte's right-hand man, a man rated by all who knew him as the best of the best. Finest drover beef herder in the business.'

Joe interrupted, 'Andy Grant, Maureen, he's no longer here?'

Maureen gave a deep sigh. 'No Joe, he was, till, when was it now, maybe a few months, a half year before you arrived. Along with Pat he had been taking a herd up the north ridge of the Sweetwater Valley. They were taking them up to the army's stockyards somewhere on the red river. Andy and another cowboy, Ben Shepherd, went to round up some strays. Sadly, from that day to this neither one of the two have ever been seen again. Pat organised a nine-day search of the area that came to no avail. My husband then employed one of the best trackers in the whole of Texas, along with an assistant Indian Comanche scout. Again, resulting in disappointment.'

Joe then asked about Stark and Eliot. Maureen replied that they were the ones who had returned the strays, telling Pat there was no sign of Andy and Ben. Joe was suspicious of the two men, what with Stark becoming top dog and not previously known in the cattle business.

Joe was eager to hear more but their conversation ended with the sound of Cookie's chuck wagon entering the yard.

The two sat in silence as they entered the yard. Cookie yanked on the rein, bringing the wagon up alongside the cookhouse door. Wearily he stepped down. He turned, looking up at Cord, who was stretching.

'We are late, boy. Best you see to the horses, I will unload.'

Cord jumped down, looking over at the corral. The shine stood watching them. Sneeze Eliot's chestnut horse was taking water. Cord whispered to Cookie, 'Looks like Sneeze is in.'

Cookie looked over at the pen. 'Yeah, so, maybe he's found Jake.' He stared at Cord. 'Let us hope he is in with him.'

Cord walked away to the rear of the wagon. He untied Jake's horse. He muttered as he passed Cookie, 'Yeah, if he's in. I'm thinking he's got a Comanche arrow in his back.'

Cookie ground his teeth and strode out, grabbing Cord by the shoulder. He whispered in Cord's ear, 'I thought we had agreed, boy. We have seen nothing, we have heard nothing. You hear me?'

Cord shrugged. 'Yeah, I'm hearing you, Cookie. I'm just a-hoping we can sleep at night knowing what we know.'

Cookie released his grip and patted Cord. 'You think about living, boy, yer future.' He winked. 'A life with Miss Kathy.' He looked over at the house, with a sad look and a shake of his head, saying, 'This ain't the place for them two fine ladies. Maureen should sell.' Looked and gave Cord a hard stare. 'Knowing what we know.'

They turned on hearing the crunch of boots coming from Joe Dupree, who was approaching them. 'Hi, you latecomers. How has your day been? You both look tired, spent. I am here for that supply list, Cookie. I am hoping to be off first light come the morn.'

Cookie slapped his thigh, a hand up to his brow. 'Oh, the supplies. Sorry, Joe, clean forgot all about them. Yeah, that list.

I will have it ready for you come tonight.' He sighed. 'Been one hell of a day.'

Joe nodded. 'You can say that again, Cookie. Yeh would not have heard what's happened up on the north pasture.' Cookie and Cord looked at each other. 'Well, a family of settlers. They got butchered by a Comanche raiding band. They got Jake Potter too, by all accounts, must have been with them. They burnt a Savannah and all with it. Stark seems to think, well, they could just be the same band that murdered Pat.'

Cord looked at Cookie, who spat, as a voice bellowed out from behind the trio, that of Sneeze Eliot. 'Yeah, poor old Jake. They got him too. Damned missed my dinner looking for that man.' He turned and walked away in the direction of the cookhouse, shouting out over his shoulder, 'I've one empty belly wants filling.'

Joe, with a shake of his head, said, 'Don't know how a man can eat after seeing such horror.'

There followed the sound of drumming coming from the canteen. Cookie shouted out, 'Yeah, that can all stop now, or there'll be no dinner and no rice pudding.' The drumming stopped. Cookie looked at the two and winked, giving a smile.

***

Some time later, sitting in the barn, as Cord was polishing the boots of Jack Stark, Joe entered. 'Don't you ever sleep, boy?' He smiled. 'Yeah, Cookie said I would find you here. Just picked up that list, the supplies.'

Cord sighed. 'I do not think I'll ever sleep again, Joe, with what I know.'

Joe put a hand on Cord's shoulder. 'This afternoon I had a sense something was amiss with you, I felt it.' Cord put a finger up to his lips, motioning for Joe to sit, before uttering in a faint voice, 'I just don't know what to do, Joe.' He sighed. 'Cookie, well, he says to keep my mouth shut. But I will not be able to sleep.'

Joe sat on a feed bag lying next to Cord. 'Maybe I can help. Tell me what's bugging you, boy.'

Cord, his eyes flashing, looking all about, whispered, 'That family, Joe, murdered on the north pasture. We, Cookie, and I, we met the man. Jake, too. I've just gotta tell the truth of what happened out there.'

Cord finished the story of the murders on the north pasture. Cord and Joe sat in silence. Cord held out a hand. 'So, you have it, Joe. There never was any Comanche raiding party. Have I done right to tell you?' Joe slowly nodded his head.

'Yeah, you have done right, boy. We've gotta get them two ladies away from here. I am meaning away, like now!' Joe removed his hat, scratched his head. 'Yeah, this is how we do it. Yes, it's the only way.' Later, after Joe had described his plan to Cord, with a hand on Cord's shoulder, he shook it.

'So, what yeh think, Cord?'

'Sounds good, Joe. You head out early for Angelo. Meantime, I take the ladies secretly down to Morgan's Point on the Angelo Road. We wait, wait for you to pick them up. Then you take them in with you. Sheriff McBane. Sounds good, Joe.'

'You got it, boy. I will see Maureen tonight. You will need a good hour ahead of me leaving. I'm through those yard gates at dawn. You gotta remember, Cord, to act like it's a normal day. Do not give any reason for them to suspect something is wrong.' He looked at Cord, staring into his eyes. 'Think yeh can do that?'

'If it means my life, Joe. I'd sooner die than let them bastards put their hands on Kathy or her ma.'

Chapter 22

RETRIBUTION

Maureen and Kathy sat with Joe on one side of a large table, in the sheriff's office on Main Street, San Angelo. Opposite them sat Tom McBane with Major George Storie and his sergeant, Sammy Simpson. Also in attendance, standing with arms crossed, was a six-foot tall Comanche Indian scout, Bold Wolf.

There was a moment's eerie silence before Tom, shaking his head, spoke. 'What Joe has just told us here today shocks me beyond words. These horrific acts of evil by Stark and Eliot have only confirmed that we have finally caught up with the two remaining members of the Brotherhood Six.' He drummed his fingers on the table. 'Just how many more lives those two murderous dogs have put paid to is no telling, I am sure.'

He looked with hands held out at Maureen and Kathy. 'I can add my friend Pat.' Tom turned to the Major and thumbed over at him. 'We are so lucky to have my friend Major George Storie along with his sergeant Sammy and chief scout Bold Wolf with us, here to listen, listen to Joe's tale of horror. George, thanks to God, just happened to be calling in on me on his way to Fort Worth.'

The Major, a well-built middle-aged man, with a drooped moustache and pointed beard, pushed back his chair and rose to his full six feet. He snarled, 'I will give whatever help is needed to destroy, aye, destroy, those two murderous bastards.' He looked at the ladies. 'Please excuse my language, ladies.'

Maureen smiling, said, 'You are excused, Major.'

The Major sat down. Joe looked at Bold Wolf. 'Don't the Comanche have their arrow shafts marked, Bold Wolf?'

Bold Wolf nodded. 'Yes, they do. I, Bold Wolf, have listened with much interest to your story, Joe. I think I can add to this.' He looked over at the Major. The Major waved to him to continue. 'Last winter season, my chief, Little Owl, asked if I had seen his son, One Knife. His son had not returned from hunting up in the Northern Territory.' Bold Wolf spread out his arms.

'His braves, they searched. They found One Knife's horse, a brown and white pinto. The mule trader, Collins told them he bought it from a Murphy ranch drover, name of Sneeze Eliot.' He looked at Maureen. 'Little Owl, he says to Bold Wolf, that his son One Knife is now with the great spirit.'

Maureen nodded. 'Yes, I remember the chocolate and white pinto. I was offered it by Eliot. He told me it was from one of the Comanche raiders. I refused his offer.' Putting a small kerchief up to her eyes, she said, 'Now I know they murdered Pat and One Knife.'

There followed an abbreviated period of silence before the Major stood and banged his fist hard down onto the table. He turned to his sergeant. 'Enough. Sam, you pick out six of your best troopers. I want them bastards taken out. I mean taken out as in final… I want them dead!'

***

It took the party less than an hour to find themselves out on the open plain on a journey back to the Murphy ranch for an extermination confrontation with the killers. Joe drove a wagon full of supplies; alongside him were Maureen and Kathy. Maureen was fanning herself against the sun's heat and pestering flies. Kathy held a parasol over them both. Maureen was deep in thought about her past life and her regrets about her decision to make the Atlantic crossing from Cork to the new world, America – especially after the death of Pat. Had not they had a beautiful and prosperous country life in Ireland, with Pat a well-respected businessman? They had a well-established smallholding which she totally loved.

Her grandfather, Thomas Brady, had left her the Texas cattle ranch. This was a challenge that she had hoped would give Pat, along with daughter Katherine, a prosperous life in the land of the free. She gave a deep sigh, remembering the night the killers brought him home. She wanted these two lying sadistic killers dead.

She looked at Joe and saw the fire in his eye; there was something mysterious about him. She had once asked Pat about Joe, only to be told that he was an Irishman who needed a job, a great friend of Tom McBane and that was all that was needed to employ him.

She found she was having feelings for the mysterious Joe; it was like when she had first met Pat and fallen in love with him. Tom had the answer to the Joe Dupree mystery; she must find the time to ask him. Tom and Sammy rode on opposite sides of the wagon, while, riding in pairs, a group of six troopers followed at the rear. Sam pointed to a dust cloud heading towards them. Tom at once took out a small telescope and had a look. He smiled. 'Don't be alarmed, it's Bold Wolf.'

Bold Wolf reined in alongside of Sammy. They spoke. Sammy nodded as the scout spoke. Bold Wolf took his horse ahead and galloped off.

Sammy turned in the saddle and shouted, 'My scout has spotted Eliot. He's bathing in the Sweetwater River. He is about a mile or so north of us. He looks to be out hunting; he is carrying the bow and arrows.' Maureen put a hand up to her mouth.

'You sure Eliot ain't spotted Bold Wolf, Sammy?'

Sammy winked. 'No way. I can assure you that scout of mine would not have been seen.' He looked over at Tom, then at Joe. 'I have told Bold Wolf to take Eliot out. His time on this earth is over. Then we go for Stark.'

Joe and Tom nodded their agreement without hesitation. Tom said, 'Yeah, just Stark, I hope so.' He looked at Maureen and added, 'That is if the rest of your boys stay out of it.'

Kathy answered, 'I'm sure our boys will stay loyal to us, won't they, Ma?'

Joe shrugged. 'Yeah Tom, it's like Maureen has told you, her boys will not interfere. Stark stands alone on this.'

Chapter 23
PLAYTIME

Bold Wolf slid silently off his horse. He then tied it to the branch of an overhanging willow. Taking a bow from the saddle horn, he then strung it, pulling three arrows from a quiver. He began to crouch as he bobbed and weaved his way up the river's bank. He stopped momentarily on hearing the voice of Sneeze Eliot, who was singing. Bold Wolf kneeled, slowly parting the tall grasses. Sneeze Eliot was naked, a soap bar in his hand. He sang as he washed himself.

'Oh, we gonna have some fun. Dupree lies dead from Eliot's gun. We gonna cut him up, ear to ear, then it is humping time, my dears. Oh, di dodo dodo does de oh.' He looked up at the sky, giving a hysterical laugh. 'Oh, Kathy Murphy, Sneezy gonna punch that pee hole of yours, la deda, la da dee.' He began to shout. 'Can you hear me, Ma Murphy? What Sneeze is gonna do to that gal of yours, yeah while you my fine lady muck, oh, Uncle Jack he gonna see to you, oh yes sireee.'

Bold Wolf, now down on his stomach, crawled nearer. He peered through the last of his cover. On the bank he saw the pistol lying out of its holster, just an arm's stretch from the singing Sneeze. Bold Wolf turned onto his back and placed an arrow into the bow. Quickly he rose to his knees and took aim. Sneeze, in a panic, dropped the soap bar and stretched for the pistol. There was a swoosh as the arrow left the bow; the aim was good as it flew into the neck of Sneeze. The blood began to pour from its mark. The ice-blue eyes of Sneeze Eliot turn black as a second and third arrow entered his body.

***

A short time later Sammy and his troop were riding a little way ahead of Tom, Joe and the ladies when Sammy, holding up a hand, brought them all to a standstill. Joe got up from his seat and stood looking into the distance, to see Bold Wolf heading towards them. Behind him he towed the chestnut horse of Sneeze Eliot; his body, now wrapped and tied in a blanket, could be seen hanging over it. Bold Wolf passed the horse to a trooper. He then handed something to Sam. The sergeant turned and shouted for Tom to ride forward. Tom rode up to Sammy. They held a brief conversation, with Tom nodding and looking back at Joe and the girls. Sammy slipped something into Tom's hand and he pocketed it. He turned his mount and rode back to the wagon. Bold Wolf gave an overhand wave before heading out.

As Tom returned Joe asked him, 'What was that all about?'

Tom replied, 'Oh, that with Sammy? Just talking tactics, yeah, now Eliot is out of the way.' He smiled, saying, 'It is one down, one to go. Sammy sent Bold Wolf ahead, just to make damn sure there are no unexpected guns waiting for us.' He turned to the two ladies. 'Seems I've got the best job.'

Maureen asked, 'And that is, Tom?'

'Why, looking after you two fine ladies.'

Joe slapped Tom on the back. 'Always knew you were one lucky guy, Tom McBane.'

Tom sighed. 'You got the hard part, my friend, seeing to Stark. I told Sammy that you would not have it any other way, that Stark was your baby.'

Joe nodded. 'Like you say, Tom… Stark, he's mine.' Joe turned to Kathy. 'You know your part, Kathy. Take your Ma and Tom to Cord, like we arranged.'

Kathy nodded eagerly. 'Yeah, Joe, I ain't forgetting. I just hope Cord ain't hit any problems, that Stark don't rile him none.'

Joe looked at the sky, saying, 'Cord, he's a smart kid, so don't you worry none.'

Chapter 24

MURPHYS

Jack pointed a jabbing finger at Cord. 'You, boy.' Cord blinked and shrugged. 'Yeh you, yer sneaky little bastard. Where's that fucking girl of yours and her Irish whore of a mother?' He spat, 'Don't yeh dare lie to me. You lie, and I will blow that silly fucking head off your shoulders.'

Cookie scrambled down from the wagon and, with his hands held out, walked up to Jack and pleaded, 'Come on now, Jack, boy's been out with me all day, yeh know we've been serving out grub.'

Cord stepped down from the wagon. Jack rushed by Cookie and stepped up to Cord's face. With an evil look Jack said, 'If I find yeh been fucking holding out on me, boy...' He stabbed Cord in the chest with his finger and spat on Cord's boot before spinning around and walking away. He shouted back at Cookie, 'I am fucking hungry, Cookie. Get some food on my table. I am a wanting to feast tonight,' Jack continued, striding briskly to the bunkhouse.

Cookie shouted, 'Give you a shout. Jack, er, didn't see Sneeze at dinner.'

Jack kept walking, shouting over his shoulder, laughing, 'That's because he is out there looking for them two whores.'

Throws his arm into the air. 'Could be with that French bastard. Now would not that just be really fucking nice.'

Cookie motioned for Cord to make haste. Cord stared after the disappearing Jack, spat into the dirt and whispered, 'Oh, you're gonna feast, boss… you filthy bastard!'

***

Kathy led her ma and Tom up the creek. She saw Cord waiting, with the horses splashing in the water. She raced into his arms. Cord looked at Maureen, who smiled. Tom nodded to him. Kathy did not want to let go of him; she was relieved that he was safe and not another Stark victim. Of course she had fallen for him at their first ever meeting, when he had given a helping hand to Cookie Warren outside that San Angelo store. Had she not nudged and whispered to her mother to employ him? He had told her of his dream, that of being a doctor, and she would see that dream become a reality.

'Let us get you all safely into the barn. I took out some boarding at the back, so you should not be seen. I will get these horses to the pen, then I will be back.'

Tom asked, 'Have you come across any problems?'

Cord answered, 'No sir, not as yet, but with Stark you never know.' Then he walked behind the horses to guide them into the pen. He pointed at the gap made in the boarding for Tom and the girls to enter. Cord then continued to pen the horses. He began to spread hay in the holding baskets.

Jack stood in the doorway of the canteen, watching him. He shouted at Cord, 'Don't you let that black get near that feed. You take him out, stable him up in the barn, you hear me, boy?'

Cord, without turning to look at Jack, shouted, 'I hear you, sir, no feed for the black.'

Jack stayed just long enough to see Cord walk the black out of the pen and into the barn. He spat before entering the canteen.

Cord entered with the black. He saw the worried faces of Maureen, Kathy, and Tom. Walking over to a nose bag that was half filled with oats, he put it over the head of the black, stroked him and smiled. 'All's well, nothing to worry about.'

Tom inquired, 'I take it that was our mister Stark we heard shouting just a moment ago?'

Cord nodded. 'Yeah, that was Stark. He is now stuffing his fat gut in the canteen.' Cord rubbed his chin and blinked. 'Did not see any sign of Sneeze Eliot though, his chestnut wasn't in the pen. Hope Joe's okay?'

Maureen answered, 'Sneeze Eliot is dead, Cord. We've just got Stark to worry about.'

Cord exclaimed, looking surprised, 'Dead? Eliot?'

Tom interrupted. 'Yeah, he is finished. He is dead.' He smiled. 'Don't you worry your head about Joe Dupree. He's ex-Texas Ranger.' They all looked completely surprised by what Tom uttered. Tom smiled again. 'Known that man as far back as sixty-three, ever since arriving here in America. We sailed the same ship over from Cork, Joe with his wife, Colette, and daughter, Janine. Those were sad times.' Gave a shake of his head.

'After that damn famine in forty-five till fifty-two took over a million Irish dead.'

Maureen put a hand to her mouth. 'Wife and daughter, Tom? You're saying Joe… he is married?'

Tom asked, 'Pat, he never told yeh?' Maureen and Kathy both shook their heads. Cord shrugged. Tom sighed. 'It was big news at the time. Sure Pat never mentioned about Joe, his family, their little homestead in Eagles Valley, Taylorville Austin?' They again shook their heads. Tom looked at Cord, who held out his arms, in a gesture saying no. 'Let us see, now, it was, yeh, must have been 1870.' With a serious look at them, he continued, 'It is not a nice story. You sure you still wanna hear it?'

They looked at each other and nodded.

'Like I was a-saying, it was around 1870.' Tom went on to tell them all about Joe finding horror, his family dead on his homecoming, his meeting with Pat, and the agonising wait, that he hoped would finally end by bringing him retribution. Tom shrugged, holding up a hand. 'So now you know all about Joe Dupree.' Tom walked to the water barrel and took a ladle to his mouth. Maureen and Kathy sat with tears in their eyes. With a sad face, Cord stroked the black.

Maureen wiped her eyes. 'Poor Joe. There must be a hole in his breast where his heart used to be.'

Kathy added, 'I am so sorry for him. He is like my father, a lovely man.'

Cord sighed. 'I did not know he was carrying such a burden. He has gotta be hurting.'

Tom nodded. 'Oh, he has been hurting ever since that day. Let us pray that after tonight that burden will ease.'

Cord asked Tom, 'So Stark and Eliot, they're the missing two of that Brotherhood?'

Tom opened his shirt pocket and pulled out a gold locket and chain. He gave it to Maureen, saying, 'Bold Wolf took that from the neck of Sneeze Eliot.' Maureen opened the locket and looked at a picture of a beautiful young girl. She handed it over to Kathy. Cord walked over and looked over Kathy's shoulder at the locket picture of Janine Dupree.

Kathy sighed. 'Oh, she's beautiful, Tom.'

Tom sighed. 'Yes, she was. That's Joe's daughter, Janine.'

There followed a moment or two of eerie silence that was suddenly broken by the sound of wagon wheels. Cord raced up to the barn door and opened it slightly, peering through the gap. He turned to them, a little excited. 'It's Joe, he is coming into the yard.'

They all hurried over to Cord at the barn door. They saw Joe driving the wagon and pulling up at the kitchen door. Trailing behind, tied onto his chestnut, was Sneeze Eliot's body. Arrows stuck out of the bloodstained body. Joe jumped down as the canteen door came flying open. An angry-looking Jack Stark rushed out, shouting angrily, 'Where the fuck have you been?' He froze on seeing the body hanging from the chestnut. With a hateful look he stared at Joe. 'What, what the fuck?' He pointed at Sneeze. 'What have you done to him, you French bastard? He's… he's fucking dead!'

Joe, unconcerned, gave a backward glance at Sneeze. Joe shrugged. 'Oh, him, found him out there on the Sweetwater. He seems to have met up with them Comanche raiders yer been warning us about, Jack.' Sighed. 'Man was dead when I found him. The chestnut, he was close by.' Joe rubbed his chin. 'Just cannot understand those Comanche leaving such a fine horse; come to think they never took Pat's, or Jake's, for that matter.'

Jack walked slowly up to the body of Sneeze and began to inspect the arrows. Stabbing his finger, he snarled, 'They ain't the same arrows that killed Murphy or Potter.'

Joe nodded. 'Yeah, you're so right, Jack. No, they did not come from the quiver of one young Indian brave name of One Knife,' shaking his head and pointing at the body. 'No, not his arrows.'

Jack reached down and pulled out his pistol. He grinned, snarling, 'Well, ain't we got one bright fucking Froggy here.'

Joe opened his coat. 'I am unarmed, Jack. Yeh gonna kill another unarmed man to add on to that lengthy list of yours?' Joe gave a quick glance at the figure of Bold Wolf, who had appeared from behind the large oak tree. He was slowly and silently creeping up behind Jack. Jack smiled. 'Oh, killing you, it's gonna be a pleasure, Dupree.' He puts a finger up to his head. 'But telling me where you have hidden them two fucking Irish whores, well, I would be a little gentle with yer.' Jack smiled. 'But if yeh don't, then it's pain, a lot of fucking pain, Froggy.'

Joe smiled and gave a wink.

'Yeh know, Jack, I'm a shaking in my fucking boots. Maybe those Comanche raiders of yours have taken them fine ladies.'

Jack snarled, 'Bullshit! Yeh know Dupree, I am a-gonna shut that lying mouth of yours for good.' He lifted his pistol; Joe blinked. The powerful hands of Bold Wolf wrapped around Jack, twisting the gun out of his hand; it fell to the ground. 'What… what the fuck?'

Jack, struggling, turned around to see the scout. He staggered forward, going face to face with Joe, stabbing a finger into Joe's chest. Joe gripped the finger, bending it back, causing it to break. Jack cried out in obvious pain. Joe pushed him away with a punch to his midriff. 'Now, you murdering bastard, I am giving you a choice. Where is Mary Beth, the young girl you took from a bank in Ulvalde?'

Jack looked at him, grinning. 'Oh, the banker's daughter. Now she did me and my boys a real good old time.' Jack gave a mournful sigh. 'Oh, she went and slashed her wrists. Yeah, just like the one in Eagles Valley, er, she was French. Not any relation by any chance, Dupree?'

Joe struck Jack hard, knocking him down to the ground. He then sent a violent kick into him. Jack rolled over and laughed. He looked up at Bold Wolf and smiled. 'That mother of hers,' Jack pointed to the scar running down his face, 'she gave me this. I slit her fucking throat.' He looked up at the now stony face of Joe. Jack continued laughing, pointing a finger at Joe.

'Why, she said her husband was a Ranger, she, that fucking French whore. She… she was his wife.' He winked at Joe. 'Oh, she was good, Dupree. I can still fucking smell her. Oh, la la—'

Joe gave Jack a kick to his face. His nose burst open, he began to spit out broken teeth as Joe continued to tear into him. Jack crawled in the dirt, spitting blood, pointing up at the body of Sneeze. He was choking with gurgling laughter. 'Hey Froggy, old Sneeze there, he broke your daughter.' Jack started to laugh hysterically. 'Punched her little pee hole.'

Joe, running, gave Jack one almighty kick to the head. Bold Wolf put his arm around Joe's shoulder to console him. Then, picking up Stark, he dragged the dazed body, lifting it onto the rails of the corral. He then threaded Jack's arms through the rails, binding them with strips of leather.

He stood back and nodded. Turning, he walked back to the oak tree and from behind produced a bow and quiver of arrows. He went over to Joe, who was down on his knees, sobbing. He helped Joe to his feet, then presented him with the bow and arrows. He whispered to Joe, 'Let's finish this, Joe.'

Jack hung through the rail. His head was unrecognisable. He was smiling through a bleeding mouth, mumbling, 'We fucked his family, yeh hearing me, Sneeze? His fucking family!'

Joe put an arrow to the bow and fired it into Jack's breast. Joe screamed, 'That's for Colette, my wife, you murderous insane bastard.' He reloaded, firing a second arrow into the top of Jack's head. 'That's for Janine, my daughter, and one Mary Beth and every other innocent man, woman, child, or beast you've fucking murdered.' Joe then sent a third arrow into the slumped body. 'That's for my friend, Pat, you bastard. Now it is finished.' Joe fell to his knees. Bold Wolf took the bow and loaded it, sending arrow number four into the lifeless body of Jack Stark. Bold Wolf nodded, turning to Joe and saying, 'For One Knife. Now it is finished, Joe.'

***

The cowhands, along with Sammy and his troopers, all came into the yard. Bold Wolf went over to the body of Stark and cut it free from its bindings. Sammy motioned for his troop to help Cookie, who came out from his kitchen to unload the supplies. Cookie nodded a thank you to Sammy. He then shouted over to Pete Russell, 'Pete, you and a few of the boys,' pointing at the bodies of Stark and Eliot, 'get this shit out of the yard. We do not want the boss and her daughter seeing this. Dig a fucking big hole and put them in it.' Pete nodded and with a few hands they hung Jack over his horse. Pete threw the reins to Crako who, with two other drovers, took the bodies away from the yard.

Maureen came running out of the barn, closely followed by Kathy and Tom. Cord was last out, walking the shine. Maureen bent over Joe and whispered in his ear, 'It is all over now, Joe. Your girls, they can rest in peace.'

Tom arrived and placed the locket into Joe's hand. Joe looked down, opening it. He showed Maureen the picture, saying sadly, 'My little girl, Janine.' Maureen hugged him. 'Yes, Joe.' She gave him a kiss on the cheek, sighing. 'She was beautiful. Tom told us. We know what happened. We are so sorry for your loss.' She squeezed his hand and again gently kissed his cheek before whispering, 'You know you have Kathy and me, that's if you want us, or is it too soon to love again?'

Joe got to his feet and hugged her. He nodded and smiled, saying, 'We can sure give it a try. They say love's a great healer, Maureen.'

Cord walked the shine over to Bold Wolf and held out its reins. 'He belonged to One Knife.' Bold Wolf with one hand gave an across the body wave to Cord. 'No, little brother, the horse, he belongs to you now.'

Cord said, 'But I—'

Bold Wolf stopped him. 'No, little brother, if you had not spoken out about these killers then the Comanche people, my people, would have surely been blamed. You, little brother, have cleared us. The horse is yours, a gift from my people.' Bold Wolf hugged Cord. The black shine neighed.

Maureen turned to Sammy who, with his troopers, has returned to the yard. 'Sammy, you and your men will rest and eat supper with us tonight. My chef, Cookie, will serve up such a feast. There are beds in the bunkhouse. We have all had a busy day.' She turned to Tom and Bold Wolf.

'Tom, thank you. Please, if you would, thank Major Storie too, when next you meet. I do not think we would have got through it all without you.' Tom smiled and nodded. She approached Bold Wolf. 'Bold Wolf, I will never forget you. Let us hope that for your people, a time will come when the buffalo returns for them.' Bold Wolf gave her a bow.

Cookie shouted from the kitchen door, 'Supper coming up, boss.' He looked over at Cord, giving him a serious glare. 'Cord, I need help here.'

Cord gave Kathy a peck on her cheek, handing over the shine's reins to her. 'Well, ain't you going to put your horse up for the night?' Kathy's eyes lit up. 'My horse? Shine is my horse?'

Cord hugged her. 'Yes, yes, yes.'

It was early evening, and the yard was filled with ranch hands along with their guest army troopers, all enjoying an atmosphere of friendship. On the White House veranda Maureen sat with Kathy, chatting to Joe and Tom. She looked out onto the yard; she nodded down to the happy throng of people, saying, 'It has been a long, long time since I last heard laughter all around this yard. I'm so happy I could cry, cry me a river.'

The kitchen door opened and Cookie came out wearing a white chef's stove hat. There was a moment of silence before they all wolf whistled, clapping and shouting. Cookie stood with his hands on his hips like a birthday boy. He nodded to Cord, who stood alongside him holding a metal prong. He was about to hit it when Joe stood, holding up a hand and asking for a moment's silence. He pointed over to a solitary male figure who was approaching them through the ranch main gateway.

Joe spoke so that all could hear. 'Allow me a few minutes to introduce you all to your new head of crew, your new boss of beef.' He pointed at the rider. 'Bull Ferguson.'

The yard suddenly exploded with rapturous applause. Cookie gasped, 'We got us Bull, we got us the man.'

Cord, taken aback, pulled on Cookie's sleeve. 'Bull Ferguson, Cookie, who is he?'

Cookie pointed at Bull. 'Who is Bull? Why he's the man, pioneer, frontiersman, you name it, he's done it all, boy. Why, he's as famous as your Davy Crockett, but then again suppose you ain't heard of him either? The Alamo, 1836... nah, before your time and Bull's too, come to think. That's a part of history, boy. One thing for sure, if had been in our time, Bull Ferguson, he'd have been there.'

Maureen squeezed Joe's arm and whispered, 'Bull Ferguson, why, he brought Pat, Kathleen, and me out here. How did you manage to employ the man, Joe? I thought he was with the wagon trains.'

Joe smiled. 'Wagons are fast on the decline, Maureen. The iron horse, the railway, is taking over the whole country. North, east, south and west. Bull, well he knew this and was contemplating going to Canada, that was, until I left a message with Major Storey. Yes, Maureen, Bull's working the beef for the Murphy ranch.'

Bull dismounted and took a few handshakes on his way to meet-up with Maureen. Joe nodded over to Cookie that he had finished.

Cookie nudged Cord, who rattled the triangle. Cookie, smiling, bowed then bellowed out, 'All please to enter Cookie Warren's fancy pants restaurant. Supper is about to be served.'

Chicago Dolls

'Four Women. Four Targets.
One Deadly Pact'

CHAPTER 1

One warm Sunday sunny afternoon on a middle-class avenue of detached one-storey homes in the Beverly district of South Chicago, what was seemingly a tranquil time for relaxation was suddenly transformed into one horrendous afternoon.

The silence is broken when a young girl of nineteen comes screaming out of one of the houses. Molly MacDonald staggers out with a bruised and beaten face, looking frightened and in despair, tears trickling down to her bleeding lips. Pain laces every step as she races towards the open garage of her neighbour, John Barlow. John's car, a Buick, sits out on his driveway. Molly races past it into the garage and crouches down in a shadow at the back, staring out at her house's front door. She sees it open and then the angry bull-like figure of her husband Ryan comes staggering, swaying out and onto the dwelling's front porch. The six-foot ginger-haired Irishman, eyes somewhat glazed, has a belt wrapped around his right fist. In his left he grips a half-empty bottle of scotch. He sways as he lifts the bottle to his lips and begins to guzzle from it.

He growls with his eyes flashing, head turning from left to right, angrily shouting, spitting his words, slurring in a strong Irish accent. 'Ye be a-getting yourself back here, bitch! I ain't near finished with ye.' He continues, with eyes blazing, 'Now! Ye disobey me, the harder you'll pay me. Ye fucking hearing me?' He lets the belt unroll, slapping it hard on a porch upright. Seeing the figure of John Barlow walking to his car, Ryan spits, and snarls towards his neighbour. He re-enters the house, still shouting, 'Get that arse of yours in here. I'm fucking waiting, bitch.' The door slams. Inside the garage John hears a clattering sound as Molly knocks over a can of oil, fortunately empty. John goes in to investigate, finding the terrified Molly cowering, going deeper into shadow, crawling before reaching the dwelling's back wall where she forms her shivering body into a ball.

She gives a sigh of relief on seeing the figure of a puzzled John Barlow enter. John holds out a hand, beckoning her to come to him. Molly puts out a hand to him. John takes it and gently begins to pat it. In barely a whisper John says, 'It's okay, girl, I heard the bastard.' He sighs. 'Quickly, now. Get into the back of my car, keep low.' Using John as a shield, Molly makes her way to the car. John opens the car door, allowing Molly to slide in and crouch down onto the floor.

He looks at her, shaking his head, at her cut and bruised state. 'Jesus, Molly, what's that bastard done to you? Best we put some distance between you and that crazy man of yours. Fuck, girl, you have to get away from that bastard of a man.' He takes down a hooded storm coat from its hook, then he clicks and closes the overhead door. Casually he slips into the driving seat, passing the coat over to Molly. 'Cover yourself, girl.' He fires up the engine and moves on down his drive, out onto Longwood Drive. He glances into his rear-view mirror and smiles on seeing Ryan MacDonald coming back out, slapping his belt and shouting. John presses his foot hard down on the accelerator.

CHAPTER 1

*

One month later

The West Chicago Center for Abused Women is abuzz with activity. Young girls dance to music coming from a transistor radio – 'Everyday' by Buddy Holly – while others play pool. Some older women sit in individual groups, talking and knitting. Others just drink coffee or smoke. Young children run around, screaming, chasing each other. Toddlers watch the dancers, trying to imitate the steps. A few small babies are being nursed by mothers, whilst in the main office three women sit around a circular coffee table. The door to the office stands partly open. On it a sign reads *STRICTLY PRIVATE. GLORIA MONROE. MANAGERES*. Gloria is sitting in a leather swivel chair and twirling a pencil. She is some thirty-five years of age, but looks ten years younger. She wears tight-fitting jeans on her super fit-looking body and a long-sleeved, checked blue shirt. Her blonde hair is cut in a military-style crew cut. She wears very little makeup.

She gives her watch a glance and looked over at the smiling face of Gina Pascalino. Gina's twenty-five and wears a bright red blouse under a short bolero black leather jacket. From a pocket she pulls out a small mirror and examines her face. It's a face with brown eyes and a Roman nose; she has long silky black hair. There's no mistaking her Italian heritage. She stands at five eleven, with a face and body that could make the cover of *Vogue*.

Opposite sits Martha Hendrick. At thirty-three, an athletic Afro-American woman, the hard lines of her looks shows that her life hasn't been easy. She smiles, glancing across at Gina, whose long delicate fingers are now combing and caressing her hair. Martha still carries a good body line, with full breasts and an hourglass figure. Her hair is cut razor short. She stands at five eight and wears an all-black jeans-and-sweater outfit. Around her neck is a crucifix.

Martha, yawns and says, 'You got a fine a head of hair there, girl. Wish I had it.' Gina nods a thank-you. Martha looks up at the ceiling. 'I did at one time. Till I met that bastard of a man.'

Gloria says with a deep sigh, 'Where the hell is Molly? I don't like it. She's late. Said she would be here.'

Gina, shrugging, says, 'If you ask me, if he's home, then …' she sighs deeply too, 'girl's taking a beating.'

Martha nods, 'The one I got is bad. He's tucked safely away.' She shakes her head and sighs. 'Not for long though. Fuck, if he ain't due out, next two weeks, I'm hearing. But let me tell you, that man of Molly's. He's a fucking animal.' The two other women look worried by her statement. She shrugs. 'Just telling it how it is.'

Gina nods. 'She wouldn't miss this night,' she says, with a worried look. 'It would have to be serious.'

Gloria nods, checking the time again. 'Look, I said seven. Let's give her till eight.'

Gina gives a nonchalant wave. 'I'm okay with that. That bastard of mine, Mario, he's at the ball game. Cubs have them damn Yankees,' she smirked. 'Him and his flunky, his cronies, they be celebrating until the morning light.'

Martha wags a finger. 'Celebrate? What if they lose, the Cubs?'

Gina gasps. 'Oh my God. I didn't want to think about that.'

Gloria shrugs, 'They lose, then our Gina becomes a punch bag.'

Gina buries her face in her hands, shakes her head and cries out, 'Please!' She turns to Martha. 'You're so lucky, baby, yours being in the lock-up.'

'Lucky? Lucky, you say? No fucking way, gal,' Martha says. 'He's due for release in ten days.' She sighs.

'Then Martha's dead,' Gina mutters.

Gloria sucks in a breath. 'That's for certain, Gina baby. See, Martha, she grassed him to the law. She put her man in there.'

Martha nods. 'He sold heroin to kids, Gina. I wasn't gonna have that. Put my sister's boy, sixteen, in the morgue.' Martha sighs deeply and leans back in her chair, and for a moment or two she closes her eyes.

*

24 hours earlier

In the car park of the Dollar Tree store, leaning over the top of a Ford Fiesta, the tall figure of Martin Hendrick stares at the approaching Martha, who carries a small bag of groceries. She suddenly stops on seeing her brother-in-law's now-grinning face. He walks towards her like some champion prize fighter. He motions to the bag. 'Let me help you with that.'

Martha squirms away, walks past him. Martin grabs her arm, pulling her. The groceries fall to the ground. He kicked the bag away. She shrieked.

'You know my brother Leroy is out in two weeks.' He smiles. 'He wants you at his homecoming party. Don't make me have to fetch you, you fucking be there. Why, you're the guest of honour.'

Martha scrambles for her groceries. Martin turns and swaggers away, shouting, 'You haven't forgotten the Shades club, have you, sister Martha? Be there.' He walks on, singing loudly, 'Oh what a night, oh what a night it's gonna be, oh what a night.' He laughs.

*

24 hours later

Gloria paces around her office, looking down at her watch. She slams a fist down on the desk. 'Jesus, we can help that baby.'

There is a moment of silence that is only broken when Gina says, 'I'm free till nine.' She shakes a fist at them. 'Hope to fuck them Cubs win.' Then she falls silent, lost in her thoughts.

*

Three hours earlier

In the Pascalino residence in Little Italy on the West Side of Chicago, Gina and Mario Pascalino sit having lunch. There is a long silence that is punctuated only by Mario stabbing his fork into the spaghetti. He gulps down wine, first swallowing, then spitting a mouthful into Gina's face. In one violent action, he bangs a fist down onto the table, making the dishes jump. He snarls, grinding his teeth, 'You buy in this'a shit. You not'a make fresh anymore, you idle slut.' He takes a handful of the pasta and throws it into Gina's face. He flicks his napkin at her. Her chair falls back, and she tumbles to the floor, trembling and crying out.

Mario is quick to react, standing up and rushing around the table, where he kicks her. She shields herself after taking a blow to the ribs. He snarls, 'You get me my meals like my mamma makes them, fucking fresh.' He strides to the door, turns and snarls, 'If the family call, you say Mario, he's at Wrigley Field. I will be late. Who knows, maybe I fuck some nice younger pretty girl.' He spits at her, 'You, you go to Roberto's, you go in his kitchen, learn how pasta is a fucking cooked. Like a succulent young girl's tits, not a like a fucking bunch of rhubarb.'

*

3 hours later

In the refuge centre, Martha and Gina sit watching the Gloria pacing. Martha rolls her eyes and nods at Gloria, shrugging. 'She's late, Glo. I'm cool with an extra hour or so. How about a coffee?'

Gloria nods. 'Give Marleena a call. Yeah, coffee for three.'

Martha goes to the door and looks out into the hallway. 'Better make that four, gal. Molly, she's just entered the building.' She swings the door wide open, and the small hooded figure slips inside. Head down, she brushes past a startled Gloria and drops into a seat without a word. Then, catching her breath, she finds her words. 'Shut the door, Martha, please.'

Martha shuts and locks the office door and sits down. 'I'm so sorry to keep you waiting, guys, but ...' she lifts her hood, showing a badly bruised and swollen face '... as you can see, I got fucking delayed.' The three gasp. Then they all try to talk at once.

Gloria holds up a hand. 'He did this to you, baby?' She holds Molly's hand and gently strokes her hair. Molly looks at the others with tears in her eyes.

'What the fuck happened, baby?' Martha asks.

Gina, shakes her head and says, 'He's home. That's what. Don't need no rocket scientist to work that out.'

Gloria snarls, 'Yeah? I'm hoping he's in a police cell banged up, the bastard!'

Molly starts to sob. Gloria holds her close, hugging her. 'Hush, baby. You're with friends.'

Molly stammers whilst sobbing, 'Yeah, he's home and he ain't locked in no police cell.' She pulls out a kerchief and blows her nose. 'I was just talking to a kid off the avenue, about getting my hedge cut.' She shudders. 'Ryan, he comes out from around the side of the house. He sees me talking to this kid. A kid who's only fucking thirteen years old.' She coughs. 'He tells the boy to beat it.' She sniffs. 'Well, his exact words, to a thirteen-year-old boy, were to "fuck off".'

She puts her head down onto the table. 'He dragged me indoors by my hair. He took off his belt, pulled down my jeans and panties, then he beat me with the buckle part of his belt.' Molly stands, slips off her coat, and eases down her jeans just enough to show them the damage. Angry red welts score her skin. The three women reach for one another's hands, their faces sorrowful.

'Oh, Ryan, he don't stop there. He starts to punch and slap me. He ... He ...' She opens her shirt and shows them cigarette burns to her breasts. 'He stabbed his joint out on me. Yes, joint – he was high on the fucking stuff.'

Gloria gently kisses the top of her head and asks, 'So how you get here, baby?'

'I ran out into John Barlow's garage. John's my dear neighbour. He was about to go out. He hid me in his car, then took me to the hospital, St Catherine's,' she says, shaking. 'John must have told the police. They came by the hospital,' she sobs. 'I told John to go. I didn't want that poor man involved. He's seventy-four years old.'

Gloria squeezes Molly's shoulder. 'The police, baby, what they say?'

Molly shakes her head. 'I was so fucking afraid, I told them I'd been mugged.'

Martha sighs deeply. 'You should've put him in the can, girl.' She looks round the table at them all. 'Well, I did with Leroy. He's due out in a couple of weeks.' She looks at the ceiling, then sobs, 'What am I saying? God forbid!'

Gina winks with a smile. 'Yeah, Martha honey, not such a good idea. Who's gonna pay for that, big time?' She slowly shakes her head. 'That Leroy, he's gonna come looking for you, and when he finds you,' she laughs, 'why, it's bye bye, Martha. You'll be dead meat, girl, that's for sure.' Gina makes the sign of the cross.

Molly still sobbing, says, 'Yeah and if I'd have grassed him up, oh my God. He'd have fucking killed me if I'd a got him time.' She looks at her friends' sad faces. 'Yeah, yeah, I'm foolish, fucking crazy. Hell, I'm so fucking scared now.' She sniffs, then blows her nose. Gina hands her a kerchief to wipe her eyes. 'So I did a runner from the hospital. I needed my friends, needed to get here.' She cries out, 'I got to get away from him, can't take these beatings anymore!' She sniffs again, then puts her face in her hands and shakes her head.

Martha turns to Gloria. 'So, this meet. What's it about? You said it was something special.'

Gina shrugs. 'Yeah, tell us girl, what's on your mind?'

Gloria looks at her watch and claps her hands. 'Yeah, sure. We're running on overtime.' She sits studying them, with folded arms.

Martha raises her eyebrows at Gloria. 'That Ryan, he'll be out, looking for Molly, Glo.'

Molly told them, 'Well if he is, he isn't going to find me here. He doesn't know anywhere but a barstool in a dirty sex den.'

CHAPTER 2

At about the same time, well into the evening, Ryan MacDonald is slumped at an alcove table in Sloopy's Cavern, a private establishment. He's sitting in a dimly lit corner booth near the front, with Mary Beth, a young topless hostess party girl. Onstage, two near-naked pole dancers are performing a sexual display. Mary Beth begins to pour from a bottle of Johnny Walker Black into Ryan's glass. She stops, looks to him. He leans over and kisses her nipple. Then, with his eyes swimming, he raises his hand in a four-finger gesture. He jabs his hand at the glass, then chuckles. 'Fill her up girl.' He burps. 'Then we'll do some sausage blowing, what ye say, girl?'

She smiles, winks, nudging him. 'Can't my big Irish leprechaun get it up tonight?' she laughs.

Ryan grabs her tit, squeezing hard and making Mary Beth gasp. Rubbing his crotch, he spits out a slurred answer. 'Your big Irish leprechaun will have you suck his dick ... lick his bollocks, while covered in a chocolate sauce.'

Mary Beth coughs. 'You know, Mister Irishman, that's gonna cost you some. More dollars cause I don't like chocolate.' She laughed to break the tension. 'How about we cool you off some with … let's say, strawberry ice cream. I love that strawberry cream. Mmm, mmm.'

She stands, taking him by the arm, helping him to rise. She looks to the bar where one hell of a gorilla-like figure stands watching. She yells, 'Bruce, I got myself a malignant here. Help me put him out. He's finished for the night.'

Bruce nods slowly. 'That's Ryan, He's rolled out early. He's a bad man sober. He can be trouble, but he's a spender. Best we let him sleep it off in Five.'

Mary Beth shrugs. 'Ain't that Annie's room?'

Bruce nods. 'Annie's night off. She's doing a special top-dollar job.'

Mary Beth scoffs. 'Why I never get them jobs? Why the shit?'

Bruce gives her a hug and a kiss. 'I like you here. Can't ya see I'm in love with ya?'

Mary Beth scowls. 'Fucking liar … Okay, let's move him while he can still walk. Take the dollars for the blow job.'

'But he ain't had one.'

'Fuck, Bruce he won't ever remember. I'll leave him though he had.'

Bruce nods. 'Just don't let him find out. He's a bad critter, is Ryan. Bad for you if he does.'

She shrugs. 'He needs taking down a peg, brother. So, let's do this. Be my problem.'

They both take Ryan out through the Private signed doorway, with Mary Beth, uttering, 'This way, my leprechaun.'

*

Back in the refuge, Gina sits, pulling down on her hair. She smiles at Molly. 'Wishing that man of yours dead. You aren't alone with them kinda wishes, gal.'

Molly gives a deep sigh. 'Yeah, look at me. Nineteen years old. I sure shook a fucking six in marrying that bastard of a man.'

'I'm thinking that goes for all of us, baby,' Gloria says. 'Yeah, like Gina says, I think we all threw that same number, baby. Why, I've got sixty-one abused members on my ledger.' She slowly shakes her head. 'All colours, all creeds. What a godforsaken life we're living.' She looks at Gina, then Martha. 'We shouldn't be taking this kind of shit off any man.' She bangs her fist down on the desktop. 'Matter of fact, off of nobody,' she snarls. She looked around the group with a serious expression while raising a finger as she prepared herself to say what came next. 'So in no way is what I'm about to say be repeated outside of this room … Is that understood?'

Each woman nods in agreement.

'Okay. We all have a personal problem. Problems that have ruined our lives. Truth is, these problems, well, they aren't ever going to go away.' She shakes her head slowly. 'Not unless we do something about them. Do we all agree?'

Gina gives a smile. 'Nail on the head, Glor.'

She looks to the others, who are nodding too.

'I think we all agree, Gloria,' Martha says, putting up a palm. 'What's on your mind baby? If it's getting rid of *my* problem, which is one Leroy Hendrick, then I'm interested.'

They all look at Gloria, waiting eagerly for her to carry on.

'Okay,' Gloria continues, 'I think we all agree that we have tied to our bodies, like blood sucking leeches, four men.' She points at Molly. 'Molly has that bastard of a husband, Ryan.' She waves a hand at Gina. 'Gina here has a Casanova Mafia killer husband, Mario.' She puts a hand on Martha's shoulder. 'Martha's looking forward to hell from her drug addict husband Leroy … Yeah, she might even get the death sentence.' Gloria shrugs. 'Myself? Well, I've got a money-taking killer, stalker Kenny Bailey.' She points a finger at her friends one by one. 'Make no fucking mistake about this.' Addressing Gina. 'Mario Pascalino is a born killing machine. A big piece of shit that's fucking every broad he fancies. One fucking high-ranking

Mafia hitman,' she snarls, 'except he's not satisfied with that, oh no. He gets extra pleasure from whipping his wife. Yeah, whipping her some. That's after using her as a fucking punch bag.'

Gina nods as Gloria goes to Molly, gently squeezing her shoulder. 'Molly is the youngest of us, our baby. Well, just look at her.' Gloria points at the injuries. Shaking her head she throws a punch into the air. 'I ask you. She fucking deserve this?' Gloria slams a fist down onto the desk. 'Look at her, guys.' Holding out her arms, Gloria gestures as she turns to each friend. 'She talked to a thirteen-year-old boy, for fuck's sake, about cutting her hedges. Yes, guys, our baby here has become Mister Ryan MacDonald's way of releasing his anger.' Gloria wags a finger at them all. 'But after tonight? It all fucking well stops.' She drums on the table with a fist. 'No ... fucking ... more. His hitting days are over.'

A moment's silence passes. 'Oh, I'd nearly forgot.' Gloria smiles before giving a wink. 'There's me.' Gloria brushes herself down and adopts a professional pose, like she's about to give a presentation. 'As you can see, I carry no bruises, no cuts, no lash marks.' She shrugs with open arms. 'You may ask: "Why is that? Gloria looks good".' She looks questioningly at them. 'Why?' Her friends turn and look to each other with nods and shrugs. Gloria points to her chest. 'That's because where Gloria is scared is in here. Oh yes, ladies, this gal's been hurt.' She sighs. 'Yeah, like you. I carry pain inflicted by a man too. Kenny Bailey. A man who took everything – yeah, everything, all that I ever loved – away from me.' She holds out a hand. 'All my money, all but a few dollars, that is. Had my first love murdered. A hit 'n' run.' She shakes her head. 'Never proved, but it was him.' She looks at the women's faces, their mouths open, aghast. 'Oh, at the time I didn't know. I found out much later. When it was too late. He broke my mother's heart. I know for sure he poisoned my dad.' Another sigh. 'Rusty, my dog. Bastard poisoned him too. He's still laughing at me from his sick little world. But one good thing about it all,' she smiles and winks. 'He does not reside with me. He's out my fucking door.' She shakes her head and points at the window. 'But he's out there, stalking me day and night. The police, they've found nothing.' She winks. 'Oh, Bailey's clever. So much so, he's got the cops into thinking I'm fucking insane. Telling them I ought to be certified.'

Gloria sees the women's alarm at the statement.

'No, no, no.' She waves a finger at them. 'I know what you're thinking. Just let me assure you he knows nothing of this place, my work, of us.' She starts nodding her head slowly. 'But I want retribution. He has to pay. Pay with his life. I want the fucker dead.' Gloria looks at three desperate looking faces.

Molly shakes her head. 'So, what can I do? It's hopeless.' She looks pleadingly to her friends. 'I can't kick that bastard out. Why, he'd fucking kill me. The police? That's a no go. You're saying that I've just got to pack up and move out, Gloria?' She buries her face in her hands and mumbles, 'That's if I ever get the chance.'

Martha nods. 'Yeah, these men of ours. There's no way we can get one over on them. I gotta fucking move too. Or I'm dead.'

Gina smiles. 'Wait, wait a minute now, guys. If you were to ask me, I'm thinking that our Gloria here, she ain't called this here meeting to sadden us more.' Gina wags a finger at Gloria. 'I think Gloria has something on her mind.' Smiling, she points to Gloria's head. 'That brain of hers. It's bee ticking over like a fucking Ferrari.' Looking at Gloria she asks, 'Am I right or what, Glo?'

Gloria, smiles and winks 'Yeah, Gina's right. We take the fuckers down.' She stares at them. 'We make them no more.'

Martha's mouth is agape. 'Ya mean fucking kill them?'

Gina gasps. 'Fucking kill them? Is Martha right in thinking this, Glo?'

Molly, suddenly alert, jumps up from the table. 'Oh please, please! But how?'

Gloria pulls them all closer. She looks to the door. Lowering her voice, she says, 'We take them down, girls. They have to die.'

Gina nudges her. 'Well, don't hold us in suspense. How, how the fuck we gonna do that?'

Gloria looks each of her friends in the face one by one and smiles. 'First, it's make-your-mind-up time. The time to say if you're in or out.' She taps the tabletop in rhythm with her words. 'If you want out, then I promise it won't be held against you. It's your decision, yours alone.' She stops her tapping, looks at each of them in turn, holding out her arms. 'Yours to decide.'

Martha speaks next. 'Okay, Gloria. Let's say we go with this – and I for one want in.' She smacks her lips. 'How we keep from walking into hell's gate – jail?' She sighs. 'Away for what could be a long, long sentence?'

Molly puts her hand to her mouth. 'The chair!' she exclaims. 'A death sentence.'

Gloria shrugs. 'Thought you'd ask that. Good question, and one that needs to be perfectly understood.' She waves them to come closer. 'First and foremost, well, there's no guarantee on this. Let's make that clear from the start. If we make mistakes,' she says, shrugging, 'then you know we gonna pay.' She looks to each face staring back at her. 'But I don't think ... what's on offer ... is mistakes?' She winks. 'We ain't gonna be making any.' She looks to each of them. 'So, my friends, do I take it we are all in?'

Molly eagerly cries, 'Count me in. I won't need no help in digging my man's grave. The sooner the better for me.'

Gina nods. 'It goes without saying. I'm ready for this. But remember, whatever's planned,' she gives a deep sigh, 'Mario has powerful connections. It will be difficult.'

Martha happily answers, 'Don't need to ask me. What with Leroy on the prowl ... I've got to take the risk. If he lives, then I'm dead anyway, that's for sure.'

Gloria claps her hands. 'Good. We gotta move fast on this. I'm thinking we take out Ryan MacDonald immediately.' She points to Molly. 'Molly will not be involved. We'll establish a watertight alibi for her.'

Gloria smiles and gently rubs Molly's arm, telling her, 'The job will be done and planned by Gina, Martha, and myself. She then holds her hand to the other two. 'Molly will know nothing of this. It ensures her full protection. What she don't know, she can't tell.' She spreads her arms, looks at Martha and smiles.

'You telling me Leroy's next, girl?' Martha asks Gloria.

'You bet, sweetie. We won't let him bite ya. He's leaving the planet … He's good as dead.'

Next Gloria smiles at Gina. 'Sorry, girl. Like you were saying, Mario, well, he's gonna take some thinking about.' She winks 'But I've got a plan. We go for him after Leroy. Me, I'm last.'

Gloria sits back, the room falling silent for a moment, before she gives a clap of her hands. 'So I can take that as a yes?'

Molly gives a weak smile. 'I don't see us having any choice. I'm wanting that piece of shit gone. Let's do this, Gloria. For me, I'd take a prison risk anytime.'

Martha goes over to Molly, gives her a cuddle, kisses the top of her head, then jabs a finger at her. 'You got more to come, girl. Will that bastard bray you some more?' Looking up at Martha, Molly starts to nod, with tears gathering once more.

Gloria coughs. 'So, let's get down to business, Molly baby. We need to know his routine, night activities. Everything about him.'

With a more serious look she adds, 'We need to know. What he does, where he goes, his job, everything, baby.' She opens a drawer and hands Molly a book and pencil. 'I want you to write everything down. Leave out nothing. That includes when he goes for a shit.' They all look at Gloria, then they laugh. But Gloria ain't laughing.

Gina looks at Gloria. 'You gotta be kidding there, aren't ya?'

Gloria shakes her head, smiling. 'Never been more serious in my life, girl. We leave out nothing if this is gonna work.'

There is a good fifteen seconds of silence before Molly points to the book. 'Ya wanting me to put this down now, Gloria?'

'Sooner it's done, sooner it's a go,' Gloria replies, before putting a finger up to them and pointing to the book. 'That book does not leave this office. When a plan is made, it is destroyed.' She smiles, pointing to her desk draw. 'I got plenty books, ladies. We leave here tonight with no outside association with each other, no matter what.'

They all nod.

'Molly can have time here in this office to give us the full dirt on Ryan MacDonald, I tell you all now.' She drums a fist.

Molly says eagerly, 'He thinks I'm hospitalised. He won't visit. He never does.' She gives Gloria a pleading look. 'If I could sort a bed here tonight, then I could get it all finished. Won't take me long. What do you think, Gloria?'

Gloria gives the desk top a tap. 'Tell ya what, baby. I'll bed down here with ya. We got blankets in the store room.'

Gina mutters, 'So, I take it we can't move till Molly puts it all down. Then what?'

Martha frowns. 'Leroy, he's out sometime in the very near future. Probably next two weeks at the latest.' She sighs. 'I need some fast closure on bad man MacDonald. I tell you what, girls, I'm worried sick. I'm wanting MacDonald. Well, he has gotta go down, like, yesterday.'

Gloria nods. 'If Molly gets it down tonight – and I must stress *everything* – then we could be a go, this coming weekend. That sound alright with ya all?' She points at Martha. 'Meantime, Martha, you gotta get yourself back in here and put what we need down on Mister Leroy Hendrick. You only do it here, in this office. The same rules apply.'

Martha nods an understanding. 'It's looking like you've got a full house tonight, Gloria.' She winks and smiles. 'Best you go into Pandora's box there, give little old me a book and pen.'

Gina claps her hands. She imitates the pull of a zip across her lips. 'Wish I could make that three of a kind, a full house,' she sighs, 'but I gotta get home. For me it's "Come on you Cubs."'

Gloria stands up and unlocks the office door and Gloria, Martha and Gina exit the office, leaving Molly busy working on the book. The trio strides out into the main hall, now deserted. Gloria looks at her watch. 'They've all gone home early, it seems.' She nods. 'Ah, I'm forgetting it's Monday, *Big Money Showboat*'s on TV. They'll not miss that quiz for anything.'

Martha nods. 'Yeah, I like to get in for it. Some dudes from Ohio chasing a quarter of a million dollars tonight.' Then she smiles. 'But I'm chasing more – a longer life expectancy. They say money don't mean nothing if you're dead.'

Gloria pulls back the latch, turns the key and opens the door to the street. 'Ya know, girls, I once had that kind of money in the Pony. Best of luck to the man from Ohio. Oh, and Gina, baby, tomorrow come dressed for work. Wear black. That's always assuming we get the go. I'm thinking it's gonna be the weekend, but come prepared anyway. Oh, that's absolutely assuming you can get away.'

Gina smiles. 'Tuesday. Mario will be up in Arlington. Tells me he's got a horse to view at the track, a filly. Out of some English Derby winner … Thinks I'm stupid. He's chasing a filly alright – name of Jasmin Cornell. But what the fuck!'

Martha nudges Gloria. 'Seems to me it's action stations. With Gina free tomorrow, then it'll be all down to Molly.'

Gina exits the building with Martha blowing a farewell kiss to her. She pushes Gloria on the shoulder. 'Can't wait to get started … I'm excited. So come on. Molly girl. Let's get back to her.'

Gloria looks out onto Main Street and watches Gina hurrying away. 'Same time tomorrow,' she shouts after her, and Gina gives an overarm wave.

With that, the two walk back into the hall, with Gloria

securing, bolting and locking the door. 'We've got this place to ourselves. It's officially closed Tuesdays. Good time to get moving on this.' She takes Martha by the arm and the pair walk back towards the office.

As they pass the pool table, Martha sends a ball into a pocket. 'Black ball game,' she mutters.

Gloria stops at a large basket, opens it and takes out six blankets and three pillows, and Martha holds out her arms and takes them. 'Just put them down in my office. I'll sort them later,' Gloria says. Gloria proceeds through a door with a sign that reads COFFEE SHOP. She turns on the light and finds a cardboard box, then fills it with a large pack of biscuits, three coffee cups. She then unplugs the coffee percolator, taking it over to the shop's sink. She fills the percolator, which she then adds to the box, along with a packet of Columbian ground beans. She then opens the refrigerator door. After a thorough inspection, she closes it, then turns off the light.

The door to the office opens and Gloria enters with the box and puts it down on the desk. She gestured at her friends, rubbing her tummy and pointing at the box. Molly smiles back.

'Looks like you've been a busy, girl,' Gloria laughs. 'All five star comforts for us, baby. We got good Columbian coffee with sugar to taste. We got biscuits from across the pond – Scottish shortbread.'

Martha gives a thumbs-up. 'Oh, I love them shorties. Better watch I don't eat the lot. What more could a girl ask for?'

Gloria nods. 'Yeah, mine too. Good. I'll make us some fresh coffee, baby.' She puts a gentle hand on Molly's shoulder. 'How's the Ryan MacDonald story going?' Then she looks to Martha. 'Best you start on the Ballad of Leroy Hendrick. I'll be mother tonight. So, leave nothing out.'

'I'm on top of it, Glor,' Molly says. 'I'm getting there.'

Gloria looks at Molly, who is now sitting with eyes closed. Then she turns to the nearby radio that's sitting on top of a filing cabinet. She turns it on. The sports news is just finishing, and the Cubs have triumphed over the Yankees. Country Music comes out from its speaker – Willie Nelson is halfway through his rendition of 'Crazy'. Gloria turns the volume down a little and hums along with the melody. Molly's eyes open and close as she says, 'Oh, I love that man. Seems Gina is in for a trouble-free night what with the Cubs winning. Come to think of it, Willie Nelson could well be about right with that ballad.'

Gloria smiles. 'Me too, baby. Relax – get some rest. Yeah, Willie, you're sure right about that. Boy, are we all fucking crazy.'

She rises and spreads out two sets of blankets and pillows, positioning them on either side of the desk. She passes the third set to Martha. She slowly eases Molly out of her seat and down onto the blankets, putting a pillow under her head. Half asleep, Molly yawns as Gloria coves her with a blanket. She turns to Martha, pointing to a corner spot. 'There you go, Martha baby. Lay your bedding over in that corner, girl. I think I'll read though some of Molly Mac's essay for a while.'

'Thanks Glor. I ain't a bit tired. May as well get on with Mister Leroy Hendrick. Just say when it's lights out, gal.' Gloria sits back at the desk. She opens the draw and hands Martha a book and pencil. Then she leans back, picking up Molly's written work, and begins to read.

*

The following morning, Gloria sits reading a newspaper. There's a selection of fruit and sandwiches on the desk. Coffee is on the go, and Molly is beginning to stir. She sits up and stretches out her arms. blinks, rubs her eyes, and looks up at Gloria. Yawning, she asks, 'What's the time, Glo?' Then she looks around the office, somewhat puzzled. 'Where's Martha?'

Gloria peers over her paper. 'Well, good morning, baby. It's eight thirty, coffee's on. Martha, she went out early. She'll be back after a change of gear.' She smiles at Molly 'Come get breakfast. You know where the John is, if you need to freshen up. There're towels if you want to shower.'

Molly rises and gazes down at the food that had appeared overnight on the desk.

She looks at Gloria, who's smiling. 'Oh, I've been out. Got us a few bits. It's raining out there. Not a nice day at all.'

Molly rubs her arm. 'I'm sore. Don't think I'll be going out anyway. Looks like you got a helper, Glor.' Gloria posed with her hands on her hips. 'You can put down that book. You got much more than enough on the life of that bastard.' She smiles, adding, 'I went through it last night. I think we've got enough.' She goes to the coffee pot and pours into two cups. 'Oh, before I forget, have you got your house key? We need it to get into your home.'

Molly nods, suddenly becoming more alert. She gives Gloria an enquiring look. 'You're not thinking of going there?' she asked, blinking fast. 'Surely not, Glo?'

Gloria gives her a reassuring pat on the back of her hand. 'Yeah, I need you to make out a list of your dress requirements for a week's vacation. Put where in the house they are. Oh!' She turned on her heel, looking down at Molly. 'Only items that will not draw him into thinking you've done a runner.' She smiles. 'Leave the fragrances, shampoo, toothpaste, stuff like that. We'll buy fresh. You walk out and he won't suspect nothing'

Molly gasps, then gives a deep sigh. 'Glo, what you talking about? I ain't got money for no vacation.' She shrugs. 'Is this really necessary?'

'Shush, will ya,' Gloria interrupts her. 'You're already booked into a spa hotel in Helena, Montana, baby.' She shakes Molly by her shoulders. 'You fly out tomorrow evening. It's all arranged. So, get on with that list. After a few days,' Gloria continues as she winks, 'why, you're going to return a grieving widow.'

Molly tries to smile but she looks worried. 'You sure about this, Glor? Who's gonna pay for all this?'

'Well, I am, baby. It's already paid. I had to use your name. Paid in dollars, cash.' She shrugs, smiles and holds out her hands. 'Don't you worry none. I want you to enjoy.'

Molly hugs Gloria. 'Thank you. I've never ever been on vacation. He's never given me one.' She sighs. 'Bastard never took me on any holidays. Never taken me with him.' Then she smiles. 'Not that I'd be wanting him to.'

She looks to Gloria, and her tears flow.

CHAPTER 3

It's early evening and all the girls are sitting at the desk. They're having coffee, and Gina, Martha and Gloria are all dressed in black.

Martha asks Molly, 'You okay, girl? I mean, with the vacation an all?' She winks. 'Wish I was a going with ya, gal.'

Molly smiles and nods. 'So do I, Martha. I just hope things go right whilst I'm in Montana. I'll be on edge, thinking about you guys.'

Gina kisses Molly on the cheek. 'You enjoy, baby. What time's your flight?'

Gloria looks down at her wrist, checking the time. 'Flying out tomorrow night. She's on the nineteen hundred to Helena Regional. She's got all the time in the world.' She turns to Martha. 'Yeah, Martha, wish I was going too.' Then she claps her hands. 'So, down to business.' She takes down the radio, handing it to Molly, saying, 'Molly, you take the radio, go into the coffee shop. I have to go through a few items with the girls.'

Molly started to protest. 'But …'

Gloria points at her and smiles. 'Remember what I said? Sorry, baby.'

Molly picks up her drink and, taking the radio, exits the office.

Martha sighs. 'Poor baby.'

Gloria tells them, 'I've checked and double-checked Molly's book, and according to her, Tuesday night Ryan goes down to Sloopy's, that private sex dive off Randolph Avenue.'

Gina puts a finger up to her brow. 'That's in the West Loop.' She shakes her head. 'Excuse me Glor', but how come she knows this? It seems funny to me. Why would she have such information? You sure on this?'

Martha slowly nods in agreement with Gina.

Gloria smiles, waving the book at them. 'Molly found out by checking a credit statement, that our friend Ryan had carelessly dumped in the trash can. The month's statement puts him there every Tuesday and Thursday.'

Gloria raises her hand and turns her wrist. 'That's, of course, on the weeks that he's home.'

Martha nods. 'Good girl. Must have a side piece there. So, Molly lives West Side?'

Gloria shakes her head. 'Wrong. Molly lives in Beverly, that's south. He does some business down there in the norm.'

Gina shrugs. 'Yeah? Well, I'm East and I ain't heard of Sloopy's.'

Gloria smiles. 'You won't. It's a private gig, with no flashing neon sign. It's where the wife-beating perverts go for a hundred-dollar blow job.'

Gina nods. 'Yeah, I'm betting that bastard Mario's a member. He'd know that place.'

'More than likely, girl,' Gloria says. Then she leans in. 'So, here's what's going down.'

*

Around midnight that night, Gloria, Gina and Martha sit in Gloria's red Chevy, surveying the homesteads along Kolbeck

Road. Gloria's in the driver's seat, Gina's beside her, and Martha's in the back.

Gloria lowers her voice to a whisper. 'It's like a graveyard out there. Nothing's moving. Best we leave the car here. Can't risk parking any nearer to Molly's.'

'Can I make a suggestion?' Gina says.

'Sure, girl. What's on your mind?'

From the front passenger seat Gina turns to face them. 'I was thinking, Gloria. You have the list. You know what to do in regards to Molly's gear.' Her friends are listening intently, waiting for her to continue.

'I think it's a risk, us walking the hundred or so metres to Molly's, don't ya think?' She shakes her head. 'It's fucking too quiet. Why, three figures in black,' Gina points over at the row of homes that line each side of the road. 'It only takes a view from one of those curtains, and I know – and I think you do too – that they'd be on that phone.'

Martha nods in agreement. 'I'm thinking Gina could be right, Gloria.'

Gloria taps the steering wheel. 'Okay, this is what we do. Gina takes the wheel. She drops us off outside Molly's. It's just over there.' She points to a clump of trees fringing the garden just off the roadside. 'Martha and me will do the house. Gina, you drive on. Give us fifteen minutes, then come pick us up. That sound good?'

'I didn't mean for me to ...' Gina starts.

Gloria pats her hand. 'I know that, girl. That was good thinking on your part.'

Martha gives Gina a wink. 'Yeah, good thinking gal. Let's do this.' She glances up and down the road 'Then we gets the fuck out of here.'

Gloria swaps seats, giving Gina the wheel. Gina rolls the car silently down the road with its headlights switched off. Gloria and Martha are watching every house as they stop at the trees.

They sit in silence, hearing nothing but the sound of the car's engine turning over. Gloria nods to Martha, and they both open their doors simultaneously and slip into the cover of the trees. Gina drives silently away.

*

The trio are back on the open highway after an uneventful trip. Gloria is back driving, and the radio is tuned to a country music channel. Gloria suggests in a most serious manner, 'I'm thinking we should mix a few colours. Looks like we've been to a funeral.' She pulls at her sweater. 'I think the law would certainly question us, if we should happen to get a pull.'

Gina turns to Martha. 'Take your top off, girl. Gloria's got a point. Look bad if we get pulled all dressed in black.'

Martha grins. 'Well, if I leave mine on, I don't think they'd notice me, sitting here in the back. Me being fucking black an all.'

They all burst out laughing.

'So, you guys you have it all?' Gina asks. 'The vacation holiday gear for our Molly?' She points over her shoulder at the large travel bag that's lying next to Martha.

Martha replies, 'Hope we have. We've got what was on the list.'

'That was a cool undertaking, no problems at all,' Gloria adds. 'Yeah, didn't expect trouble back there. Unbelievably smooth. Now comes the hard part.'

There's a moment of silence, and Gina puts her hands together in a prayer-like fashion. 'Let's pray part two goes down just as easy. Do you know, I'm getting very excited about this kind of work. Like I've been doing it all my life.'

Gloria looks a little surprised and concerned at her friend's statement. 'Hey, it's all new to me,' she says, then coughs. 'Not sure about you two though. I'm thinking could I be riding with a couple of established killers.'

'So you had better watch your back now, Gloria Monroe,' Gina deadpans, before they all laugh.

'I think Molly will be pleased,' Martha says.

Gina laughs. 'Pleased? Pleased? Well, I sure would be. Can't wait for my vacation, and Mario's annihilation.' She smiles. 'You know Mario, he was named after the singer Mario Lanza. The Italian movie star.' She laughs. 'Often I think of the ballad – "I'll walk with God" Beautiful. One of his father's favourites.' She sighs. 'Well, Mario Pascalino, I'm afraid for you it's not God you'll be walking with. It'll be the man downstairs. The fucking Devil.'

Gloria and Martha clap.

Gloria turns to Gina. 'Gina, I'm worried about your man Mario. He's no Ryan MacDonald. He's smarter. I'm going to be interested in your book on him.'

Gina nods. 'Unlike MacDonald, he's not a man you can set your watch by. He's so unpredictable.' She sighs. 'We could have problems. But in saying that, I can only put down the way it is, girls. Take right now, for instance.' She waves a hand over her head. 'I'm free of him for a few days. He's down in LA. His Don, Vincent De Generio. Well,' she shrugs, 'you don't want to know him. Not a nice face to know. He controls the east side for the family.' She smiles. 'Well, yesterday the Don sent Mario to contact one Korky O'Dell.' She shrugs. 'Seems old Korky's been creaming off their interest.' She shakes her head. 'In the Family, that's a death sentence. You steal from the family, you pay with your life.'

*

Later, Gloria and the team are back in the refuge centre contemplating their next operation.

Gloria addresses her friends about what could be a major problem concerning the extermination of Mario, having already solved Martha's dilemma.

'Yes, I know we have to tread very carefully with Mario. We make a mistake, then it's good night, Vienna.'

Martha shakes her head, saying, 'Jesus. And I thought *I'd* got the problems.'

Gina continues, 'The Don wants Mario to rub out – kill – Korky. He's asked for closure.' She stabs a finger at the table. 'What the Don wants, the Don gets.' She smiles. 'The Sicilian God orders Mario to take off his head, to bring it home to Chicago,' she grimaces, 'in a fucking basket.'

Martha puffs out a breath. 'Wow. Urrrgh. That sure is some heavy shit.'

*

The girls sit in the car. They watch Molly, who is pushing her baggage cart through the terminal doors. Gloria pulls away, driving the car back onto the main highway, heading back towards the city.

Gina speaks with a clap of her hands. 'Well, the baby's on her way.'

Martha shrugs. 'I thought she looked kinda sad.'

Gloria nods in agreement with Martha. 'Yeah, I thought that. But she had to travel alone. But yeah, baby, she was certainly missing us, from the moment she left the car.' She slaps the palm of her hand on the dash. 'But she I'm sure will be fine. Knowing that's the last of her life with MacDonald.'

Gina gives a meaningful look at them both. 'We hope.'

Gloria stabs a finger at the Italian. 'Don't be so negative, girl. We're gonna do this. He won't know what's fucking hit him.'

Martha wears a look of excitement. 'Bring it on. I want to do this now.' She nods in the direction of a plane in the distance, coming in to land, as the red Chevy got further away from Chicago's Midway Airport. 'For Molly.'

Gloria adds, 'Look, Molly has no idea – no knowledge at all – of where, how or when we're going to hit that bastard.' She gives a nod to Gina. 'You clear with Mario, girl? He ain't gonna surprise you by getting home early now?'

Gina gives Gloria a serious look. 'You gotta be joking. He don't even give me a call. Would he notice me missing? The answer's no.'

Martha reminds them, 'It's Thursday. That's one of Ryan's Sloopy days, girls.' She smiles. 'Good day to die?'

Gloria nods. 'Could well be, Martha honey. Could well be.' She turns on the radio. Bruce Springsteen had just starting his ballad 'The River'.

'Springsteen, he's good,' says Martha. 'But so is Smokey Robinson. You gotta get a little soul, girls.' She sways her shoulders, her hand brushing her cheeks as she melodically hums, then points to her face. 'Mmm, mmm, mmm ohhh, see the tracks of my tears.'

Gina nudges Gloria and nods at Martha, then winks. 'When it comes down to song, the blacks sure outshine the whites.'

Gloria nods. 'One hundred per cent they sure can at that. Dance too – they can really grind it out, with that ass shaking and those hips swaying.'

Gina and Martha laugh at Gloria's attempt to do a car seat wobble.

Martha says with a wink, 'Hey, you two. Ya wouldn't be trying to pull my leg? Remember this, girls. All the American champion athletes are black. The fighters too – Ali, Tyson, Forman, Hagler, Hearns. Ain't that proving a point. I love boxing.' She laughs. 'Big men hurting each other.'

They laugh, Martha looking out through her window.

The car slows in passing a floodlit building complex.

'Hey, what's about here?' Gina points out at a large construction site.

Gloria replies, 'Oh, that's gonna be the new mall. Cost a few million dollars. Big consortium. Blood-stained. Contracts.' She smiles at Gina. 'Maybe your Mario knows? Rumour has it there's Family involvement.'

Gina scoffs. 'Don't surprise me none. They just about control every damn thing in this city. Only thing they ain't into touching is drugs. The Don won't have them in his shed.' She shakes her head. 'Not after Angelina – his granddaughter – overdosed on some nasty shit.' She looks at Martha. 'Who knows, gal – probably came from your Leroy Hendrick.'

Gloria slaps her hand hard down on the dash, smiling. 'Jesus! Why did I not think of that? Why, it's perfect. It's a problem solved.' She turns to Gina 'Get that added to that book of yours, Gina. The Don's granddaughter. I have an idea.' She smiles and winks at the two of them.

Martha laughs. 'Sounds like you won the lottery, gal.'

Gloria nods. 'I just may have done that, ladies. Could well be near perfecto.'

*

The three girls sit in the office drinking coffee. The remnants of a takeaway lies on the desk, along with Molly's exercise book.

Gloria looks at her watch. 'Well, ladies, now is the time to get our arses moving on Ryan.' She picks up Molly's book and waves it. 'According to baby's notes, Ryan works on those restroom hand-drying machines. He works three weeks on and a week off for Grants, the vending machine people.' She laughs.

Martha shrugs. 'Yeah, every shithouse has a Grants. With a shithouse working for them.' She slams the table. 'Say, Glor', so come Monday, MacDonald, he could be away for three weeks.' She shakes her head. 'Jesus, we've got till Sunday to see him dead. Leroy, Glor' – he could be out next fucking week.'

Gloria looks into Molly's book. 'Or could be Sunday night. Molly says he sometimes has to drive overnight if he's working distance.'

'So we've got until Saturday,' Gina says. 'Time's not exactly on our side, Glor'.'

Gloria sighs. 'No, it's not. We got to grab some rest, and we hit him tonight.'

Martha and Gina look at each other and simultaneously utter 'Tonight!'

Gloria gives a deep sigh. 'I don't think Baby Molly can wait another day. Come to think, Martha certainly can't.' She gives them a deadly serious look.

Gina smiles. 'We fucking well know that she can't.' She looks at them both for some sign.

Martha answers. 'We gotta do this, Gina.'

'Okay,' says Gina. 'How, when and where tonight?'

Gloria shrugs. 'We gotta do it while he's out at Sloopy's Cavern. Gotta do this while he's gone. It's gotta be tonight.' She points to the book. 'Molly's saying if he's doing a long haul, then he'll leave Sunday.'

Gina holds up a palm. 'Let's get this over and done with.'

Gloria nods. 'This is what I feel we must do. We got one shot at this, and we can't afford any mistakes.'

Martha adds, 'I'm thinking here, Glor'. Wouldn't it be better to hit him while he's out on the road?'

Gloria gives a shake of the head. 'Yeah, would be great if we could all spend time away. To know where he's at. What town. City.' She smiles. 'Sorry, but without looking into his diary, it's gotta be a no, no, it's got to be now.'

Martha sighs. 'Yeah, that's the when and where. But you're not saying how, girl.'

Gina nods. 'Yeah, how we gonna murder the bastard? Shoot, knife, how?' She shrugs. 'Glor'?' Gloria waves a hand. 'Nothing like that. What we needing is a silent killer.' She points to a locker standing in the corner. She goes into her pocket, takes out a key, and hands it to Martha. She motions to them to go take a look and smiles. They both stand and walk over to the locker. Martha puts in the key and opens it, standing back to allow Gina to view its contents. They both gasp at a prominent bottle of tablets labelled DEADLY POISON: CYANIDE SALT, with a skull and crossbones under the words.

Gina gives a puzzled look. 'But cyanide, Glo? Is that what's in that bottle? Because if it is, then how the fuck are we going to administer it to that bastard? Am I right into thinking we're going the full hog and poisoning MacDonald?'

Martha puts hand up to her mouth. 'Yeah. But how we gonna get that bastard to take it? If we miss on this, then we have problems.' She sighs. 'Or Molly has.'

Gloria calls them back over and smiles at them. 'Remember I told you that Kenny Bailey, he done my dad? Yeah, with that very poison. How do I know this?' She smiles and points at the bottle that Martha is holding out. 'From out of that bottle came just one of those tablets. They're cyanide. Bailey got them – God knows from where – and he gave my dad one.' She shrugs. 'One was enough, killing my dad in seconds.'

Gina holds up a hand. 'But the police. They didn't come to arrest this Bailey?'

Gloria sighs. 'Oh, he was a smart mister. He was someplace else. A motel somewhere in St Louis.' She nods. 'Strong alibi. He'd paid someone else to administer it.'

Martha blinks. 'This bottle here ... that I'm holding? How?'

Gloria takes a moment to reassemble her thoughts. 'How? How I come by it? He carelessly left it under my dog Rusty's blanket. Yeah, in his outdoor kennel. Rusty brought them to me in his mouth.' She points at the bottle. 'Me, well, I swapped them over, putting the same amount back with a similar looking painkiller – aspirin.'

Gina stammers, 'But, but ...'

Gloria sighs. 'He must have gave Rusty the full bottle of them painkillers. Mixing them into his food.' She gives a deep sigh. 'Next day, Rusty was dead. Yeah, there was no way he was wanting Rusty to find and bring out the evidence.' She smiles

'But his mistake was in thinking the poison was safe. That my dog had swallowed it.'

'The evil bastard!' Martha snarls.

Gloria shrugs. 'Yeah, the bastard stood, watched me burn Rusty's kennel. Standing there with a sick smile on his face.' Gloria has a sad expression on her face as she remembers. 'It was a pile of ash when I left. I watched him through the kitchen window. He was poking the ashes.' She smiles. 'He didn't suspect. He thought all the evidence had been destroyed.' She looks at Martha and shakes her head.

Martha winks. 'That's nice thinking, girl. Wow. You sort of saved them for a rainy day.'

Gina nods too. 'We think we know why you're about on with this, Glor'.'

Gloria taps her desktop. 'Good, because it came to me, while coming back from the airport. This is how it's gonna happen.' She holds up Mollys book. 'According to Molly's little black book,' she smiles, looking into their fully attentive faces, 'Our Mister Ryan MacDonald likes to sniff a line or two of the White Dragon.' She winks. 'So, here's how it's gonna go down for us.'

CHAPTER 4

The red Chevy stands parked in a dark secluded corner that looks into the large Frystone Avenue parking lot. In the lot are a large selection of top-of-the-range vehicles from high-class vehicles, both American and European: BMWs, Mercedes, Bentleys and Rolls Royce. A notice informs any non-members of the Sloopy's Cavern that their car will be clamped and removed. Gloria is looking through a pair of binoculars at Sloopy's hole-in-the-wall entrance. She turns to Martha. 'That dark blue Honda Civic.' She passes the glasses to Martha. 'Over there near the corner. It's standing next to the White Merc.'

Martha looks through a pair of night vision binoculars. 'Yeah, I've got it.'

'That's MacDonald's Honda,' Gloria whispers. 'We let you out here. Walk all around the park to it.' She points at some bright lighting and a single security camera. 'Keep out of that brightly lit section. Well away from that camera.' She smiles at Martha. 'Lucky for us, he's parked away from it.' She puts a hand on Martha's arm and gently squeezes. 'Keep your eyes peeled over at our car. Watch for a single headlight flash from me.' Her hand moves onto Martha's shoulder, she pats it. 'That's to tell you that he's on his way and alone.' Gloria looks at her two friends sternly. 'If I don't flash you, abort, girl. Wait, get out of sight. I'll flash you when it's safe to return.'

Martha nods. 'Yeah, I've got it, I'm good.'

Gina adds, 'If you hit any problem, girl, I'm watching your back.' She smiles at Martha, pulling out a long stiletto knife. 'I'll be fucking good.'

Gloria gasps. 'I'm hoping, praying, we won't be needing that.'

*

Martha is standing in a dark section of the park. She's wearing a black cloak and is some ten metres from the blue Honda. Her eyes are fixed on the area where the red Chevy stands.

Sitting in the Chevy, Gloria and Gina are still watching Sloopy's hole-in-the-wall entrance. There's a sudden movement as the large figure of a man comes out. The man looks to be a little unsteady on his feet. Gloria puts on her glasses and looks over at him. She then pulls out a small photograph and looks at it. Smiles, she nudging Gina, then points. 'That's him.' She hands the photo and glasses to Gina to look.

Gina squints, then turns to Gloria, smiling. 'Yeah, he's our boy, the fucking wife-beater. You gonna give Martha a flash?'

Gloria nods 'Yeah, but let's make sure he's on his own. By the looks of him he's well and truly wasted. Let's get him over some, nearer to that corner.'

Gina nods. 'It's now or never, Glor.'

Ryan MacDonald staggers towards the Honda, and Gloria gives a quick flash on her lights. Seeing the flash, Martha takes off her cloak and steps out. She's looking invitingly good in a low-cut, skin-tight orange jumper with black leggings. Her breasts stick out. She wears a grey-streaked wig.

She's wearing gloves. She walks over to the Honda and takes from her purse a small transparent blue bag and mirror. Putting down the mirror onto the Honda's hood, she begins to lay a line of powder on it. She puts the bag back into her purse. A staggering Ryan approaches, then stops when five metres from her. He blinks and watches Martha chop the powder with a razor, then sniff up the line.

Martha turns sharply on his approach. She holds out her arms, shakes her head and blinks rapidly, gasping in surprised manner. 'Oh, oh fuck! You've caught me! You're not ... You're not the fucking fuzz, are ya?'

Ryan sways, struggling to keep his balance. 'That's my ... my ... fucking car you're on. What's that shit you're sniffing off my hood?' He looks at her body and his glassy eyes light up. He smiles, wagging a finger at her and shaking his head. 'Now you're a very naughty girl.' He begins to unbuckle his belt. 'Naughty girls ... well, they gotta be punished. They gotta pay for being fucking naughty, using my car to cut your fucking lines on and feed your filthy habit. Oh, you're gonna pay, girl.'

Martha is wearing a well-practised worried expression. 'What ... what ya doing? What ya gonna do?'

Ryan staggers closer and jabs a finger down on the mirror, grinning. 'Well first, ya gonna give little old Ryan here some of that shit you've been a snorting. Then, when I'm really high,' he gives her a wink followed by a sick smile, 'You're gonna give old Ryan a nice blow job.' He puckers his lips. 'Yeah, with those fucking big lips ye got. Then, oh then, girl,' he snorts, 'I'm gonna fuck that fine ass of yours.' He gives the Honda's hood a little pat. He staggers forward and grabs her arm, pointing to the hood. 'So, lay me a line on my hood there. Let's get down to having some fun.'

With a frightened look, Martha dips into her purse and pulls from it a small transparent bag full of white powder. She tips some power onto the hood and then carefully chops and breaks it up with her razor.

'Hey, stop the fucking chopping on my car. Throw that fucking blade away,' Ryan protests.

He points at some bushes. 'In there. Like, now. Never trust a fucking woman with a blade in her hand.' He chuckles. 'I wanna get high. High as fucking Mount Everest.' Hustling forward he pushes Martha away from the line 'So get the fuck out of my way.'

Martha stands back and presents the line to him. He moves hunches over and sniffs. He takes in the whole line, his hands stretched out, pressing hard on the hood.

He begins to choke, he staggers back. His hands go to up to his throat, as he gasps and wheezes. He falls down onto his knees, foaming at the mouth. Blood begins to trickle from his nose. He turns to look at her. But Martha is walking away. He falls forward onto his face. His body trembles, then his eyes close.

Gloria and Gina look through the windscreen as Martha scurries towards them from out of the shadows. Gina leans over and opens the rear door, and Martha, once again wearing the black cloak, climbs in.

'How'd it go, baby?' Gina asks excitedly.

Martha nods and smiles. 'Let's get the fuck out of here. Hit that gas, Glor.'

Gloria turns and pinches her. 'Okay, but we watch the speed. Can't afford no cop interruptions. We take the back roads home. We don't want no cameras picking us up. The route's all planned out, girls.' Gloria fires up the Chevy, then claps her hands and turns to Martha. 'So? How did it go?'

Martha looks at them both. Her eyes drop to the floor and she looks glum.

Gina and Gloria look at each other, confused.

'What, Martha gal? What the fuck?' Gina asks anxiously.

Martha slaps her thigh and grins, winking at them. 'Like a dream, girls! He went full throttle for it. I left him gasping for breath.' She sighs, putting a gentle hand on Gloria's shoulder. 'He was a-gasping so much, he done run out of fucking breath. But it hurts me to say, Glor … your father … he must have suffered.' Putting a hand up to her mouth she does a fake yawn, gives a shrug, and opens her arms to them. 'Oh, you gotta believe me, sisters. That MacDonald is dead. Dead as a dodo. He's fucking no more, girls. I cannot wait to see Baby Molly's face we tell her she's a free bird!'

Gloria and Gina punch the air.

'Okay, girls, let's move,' Gloria says. She looks to Martha. 'Now, Martha, baby. Ya remembered to put yer gloves on? You didn't touch anything without em on? Tell me, honey pot – ya wore ya gloves, all of the time?'

Martha nods, then puts a finger up to her brow.

Gloria pulls the Chevy out of the parking lot.

Martha remembers something. 'Just one thing, Glor,' she says. Gloria brakes and looks to Gina, and they both turn to Martha.

'What's the one thing, girl?' Gina asks

Martha sighs. 'I don't think it's … it's nothing really. It's just that I was cutting the dope …'

'Go on,' Gloria says anxiously.

Martha waves a finger. 'I had my gloves on when … well, that bastard, he told me to throw the blade. I had to hurl it into some bushes. I don't know where the fuck it could have landed, but I can assure you my gloves remained on.'

Gloria gives a sigh of relief. 'I don't see a problem. Why, those blades, they're ten to the dollar. You can buy them almost anywhere. As long as you cut with gloves on, you're safe, girl.'

Gina gives Martha a sympathetic smile.

Gloria takes her foot off the brake and moves the Chevy on.

'Hope you got that little book filled and ready for inspection, girl!' Gina shouts over her shoulder at a silent Martha. 'That Leroy Hendrick, he's next.'

'Oh, it's ready,' Martha says, giving Gina a friendly push. 'Been ready some time. His story reads like a Mark Twain novel.' She squeezes Gina's shoulder. 'It's one of those reads you'll just not want to put down.'

'Get that date,' Gloria says seriously. 'We need to know when he's out.'

'Do we hit him with the cyanide too, Glor?' Gina asks.

Gloria gives Gina a push. 'Now, Gina baby, ain't ya forgetting?'

Gina blinks and looks at Gloria with a tell-me expression.

'We don't discuss it in front of Martha. Besides, we wait for Molly getting back. What I need is that Hendrick release date.' She looks at Martha in the rear-view mirror. 'Release date and Martha's book.' Her eyes sparkle and she smiles at Gina, then back at Martha. 'You two. Ya must have heard the old saying "kill two birds with one stone"?'

Martha leans forward and clutches Gina's shoulder affectionately and whispers, 'Now, what the fuck ya think Miss Monroe's thinking on, Gina baby?'

Gina half turns, and winks. 'I can't wait to find out, girl. But I have a feeling it's gonna be a cracker. She's wearing that look on her fucking face.' She points at a smiling Gloria Monroe. 'See?'

CHAPTER 5

It's early morning in the parking lot of Sloopy's, and Lieutenant Charlie Black stands with coroner's assistant head Joe Logan over the body of Ryan MacDonald. Officers of the Chicago police are busy searching the locality. Charlie rubs his chin, then strokes his full head of grey hair. At six two, the clean shaven, middle aged, handsome officer nods to the body. 'So what ya got for me, Joe?'

Joe shrugs. He's five six, in his early sixties, balding with a neatly trimmed beard. He tucks his paunch into his belt and gives a shake of his head. 'I'll know more when I get him back to the table.' He looks at Charlie. 'I'd say he's been dead about … well, no more than four hours, could be less. In his early thirties name of …' he looks down at his paperwork '… Ryan MacDonald. It's all with Captain Tom O'Flynn.' He points to the captain, who's talking to one of his officers. 'Yep. Ryan MacDonald. That's the name on the credit cards, found on the bod, along with a hundred and ten dollars in his wallet. Rolex on his wrist. I'm thinking that rules out robbery.'

Tom O'Flynn walks over and Charlie nods a greeting 'I'm told we can rule out robbery, Tom. How'd ya think he caught it? Any thoughts?'

Tom gives a slight sake of his head. 'Seems to me it was a bad bit of horse he's been a-sniffing.' He points down at the white powder that's under MacDonald's nose. 'See the snow on his nose?' He sighs. 'Mixed in with the blood. His car,' he says, nodding over at Ryan's blue Honda, 'sorta confirms for me that it was self-inflicted. Keys were there in his pocket, Charlie.'

Joe gives a shrug and nods 'I'll go along with that. The bad snow. Could well be. But like I told Charlie here, I'll know more once he's on my table. Looks self-inflicted.

Charlie gives a nod, puts up a finger, and looks at Joe. 'Okay, Joe. Keep me informed on that, will ya?' Charlie bends down, taking a close look at Ryan's nosebleed.

'Sure thing Charlie,' Joe says. 'Soon as I know, you'll know.' He turns to the ambulance team. 'Right, I'm done here. We can move him now.'

'Oh,' Tom says, pulling out a plastic evidence bag, 'one of my boys found a razor blade in those bushes over there.' Tom points to a large clump of wild gorse. Charlie rises, rubbing his chin. 'It's in the evidence bag, Charlie. I got men doing a search, looking if we have a witness.'

Charlie slowly scans the whole of the parking lot. Its only occupant is the blue Honda. He stops, nudges Tom, and points up at a camera pointing at the club's entrance. 'That camera. Is it working, Tom?'

Tom nods. 'Sure is. But the first pass showed up nothing. We got MacDonald coming stumbling on his walk to his car, then we lose him.' Tom sighs. 'He goes out of shot. Cameras only viewing fifty per cent of the lot, stopping well short of the Honda. Its view ends there,' He says, pointing at a spot some ten metres away. 'Just one thing, Joe.' Tom redirects his hand over to a spot about forty metres away, in a direct line opposite Sloopy's entrance gate. 'Strange, but there was another occupied vehicle situated just on the outside the lot. Same time as MacDonald's exit walk.'

Charlie anxiously asks, 'Well, let's have it, Tom. We have a witness? You get the plate off the vehicle? Who's our witness?'

Tom shrugs. 'Not so, Charlie. It was flash of a headlight. Seconds after our friend MacDonald staggers over to the Honda,' he points over the lot, 'a flash came out from the northern corner. Gotta be some kind of signal. What ya think, Charlie? Tape's showing three a.m.'

Charlie shakes his head. 'I'm thinking that you may well have something there, Tom. Let's take it down town.' He looks at his watch. 'I got seven forty-seven. Looks to be four hours since he left this world.' He looks over at Joe, who's moving the body into the coroner's wagon. 'Yeah, looks like Joe was spot on with his time of death.' He sighs. 'But I'm not sold on his self-harm. We gotta take a long hard look at the tape.'

Tom nods 'Let's meet up later, Charlie. I got this court thing. That David Stone case. I'm meeting the DA for lunch, but after that I'm free.' He throws out his arm and smiles.

'Okay, Tom. Let's say fifteen hundred hours, fifteen thirty? You okay with that?'

Tom gives a smile. 'Fine. I'll get the boys on it. Could have more for you by then.'

*

Back in the refuge centre the girls are sitting around the office desk drinking Irish cream and Jamesons coffee in celebration of their success.

Gloria gives a smile and offers her coffee for a cheers. 'Must say, seems to have gone off without a hitch.' She touches each of the girls' glasses in turn. 'What you say, girls?'

Martha stamps her feet rapidly. 'Bring on Leroy Hendrick. Let me get into my little black book. I've not got much more to say.'

Gloria rubs Martha's hair. 'His execution, I've already planned it, Martha baby. Read enough of what we've to do with

Mister Leroy Hendrick. I don't need any more than you've already given.'

Gina smiles, nodding. 'Two birds with one stone, Glor?'

Gloria nods. 'You got it, sweetheart. Two for one. We don't even have to leave base for this one. Molly and I can handle it.'

Gina's face wore a somewhat surprised look 'Wait … wait up, Glor. You cutting me out on the Leroy Hendrick job?'

Martha shrugs. 'What gives, Gloria? No Gina, no disrespect. But Molly, I'm thinking … well you'd would be stronger with Gina. Molly, she's a bag of fucking nerves, gal.' Martha leans forward putting her face in her hands and slowly shakes head.' You just don't know what kind of an animal Leroy is, Gloria.'

Gloria's face is serious as she looks at them both. 'You got to trust me on this, girls. Molly, she'll have very little to do on this.' She sighs and puts a hand on her heart. 'You just gotta trust me on this, girls.'

Martha shrugs, spreading out her arms. 'Yeah, we trust ya, baby, goes without saying. It's just that … well, no Gina?'

Gloria wags a finger. 'Like I say, it's sorted.'

*

Later that evening, in an upstairs office of La Napaloni restaurant, Vincent De Generio sits at the head of a large conference table. He looks down on a gathering of six soldiers of the Mafia. His finger begins to tap the table rapidly. The soldiers stare at their Don expectantly. Vincent opens his arms wide, shakes his head, and speaks. 'How, after all this fucking time?!' He bangs his fist down. 'It's nearly a year since my granddaughter, my Angelina, overdosed.' He continues to bangs down his fist. 'How is it I receive mail, only this fucking morning, a message telling me,' he shouts out in anger, 'who was fucking responsible?' He growls, 'who it was that administered that shit to her?' He snarls, 'Who? A fucking Waterside Snake, a black bastard pusher … a fucking candyman. One Leroy Hendrick. A fucking nigger!'

The soldiers look to each other. One, by the name of Giovani Septico, coughs and looks at his Don. The others mumble. Giovani shakes a fist. 'He is dead already, my Don. We will see he suffers. I will bury him alive. No, *we* will.' The soldiers nod in agreement.

The Don holds up his hand. Vincent snarls and says in anger, 'I want to see him suffer. I want to inflict an unbearable pain. Yes, "we".' Vincent picks up a sheet of paper from the desk, crushing it in his fist. 'Crush this bastard, bury him alive. Along with all the rats that worship him. There will be no rest … till all the Waterside Snakes are dead.' He hurls the paper ball across the room. Then he growls, 'You all know my feelings on drugs.' Again he bangs down hard onto the table. 'We don't do this drugs shit. We don't fuck up little children's lives.' With menace, he gives a under-the-eye look to every face. 'I want this bastard and his entourage off our streets.' Giving a loud clap, he dismisses them, but he shouts after them, 'Save Hendrick for me. He will be mine. I want him alive.'

*

Back in the office of the women's refuge centre, Gloria pours Glenfiddich malt whisky into Martha's glass. Martha eagerly downs in one shot. She holds out the empty glass and motions for Gloria to refill. Gloria shrugs and obligingly pouring another shot.

Gloria looks to Molly and Gina, but they decline her offer of the whisky. Martha once more downs the drink in one gulp, then draws her hand across her lips and sighs. 'Must say, Glo, Jesus I needed that. Best damn whisky I've ever tasted. So smooth. It's a malt, right?'

Gloria smiles. 'Sure is, gal. Brewed only with water from a pure Scottish mountain stream. The best – but go easy on it.'

She rubs and pats Martha on the shoulder. 'Our plan for Leroy Hendrick is already on the go. This is out of our hands, but it's gonna be so easy.'

Martha puts up a thumb. 'Easy, wish it were so, girls. That bastard, he's fucking out tomorrow.' She shakes her head. 'He's already got his people out looking for me. I can't fucking hide from them forever. My aunt over in Gary, well, she's scared.' She lets out a deep sigh. 'Guess I am too. Me staying over there is giving her and me the fucking williess.'

Gina nods 'Just a couple more days, baby. Best she stays here, Glor'. She ain't safe in Gary, Indiana, that's for sure.'

Gloria pats Martha's shoulder and winks. 'She's welcome to stay. If any of our crowd asks me why she's staying, she's training for management.' She smiles, nudging Martha. 'But not to worry, baby. All will be over soon. Gina tells me the Outfit's wheels are turning on Leroy Hendrick.'

Gina Smiles. 'Yeah, that's right. Friend of Mario tells me the Don wants Hendrick. Cannot be a business deal – the Don don't do drugs. So it's something else that's going down. Let me tell you, what the Don wants, he gets.' She sighs. 'Mario returns tomorrow with Korky O'Dell's head in a basket. Then it's back to punchbag hour.'

Gloria rubs Gina's shoulder. 'Not for long, baby. That's when we turn the screw on Mario.'

Gina gives a deep sigh. 'I just hope whatever you've planned for him is solid, baby. Because if it ain't,' she shakes her head her eyes looking up to the heavens, 'it's bye bye, Gina. It's God help us all.'

CHAPTER 6

*Later that night, outside the gates of the
Big Muddy correction centre*

The gate opens to allow four men to walk back into society. There's a moment of hand-shaking and back-slapping before each man waves and walks in a different direction. They head towards individual family groups that are waiting. The tall muscular athletic figure of Leroy Hendrick smiles as he is greeted by two black men. The men hug and dance with him. One – the younger of the two – grabs his bag and races to a big Lincoln with the engine running. The other walks with his hand around Leroy's waist. They laugh on entering the rear seat of the car.

The young man slams the door shut. He gets into the drivers seat and then slowly spins the car around. He gives a finger to the prison before speeding away.

Leroy is handed a large flute of champagne and a pre-cut Havana cigar. His companion smiles and flicks a lighter. Leroy puffs on the cigar and it glows. His eyes half close as he lets out a plume of smoke. Leroy lays back in the seat. 'Fuck, fuck, fuck, it's good to be out of that shit hole.' He looks his companion up and down and smiles. 'You're looking good, brother Martin.'

Martin smiles and punches Leroy's arm. 'You too Leroy.' Then he pats him on his stomach, smiles and nudges him. 'Little bigger, I'd say. You put on weight?'

Leroy shrugs and nods. 'Yeah, buts it's all muscle, Martin. I was in control in there, the screws under my thumb. That cunt of a warden was scared of me.'

Martin smiles. 'Oh we got to him, Leroy. A little pressure on his family situation was all that was needed.'

Leroy drains the flute in one swallow. Martin is quick to refill. Leroy winks. 'What about the grass? She still on the block? I'm hoping you gone done like I instructed. Left for me?'

'She's around, man. She's nowhere to hide. She's yours, brother. You just whistle.'

Leroy nods. 'Oh I am whistling, brother. I've got plans for sweet Martha. She'll be begging on the streets.' He snorts. 'She's fucking dead meat already. But I got to play with her a while. Yeah, before I cut her limb from fucking limb.' He laughs, swallows more champagne. 'Oh, she gonna pay for putting me in cell 491.' He claps his hands. 'Now, the club. Take me to my club.'

Martin smiles. 'All's in hand, brother. We've a welcome-home party waiting.' He slaps his thigh. 'Yeah, brother, some new young untouched flesh ready to ride.'

CHAPTER 7

In the upper office of the La Napaloni restaurant the head of Korky O'Dell sits in a linen basket on a long table. The door opens and members of the East Side Outfit slowly enter. Their eyes flash briefly as they catch sight of the head. They grimace before giving a forward glance at the sombre face of Don De Generio as he glares back at them. The men bow to the Don, nod to the man sitting alongside him – Mario Pascalino, who watches as each man takes his seat, according to their rank. They look down at a photograph that sits in front each member. Some seventeen in all.

A silence hangs over the room. Don Vincent De Generio breaks it. 'You see before you the head of Korky O'Dell. He, as you are aware, ran our business end in LA. But he couldn't keep his fingers from dipping into our honey pot. So, you see what happens to our little embezzling thief.' He points at the head. 'That piece of shit will be buried with tonight's pour at the new mall.'

He spreads out his arms. 'But enough. We are not gathered here this evening to discuss Korky O'Dell.' He shakes his head. 'Oh no. You are here to end the poison that floods our streets.

To put a final end to the so-called Waterside Snakes. The blacks who hand out death to our young, by way of heroin and all its offshoots.' He again shakes his head. 'We, the Family, don't sell death. But there comes a time when we, as a family, can administer it.' He points at the head of O'Dell. 'Just like you see.' He looks down at Mario. 'Mario.' Mario stands and bows to his Don. 'We strike tonight. The Shades club. It will be full to its capacity.' He smiles. 'All will be there. A party for the return of Leroy Hendrick.' He looks to his Don, who gestures for him to continue. 'Hendrick,' Mario continues, stabbing a finger at the air, 'must be taken alive, while his entourage all must die.'

Vincent interrupts. 'Hendrick alive? I want him taken to the new mall. Take him up the Reece Tower to errr ...' He looks to Mario.

'Level forty-eight, my Don,' whispers Mario.

'Ah, yes, level forty-eight. That black bastard, he's mine.' He gestures for Mario to continue.

'We leave in three limos, six to each vehicle, armed and loaded automatics.' He bangs down his fist. 'Fucking empty them. No witnesses. No one leaves alive. Except Mister Leroy Hendrick.'

He holds up his photo of Leroy. Mario points to it. 'This is he,' Mario says. 'We take him alive. I have it from a watching soldier that the music is playing.' He grinds his teeth. 'The drinking is at a peak. I think now,' he looks to his don, who is nodding. 'Yes, now is the time.'

*

In a closed darkened office of Police Special Homicide Squad headquarters, Charlie Black and Tom O'Flynn sit alongside officer Bill Harris, looking at images of the Sloopy's parking lot on a monitor. Bill stops the film and points to the flash that's clearly showing on the tape. 'There. That's a signal if ever I saw one.' He looks at Charlie, then Tom. 'Come on now, guys. Why, it's as plain as day.'

Charlie slowly nods 'Wouldn't argue with that, Bill. Tom?'

Tom nods. 'Got a couple of the boys on it, Charlie. Let's hope we can get some tyre castings. Who knows, we may just get lucky.'

'Yeah, let Gilmore have a go at any you find, Tom,' says Charlie. 'He's your man when it comes to tyre mouldings.' He wags a finger. 'Run it through again, Bill.'

*

It's party time over in the Shades club. The floor is packed with intertwining bodies rolling, swaying to a soulful sound coming form a four-piece band. Bunting hangs overhead with banners reading 'WELCOME HOME LEROY'. Across the room in a central booth, Leroy sits in a white and silver suit. Under it he wears a purple silk shirt unbuttoned to his waist, several chains of gold around his neck. His arms are wrapped around the shoulders of two young topless girls. His knuckles sparkle with carry gold rings studded with diamonds. A gold watch encircles his wrist loosely. The girls sit either side of him, kissing him, moaning and pawing him. To his left Martin sits with a young girl on his knee, pouring champagne into his wide-open mouth. Leroy winks and nods to Martin. 'You sure gone and done me proud, brother M. You held the fort well while its king was away.' He smiles. 'Yes sir. I tell ya, man. You done good.'

Martin bows to him and smiles, before pressing then kissing the nipple of the young girl. 'The night's still young, brother.'

Leroy rubs his hands. 'Yeah, but where's the star attraction? Where is the grass, brother?'

Martin gives a wink and smiles. 'Don't worry so much. I got the boys out looking. She ain't run, that's for sure. She wouldn't make it a mile.' He holds out a hand palm up. 'I got my brother

Sam and two of the boys out there. They're on with it, Leroy, anytime now.' He points at the two girls. 'Relax. Enjoy, brother.'

*

Just a half block away from the Shades sit three large black limousines. It's raining. Inside of the lead car Mario sits looking at the flashing lights coming from the club. Two big bodyguards stand at the front entrance, smoking. He grunts and turns to his men. He looks to one soldier in particular, saying, 'Roberto, step out and do a walk by. Take your pistol. Fit the silencer. Take them both out, headshots.' Next he taps the shoulder of a young man who is sitting alongside the driver. 'Antonio, you will follow Roberto. Drag them into that side alley.' He nudges his driver. 'Piero, get out. Go tell Giovanni and the rest what's going down. Tell him we all go in as one. To mask up.' Then he turns to his youngest soldier. 'Joey, you are outside on this. Take down all who attempt to leave. Stay safe at all times.' The young soldier sighs then nods. 'Okay, Roberto. Go. Antonio, give him backup. Stay with him discreetly.'

They all look out over Mario's shoulder at the drunken staggering act of Roberto approaching the club. 'Boy, that Roberto, he sure can act. Like a Valantino, yes?' says Mario. They all laugh.

Roberto stumbles towards the doormen. The bouncers nudge each other and make for Roberto. One of the bouncers with arms spread opening wide says, 'You on the wrong block, man. You looking to get turned? Get that fucking ass of yours moving off Waterside. Whites ain't welcome.'

The other bouncer points and shouts to his buddy. 'Hey Ray, looks like another coming this way. They fuckin' stupid or what?' He points to the ambling figure of Antonio, who's closing in on them.

Ray laughs. 'They sure as hell picked the wrong street, Errol my brother.' Ray makes a grab at Roberto who, straightening up, takes out a pistol. He fires two quick bursts into Ray's head – pop-pop. Errol goes for his gun. There's another quick pop-pop, and he falls too. Antonio races up and they each drag a lifeless body down into a side alleyway.

The limo doors fly open and the heavily armed soldiers race to the club's door. Mario is shouting, 'Go, go, go! Get me Hendrick!' He turns to Joey. 'If any escape, they'll be coming out of this alley. Take 'em down, Joey.'

He pulls one of the passing soldiers aside. 'Tony, you help Joey. No fucker leaves alive.' The sound of rapid automatic gunfire comes from within the club. Mario and Giovanni wait at the entrance. They hear women screaming. A screaming girl races out, straight into the path of Mario. She grabs him and clings on for safety. Mario smiles and pushes her away, before firing a bullet into her head. She falls at his feet, her blood oozing out onto his shoes. Giovanni takes out a silk kerchief and, bending, wipes the shiny leather clean. Lots of the Waterside Snakes gang are trying to make it out by using the emergency exit doors, only to be met by a crescendo of rapid gunfire coming from Joey and Tony's automatics. Moments later the gunfire subsides. A soldier comes out into the club's entrance hall. Mario raises his eyebrows at the man, awaiting news. The man smiles and winks. 'They are finished, Mario. No one lives.'

Mario pushes past him into the heart of the battleground. He's snarling while he surveys the scene. His men walk amongst the fallen, accompanied by the pop-pop of automatic gunfire as they silence every groan. Bodies of the Waterside Snakes empire, male and female, oozing blood. Some two hundred souls are dead.

'No one?' asks Mario anxiously. The soldier points at the dazed figure of Leroy being dragged towards him and smiles. 'Only Hendrick lives, Mario. We've given him some an anaesthetic. He will give you no trouble. He's bound and being dragged like a dog through his dead loyal followers.'

A dazed Leroy is dragged onward, towards Mario, until he's next to him. Mario puts up a hand. The soldiers stop. Mario grabs Leroy's hair and pulls back his head. He then spits into the face of the unconscious King of the Snakes. Mario nods and smiles. 'Get him into the limo. Let him sleep it off in the trunk.' He stabs a finger at Giovanni. 'Tell the boys to fire this fucking nigger's den. Make it no more.'

Giovanni walks by, patting Mario on the shoulder. 'Consider it done. I'll see to it, Mario.'

*

The soldiers drag Leroy out onto the street. A limo drives up at speed and stops. The driver exits and opens its trunk. Leroy is stuffed inside, the trunk closed.

Mario climbs into the limo. He quickly waves to Joey, who's running to join Mario in the back. As he gets in, there is a series of explosions. The soldiers race by, whooping and hollering, diving through open doors of the slow-moving limos. Mario's smiling face is illuminated as he peers out of the limo window at the Shades, which is now a theatre of fire. The limos drive off at speed, each taking a different exit route.

As the fire rages, three black men emerge out from the shadows of a nearby alley. Sammy James, Sonny Boy Floyd and Marvin Rolands stare at Shades, now engulfed with flames.

'Our brothers, sisters … They were in there. Oh my God. What the fuck's gone down here, Sammy?' says Sonny.

Sammy's eyes are flashing. 'Looks like we upset the mob, Sonny. They've taken Leroy. What's he done to cause such fucking anger?' he gasps. Then he grabs Sonny's shoulder and shakes it, staring into his friend's eyes. 'My brothers. Leroy. Martin. Maria, my girl. Fucking sweet Jesus, Sonny. Leroy … it's his first day out of the fucking can.' His body jerks about in a frenzy.

Marvin grips Sammy's shoulder. 'Not just them, Sammy. Fucking all of them. Our families, our friends. They've murdered the lot.'

Sammy sobs. He turns to them. 'Oh no,' he snarls, shaking a fist. 'That's where ya fucking wrong, Marvin. They ain't got us. We still remain.' He growls, voice low and fierce. 'The three fucking musketeers.'

Marvin asks, 'What's on yer mind, Sam?'

'Mario. That bastard Mario. He's on my mind. Oh, he thinks this is all over. The fucking De Generio outfit – they will fucking die.' He grabs Sonny and Marvin by their collars and pulls them to him. 'We take Mario first. Then the Don.'

Down the block, people start emerging cautiously into the street. They huddle together gazing open mouthed at the blazing Shades club. Sirens can be heard in the distance getting louder by the second. The red and blue flashing lights of the services come racing down the avenue – ambulances and fire engines, followed by screaming police cars.

Sammy, Sonny and Marvin sink back into the shadows and quietly retreat from the flaming carnage.

CHAPTER 8

In the large open-plan special units crime office, desks and consoles line two long rows. Detectives work in a hum of activity, the men in shirt sleeves and the women in jeans and jumpers, or blouses. The office phones are constantly ringing. Almost as one, officers pick up the ringing phones, listen, put the phone down again fast.

Squad members begin to hurry, taking guns out of drawers and coats off hangers and the backs of chairs. They race towards the exit. The door to Charlie Black's office opens and Charlie pokes out his head, a worried look on his face. 'What's going down, Gerry?' he calls to his workmate.

Squad officer Gerry Small sighs and holds out his hands. 'We got a situation, Charlie. Down on twenty-first. Shades club. They got a fire out of control. You coming?'

Charlie nods. 'Yeah. I'm on it, Gerry, give me a sec.' He turns and re-enters his office, going for his coat and hat. He glances at Tom O'Flynn, who's seated on the other side of Charlie's desk.

'What's the commotion, Charlie?' asks Tom. World War Three started?'

Charlie smiles. 'Looks that way, Tom. Grab your coat. We've got a fire that's raging, down on twenty-first. Shades club.'

Tom laughed. 'Couldn't have happened to a nicer den. That's the Snakes' hideaway. If you ask me, Charlie, I wouldn't rush to save that shit hole.' He stands and grabs his overcoat. 'Okay, let's go take a look at her. We'll take my car. More official. I'll drive.'

*

On Twenty-First Avenue, Charlie and Tom stand looking at the uncontrollable fire that's almost completely destroyed Shades.

'What you got, Pete?' Tom asks fire chief Pete Wiseman.

Pete shakes his head. 'We lost this one, Tom. Gotta just try to contain the spread. Don't want it hitting those apartments to the right.' He points over at a fountain of hoses that are spraying the joint. 'Joint was full, by all accounts. Big homecoming party for the Snake King, Leroy Hendrick. Over two hundred souls, so I'm told.' He sighs. 'We'll know more when we can put the fucker out. Sometime tomorrow. Then let the forensics go through it. Seems heavy gunfire was heard.' He looks at them both. 'Oh, by the way, nobody walked out.' He shakes his head. 'There'll be one hell of a heap of dead in there.'

Tom sighs. 'Thanks, Pete. Let us know when you've got something.'

Pete waves a hand and returns his attention to the fire.

Charlie takes out a cigarette and flicks his lighter. 'What the fuck. This is serious shit, Tom. Real heavy duty that's gone down here.'

Tom sighs. 'Yeah. We got no luck on the tread. Boys found a big mamma of a truck had parked over the area since the fire started. Looks like one job at a time, Charlie.' He shrugs. 'All previous markings gone. Spud Wilson, he never taped the area off. I've given him a rollicking. Right now, they're checking all highway cameras. Fingers crossed. Could really do without this – what looks to be arson. But fucking gunfire with over two hundred souls and no witnesses? I tell you, we have problem, Charlie.'

Charlie shakes his head. 'Yeah, not a good day for the crime fighters. Whoever took this on, they were big-time players. My feeling is Mafia, the Outfit.' He points at the gathering crowd. Tom looks over where Charlie's pointing – at a huddled section of the locals. 'Just look at them faces. Man, they're so fucking scared. Looking like we're running on empty in regard to Mister MacDonald.'

Tom sighs. 'Let's hope we get a break from somewhere. On that one, Charlie, I'm thinking it's best we concentrate on the Shades fire.'

*

In the small blacks-only diner sits what's left of the Waterside Snakes: Sammy, Sonny and Marvin. Marvin is constantly twirling a spoon in a mug of hot coffee.

Sammy's bangs his fist on the table. 'For fucks sake, Marv. I can't fucking concentrate with you and the spoon.'

Marvin puts his hands up. 'Sorry, Sam. Seems we're on our own with this revenge play.'

Sonny nods. 'Yeah. I asked Jersey Boy Ross to help, with a few of the Ravens.' He shakes his head.

'Those black bikers ain't interested. They don't wanna know, Sam. Like Marv says, we're on our own.' Sammy grunts. 'He's just one man without his crew – well, he's fucking nothing. Better to ask Toby Lewis.'

Marvin looks over at Sonny and shrugs. 'Toby. Toby Lewis?' He laughs. 'Why, Toby must be sixty-five if he's a day old. You gotta be joking. Why Toby, Sam?'

Sammy smiles, nudging the two of them. 'Why Toby Lewis? Why? Because he's janitor up at that fancy school.' He repeats the nudge. 'Ain't that just where Mario takes the De Generio kid to learn his reading and writing?'

Sonny and Marvin both gasp. Marvin can't believe what he's hearing. 'Wowwww. Now, Sammy, no way we're taking on the Don.'

'That's a no, no, Sammy,' Sonny agrees. 'We can't go there. Vincent would kill every black ass all along the Mississippi.'

Sammy growls. 'Don't ya think I don't fucking know that? No – we wait till he's dropped the kid off. We follow the bastard and take him down in the limo.' He smiles. 'Then I get to burn the bastard, like he done my brothers, my Maria.' He jabs a finger at Marvin. 'You see, with Toby, we get to know all you can from him. Times, route he takes leaving. Toby may work for the whites but his heart's all black.' He turns to Sonny. 'We've got one chance on this. Let's make it a good.'

*

The following day back in the refuge centre

Gloria, Molly and Martha sit with eyes glued to a news broadcast on the office TV. The report is saying that it's believed that over two hundred souls had perished in the Shades fire. the reporter adds that the bodies were burnt beyond recognition, and the missing were being identified by dental records items of jewellery and the like.

Molly's mouth was agape. 'Jesus, Gloria. I never dreamed that Gina's Mario would go this far. I feel sick. All those poor people dead.'

Martha let out a deep sigh. 'I'm sure they'll recognise Leroy. He carried a sackful of gold on his body, his mouth too.'

Gloria looks at her watch. 'Where's Gina? I thought she'd be here by now. I thought they'd just go after Hendrick, not the whole fucking Waterside Snakes. Jesus Christ. What fucking happened?'

Martha smiles, gazing out into the hall. 'We'll soon know. Gina's just arrived. She'll know more than that CNN report.'

Announced by the sound of her high heels clicking down the hall, Gina dashes in, looking depressed.

'Gina, thank God you're here,' Gloria says anxiously. 'You okay, baby?'

Gina shrugs. 'Fuck, Glo'. How can I be smiling at what went down?' She points at the TV. 'It's on non-fucking-stop. That bastard Mario, his godforsaken crew, they sit admiring their work, like it's some Michaelangelo's David. I feel responsible, Glor.'

Gloria gives Gina a hug. 'Yeah, we all feel the same, baby. But what's done is done. Now we really got to take that bastard down.' She shakes her head. 'Word's out the press, TV, police. They all know it's Mario. It's …' Gina raises a hand. 'Hold up now Gloria. The police – you think that's gonna do it? Let me tell you, he'll never make trial.' She looks at her friends, shaking her head. 'Why, you ask?' She pulls on her hair. 'Why? Because, my dear friends, Vincent has the law in his pocket. He would see to Mario's freedom. Some other stooge would take the fall for Mario's action. Yes, I would forever remain his punching bag.'

There are a few moments of silence before Gloria brings out the scotch. 'Let's have a drink and think about this. Gina, well, she's right. We should have heard of Mario's arrest by now, according to Gina. Seems the Don is holding a loaded gun to the Mayor's head. Vincent De Generio is a powerful man. But you know we can't stop now.' She smiles and winks. 'We still have two to go.'

CHAPTER 9

On the top floor of a tower block on a building site, paint cans are stacked across a freshly plastered back wall of a near finished apartment. Under the frying light of an arc lamp Leroy Hendrick sits with his hands and feet bound to a chair. His eyes are swollen and badly bruised. All his jewellery has gone. His gold teeth have been torn from his mouth by a pair of pliers that sit on a military-issue table. His eyes are closed to the powerful beam that's set shining into his face. A pail of water is flung out from the shadows and into his face. His head flies back, but his eyes remain closed. The voice of Vincent De Generio breaks the silence. 'Nigger, motherfucker, open your eyes or lose them. The choice is yours.' He slaps Hendrick's face. 'Don't waste my fucking time, you black piece of shit.' Leroy opens his eyes and blinks into the full beam. 'A wise choice,' Vincent tells him.

Mario walks out from the shadow and confronts Leroy with a photograph of a beautiful young girl. Leroy looks, then turns away. Through cracked lips he whispers. 'Whooo is sheee?'

Vincent slaps Leroy's face. 'She's my granddaughter. Seventeen years old. She's dead, nigger, thanks to some very bad shit you shot into her veins.' The don shouts then summons Mario, who walks forward and puts a brass knuckle duster onto his boss's right hand. He makes a fist before punching Leroy on his nose. Blood begins to pour as Vincent continues to interrogate Leroy. 'Remember, you bastard? Shit heroin you injected, after you fucking raped her.'

Leroy coughs up blood. 'Like I'm a saying, brother,' he splutters, 'I don't know the girl.' He coughs again. 'You caught the wrong fish, man.'

Vincent scowls. 'Oh you'd like to think that. One thing – get it in that black head of yours – I ain't your fucking brother. But I've waited a long, long time to hook you, black boy. Your fucking pond days are over.' He gestures to Mario, who once again strikes Leroy's face. His head snaps back, then hangs down on his chest. Mario turns to accept another pale of water from a soldier and throws it onto Leroy's head.

Leroy shakes his head and then slowly looks up at his captors, knowing his time on earth is over. 'Come on you bastards!' he shouts. 'Let's get this over with. This black boy ain't gonna cry for no fucking high school bitch. So come on, let's do this.' He laughs 'She wasn't even a good hump. Laying like a sack of sand.'

Mario pulls out his pistol and puts it to Leroy's head, turning to his boss to get the go-ahead.

But Vincent waves a hand. 'No, no, Mario. I've got plans for our nigger.'

Mario re holsters his gun. The Don walks into the light. He pulls back Leroy's head by gripping his locks. Then he stares into the black man's eyes. 'Look at me, you piece of worthless shit. Look. Because I'm the last face you're ever gonna see.' With that, Vincent takes from his coat a long thin bladed stiletto knife. He sticks it into the socket of Leroy's left eye. cutting it out, then the right, while Leroy shrieks. 'You nigger, you fucking talk too much,' Vincent says. Then he nods to

Mario, who wedges Leroy's mouth open with his pistol. Vincent takes a pair of wire grips from the hand of a soldier, and uses them to grasp Leroy's tongue. With one fast slice he cuts it out. Blood, thick like jelly, pours out, and Vincent begins to laugh. 'What's that you just said, nigger? I can't fucking hear you.' Vincent throws the tongue to the floor. The soldier takes the grips off his don and hands him a screwdriver. The Don smiles as he drives it deep down into each of Leroy's ears. 'Oh, and now, nigger, here comes the fun part. We take you down to the street.' He giggles. 'Oh, but you can't fucking hear me, can you?' He motions for Mario to untie Leroy. Two soldiers appear, lifting the now groaning Leroy to his feet. They drag him to a half finished balcony, with Vincent following close behind. The Don gives Leroy's back a gentle push.

Leroy falls the forty floors, landing hard on the upright steel rebar of an unfinished concrete footing. Vincent walks to the service lift and turns to Mario. 'Clean it up. Put him in the next pour.' He enters the lift and Mario follows, turning to Giovani. He waves a hand over the blood-soaked floor, Leroy's eyes looking up at him, Leroy's tongue laying alongside, like a blob of jelly. Mario shrugs. 'See that all is done.'

Vincent smiles, patting Mario's shoulder as the lift descends.

*

12 hours later

On an open country road, the black limo is making its way onto Paradise Drive, passing through the green pastures associated with the many stud farms of Chicago's horse racing fraternity.

Mario sits in the back reading the *Tribune*, following its ongoing story of the East Side fire. He smiles, leans forward and brings a glass of bourbon to his lips.

The car suddenly brakes, throwing Mario forward, and the drink spilling from the glass.

'What the fuck, Piero!' Mario shouts. 'Have we hit somebody?'

'No hit, Mario,' Piero says. 'There's a couple of black assholes with hand carts, blocking the road. Looks like one cart has a wheel off.'

Mario curses. 'Well get the fuckers to shift out of our way. Give them a hand if need be. I've a fucking schedule to keep.' He smiles, uttering himself, 'She won't want me to be late.'

Piero exits the car, walks up Sammy and Sonny. With his thumbs tucked into his belt. He nods at the carts. 'Hey fellas. Come on now. You're blocking the fucking road.' He waves his hand. 'Get your carts to one side, let me help ya.'

Sonny pulls a gun with a silencer out from his cart, putting two rounds into Piero's head. Piero falls. Seeing the attack through the windscreen, Mario draws his pistol and ducks down out of sight. Carefully he clicks open his door. Sweating, he lifts his head to see Sammy aiming a bazooka at the car. With eyes wide open, he gasps as he sees a missile flying towards him.

One giant boom and the car explodes into a ball of flame, sending metal and body parts in every direction.

Sammy stands, the smoking bazooka still resting on his shoulder. Sonny gives Sammy a hug. Sammy winks. 'That was for my brothers. For Leroy and Martin. For my Maria. For all my friends, you bastard. Go to your place with Satan.' Sammy is shoulder marching the bazooka Sonny leans to it kissing it. 'What a fucking baby you are.'

CHAPTER 10

In the refuge centre, Gloria, Molly and Martha have eyes glued to the TV. CNN is showing pictures of the fire on Twenty-First Street. A 'breaking news' bulletin cuts in, showing the burnt-out remains of Mario's black limo, the voiceover giving a short report on the deaths of Mario and his driver. It ends with a promise of more news later. The picture returns to the fire and a request for witnesses to come forward.

The office door opens and Gina enters. They turn to her, mouths agape. Gina holds up a hand. 'Okay, I'm sorry for being late. Found it hard to get away.' She smiles. 'But Lady Luck smiled on me. Mario left a message saying he'd be late home … So here I am, girls.'

Gloria turns to the others and points at Gina. 'She doesn't fucking know.'

'Know what?' Gina says with a puzzled expression. 'That Leroy's dead, and it's two to go? That Martha can live again?'

Molly shakes her head. 'Yeah that's right, Gina, but it's three down and one to go.'

Gina nods at Gloria. 'You got your man, Glo? He's fucking dead?'

Martha smiles. 'No, baby. Gloria ain't got her man … Mario, he's dead.'

Gina is completely taken aback. 'But … but …' She puts a hand up to her brow. 'When? How?' She turns to Gloria for an explanation. 'This true, Glor'? What Martha's saying, that he's dead? Mario?'

Gloria's nods and smiles. 'Just been breaking news on the TV, baby. We were waiting for more when you came in the door.' She puts her arm around Gina. 'Seems someone blew his limo to pieces. Two dead: Mario and his driver, one Piero.' Tears flow down Gina's cheeks. 'Gina, it's over. You're free. Don't fucking cry, baby.'

Gina smiles. 'I'm fucking crying tears of fucking joy, baby. Tears of joy. Just one to go. You know what, I think we've done it.'

Martha's claps her hands once. 'Leroy dead, I ain't fucking crying along with all of his associates. No doubt on it being the mob's doing. Just sorry they had to take out the women. Hope my sister's safe. Come to think of it, she'd never go to a party for that child killer.'

*

In Chicago's West Side coroner's office Charlie Black sits looking at a report. Joe Logan enters with two cups of coffee.

Charlie nods and scratches his chin. 'Say Joe, how long would it take for this cyanide to roll MacDonald over?'

Joe hands him a coffee and Charlie nods a thanks. Then Joe smiles. 'With the hit that MacDonald got? It'd knock down a fucking herd of elephants.' He holds out a hand. 'Would be instant, Charlie. Inside of a minute, maybe less, he'd be convulsing.'

Charlie puts down the report. 'Yeah, that's what I thought, Joe. He'd have had to have taken that line there at the scene.'

Joe nods.'You can definitely add a yes to that, Charlie.'

Charlie nods slowly. 'So how come we find nothing, at the scene of the death, Joe? Parking lot was as clean as a whistle.'

Joe shrugs. 'Just that blade in the bush. The one Tom's guy found, Charlie.'

Charlie nods. 'Mmmm, yeah, the blade.'

Joe remembers the report. 'We had traces of the mix on it, Charlie. It was the one used.'

Charlie shakes his head. 'Just the blade. Nothing but that blade. I tell ya, Joe, this ain't no self-harm. This is a fucking murder.'

Joe sighs. 'If you say so, but you're the detective. I'm just the body cleaner.'

Charlie winks. 'MacDonald he was taken out by a professional, Joe.'

Joe nudges him. 'Or a woman, Charlie.'

Charlie stands and makes for the door, but he turns, wagging his finger. 'You know, Joe Logan, you may just have hit the nail on the head. A woman.' He waves, opens the door, and leaves the office.

Charlie's drive back to the police headquarters gives Charlie time to analyse the situation. Before the death of Mario Pascalino, he was seriously contemplating labelling the MacDonald murder a cold case. He feared that the massacre of the Waterside Snakes was far from over. The murder of Pascalino had confirmed his view: the mob were responsible for the burning down of the Shades club and the deaths of over 200 souls.

But the body of the one-time king of the drug-pushers, Leroy Hendrick, had not yet been found, despite forensic examination of the now completely destroyed building. Charlie would need to organise his much-overworked team to put all of its efforts in to ensuring that these recent horrific incidents would not be allowed to turn in to a full-scale war. The days of Al Capone and the gangland murders could never return to the streets of Chicago. Tom had already warned him of reports of heavy-duty weapons being acquired by an all-black army of bikers. He must not allow this to situation to escalate.

His phone begins to beep, he answers to a call from Captain Tom O'Fynn. Tom tells him he'd better get over to the La Napaloni restaurant, that there had been another major incident.

'La Napaloni,' Charlie muses. 'Tom, ain't that the one used by the Don De Generio outfit?'

'Yeah, the right-hand man of the boss, Don Vincent, who has a hand in everything except drugs.'

'Tom, you're talking like Don Vincent ain't around any more.'

*

Four hours earlier

It's late evening in the La Napaloni, and Don Vincent sits at a celebration dinner table with all his entourage – twenty-eight in total. To his right, one chair is empty.

The Don stands and a silence falls over the restaurant. He holds his arms out and begins to speak. 'Welcome, my family, my friends, my army generals. We are here to celebrate the life of my brigadier Mario Pascalino, who will be sorely missed. But he will be avenged. Those black bastards who have taken him from us will pay. Their families will pay.' He gives a deep sigh before continuing. 'My little princess … my granddaughter … has finally been avenged with the extermination of Leroy Hendrick. We have saved countless young lives. So, enjoy your dinner.'

Giovanni stands and says to his Don, 'Please, allow me, my Don.' Vincent nods and waves his permission. 'Thank you my Godfather. We drink a last toast to our comrade Mario and offer our everlasting love for a long life for our Godfather Don Vincent.' With that, he raises his glass and cries. 'God bless our Godfather Don Vincent De Generio!'

At that moment, Marvin and Sonny open fire with suppressed pistols, cutting down the two mobsters guarding the Don. Sammy steps out of the saloon car cradling a loaded bazooka, waiting until Sonny and Marvin draw their rapid-fire automatics. Then the three Snakes stride into the restaurant's main dining area, guns roaring. Sammy squeezes the bazooka's trigger, sending a round straight into the head table where Don Vincent De Generio sits. The Don and his guests vanish in a violent blast. The rest of the diners are mown down in an unrelenting hail of bullets. Moments later, silence hangs heavy, until flames erupt from gasoline poured across the floorboards. As the fire takes hold, the black sedan tears away, Sammy leaning out the window to blow a mocking kiss.

*

Charlie can see the flames lighting up the sky as he approaches the restaurant. He pulls over to make way for a fire engine that comes screaming by. On the scene, Tom is standing with fire chief Rod Willis. Hoses are shooting water at a fire that looks to be out of control.

Charlie walks up to the pair, shaking his head. 'What the fuck, Tom? We have problems. What's going down next? I can see the ghetto in flames. The Family ain't going to take this eye for an eye shit.' He sighs. 'We have to put an end to this, Tom, and we must start today. Otherwise the FBI are going to be on our fucking patch.'

After a beat, Tom adds, 'I've got the team asking around. We have a few grasses on our books. They owe us, Charlie. They stay silent on this and they'll feel our wrath.'

Charlie nods. 'Let's get on it, Tom. I don't see anything more we can do here till that fire's out, then we will lose time, relying on the time our forensics is going to take. We have got to move with this, baby.'

'MacDonald, Charlie?'

Charlie shrugs. 'I spoke with the neighbour, a John Barlow. The man told me that MacDonald was an evil piece of shit who'd give his wife regular trips to the hospital. He got what he deserved, according to Barlow. We have nothing, Tom. It's winding up to be a cold case. By all accounts the man was a bastard, a wife-beater, a fucking no-good sex-den regular with a drug problem. A man whose killer I'm not inclined to waste time pursuing.'

He sighs, pointing at the fire. 'I think we have more of a problem sorting this lot out, don't you?'

Tom nods. 'I can go with what you've said, Charlie. Let's do this.'

CHAPTER 11

I t's early evening. In room 1708 on the 43rd floor of the San Mon apartment block, Kenny Bailey lounges on his sofa, watching a football game. The Chicago Bears are on the ten yard line, pushing for the end zone. The Minnesota Vikings are down 22-16. Kenny leans forward and shouts, 'Give Jameson the ball! He's our best receiver!'

The Bears' quarterback calls a play. They line up, the ball is snapped, and he fumbles. The crowd erupts as the loose ball lands in the hands of a Viking, who charges forward for twenty yards. Kenny leaps to his feet, yelling, 'Oh, you fucking idiot! You piece of shit!'

He walks over to the fridge and takes out a beer. The doorbell rings. 'Now, who the fuck's this?' he snarls. 'I'm at Soldier Field, for fuck's sake!' Going over to the door, he opens the peephole. Molly's outside, wearing a bright green jacket and cap. 'Yeah? What is it?' he calls. Molly stands holding a parcel in front of apartment 1708. Out of sight on either side are Gloria, Gina, and Martha. Smiling, Molly says, 'Parcel for Mister Bailey. Needs to be signed for, sir.'

There follows a few moments of silence. The door opens on

its chain. Kenny peers through its gap. He smiles. 'Must say, I wasn't expecting no parcel, not at this time of night. You're interrupting my ball game.' He unhooks the chain and looks Molly up and down. 'Now, if you were my daughter, I'd be bathing you every night.' He takes the parcel off Molly, puts it down on a side table. Then he gives it a puzzled look.

The parcel has no name or address on it. He turns, only to find Gloria and the girls rushing in and pushing him back into the room. Gloria presses a pistol to his chest. She snarls at him, 'Sit down, Bailey.'

Gina walks past him, pushing him down onto the sofa. She goes to the TV, turning it up a little more. Kenny gives a nervous laugh, points to the gun, grits his teeth. 'You wouldn't fucking dare, girl.'

Gloria winks. 'Nothing would give me more fucking pleasure.' She nods to Martha, who comes from behind, produces a syringe and stabs it unceremoniously into Kenny's neck. She presses the plunger. Moments later, Kenny's limp figure sprawls across the sofa.

Martha smiles. 'Jesus, Glo'. What'd you put in that there syringe? Put him out like switching off a light. Definitely the Go To Sleep Killer.'

'Go to sleep,' Gloria repeats, winking. 'It's what vets use to put a dangerous animal down. I just added a little extra for that dangerous creature.' She points to Bailey. 'He'll be out for a couple of hours. Long enough to clear this apartment of everything that belongs to him ... and I do mean everything.'

Gina's voice is anxious. 'We can do this now Glo'. Let's do this and get the fuck out of here.'

Gloria shakes her head. 'No. We wait till dark. After midnight. If he wakes, we give him another shot. I'm taking him from here.' She stabs a finger at him. 'I want him to know he's gonna die. I want him to feel the pain.' She pokes him with the pistol. 'Like I've had to bear over these past years.' She nods. 'Feel the same as my daddy felt, my dog.'

She gives a deep sigh. 'My daddy's body was never found. I want his killer to tell me where he is.' Turning to Molly, she says, 'On the stroke of midnight, we move. You and Martha will go fetch the wheelchair. Don't be seen. Use the fire door. Take the service lift back up to this floor.'

She nods to Gina, smiling. 'Gina, rustle up some food. We've got a long wait. I'm sorry, but we've gotta stay positive on this. We've come too far to fuck it up now.'

Gina pats Gloria's hand. 'Yeah. Sorry, baby. You're right, of course. Silly me. Sorry.'

Molly sighs. 'We've got over six hours to wait. I'm not watching fucking football. There must be something better on TV.'

'Nobody's watching anything,' Gloria says. 'We've got some clearing up to do.' The girls look at her. 'Yes, cleaning up,' she continues. 'I want this place looking unlived in. All his shit out. Pack everything. Clear the fridge. Leave nothing to say Mister Kenny fucking Bailey was ever here.' She grins. 'Oh yes, after tomorrow it'll be mission complete.'

*

In Charlie Black's office, the Prime Unit of the Special Crime squad sits waiting, their gathered reports stacked on the table. Charlie stands at the window, gazing out over the city, fingers drumming lightly on the glass. Tom and Gerry are going through the reports, pulling out the ones that they think are most important.

Charlie sighs, then turns to speak. 'We all know Vincent De Generio, the Outfit, the fucking East Side Mob. They're the only ones with the balls to wipe out the Waterside Snakes, for Christ's sake.'

Tom raises a hand to cut him off. 'Not all, Charlie. Who accounted for our friend, Mario Pascalino?'

Charlie shrugs. 'We'll know that when the body checks are all finished.' He smiles at them both. 'Let's say in a year or two.'

Gerry nods 'Yeah, Charlie's right, Tom. We need to hit the street to find the Snakes that survived the big party.'

Tom points over at the window and the bustling city outside. 'We've got the squad meet later today. I'll add that to our enquires.'

Gerry's voice hardens. 'We've gotta crush this before it turns into a heavy-duty situation, Charlie.'

Charlie spreads his arms. 'Don't ya see? There'll be no shit on the streets. Heroin and its offshoots will dry up. The users will go fucking crazy.'

Tom slowly nods. 'Gerry's right. Somebody's gonna have to bring it in. I'm thinking that they'll float it up the river from New Orleans, out of Mexico. Then across country, Frisco and LA, up the old mother road. Route 66, straight to Chicago.'

Gerry adds, 'Yeah, on to Twenty-First West to East. There's a run of twenty blocks, with dealers and their goons standing on every corner.' He shakes his head, walks to the window and points to the city below. 'Sharks, Wolves – just two of the crews ready to fight for colours now the Snakes are gone.'

Tom scratches his chin. 'The Snakes … well, they were top drawer. Respected, feared. If I had to guess, I'd say the Brewers.'

Charlie frowns. 'Brewers? Ain't they South?'

Tom nods. 'Sure. But they're Irish. They'd invade. The Mafia's changing, Charlie. Prostitution, gambling … they're small change compared to what drugs bring in, especially with the Outfit finished. There's room to move in.'

Charlie raises a finger. 'I'm thinking crystal meth. Those labs will be running overtime. And Vincent De Generio? I always figured he was against drugs. Same with the cartel.' He turns to Gerry. 'Find out what's going down. Put the fear of God into those snouts. This fire, we put it out before it takes hold. And bring in the grasses. Someone out there knows something, and we're gonna turn the screw until they talk.'

CHAPTER 12

San Mon apartment blocks rear entrance

At around 1 am, the fire door opens. Molly, hood up, pops her head out. She opens it wider, allowing a hooded Martha to come out with Kenny Bailey in a wheelchair. Kenny's breathing is shallow. They cross the back road toward a wooded area. A black Ford Transit van pulls rolls up and stops. Gloria's at the wheel, and Gina rides shotgun, holding a pistol. They both jump out and hurry to the van's rear doors. They open them and Gloria pulls out a ramp. She whistles, the sound bringing Molly and Martha running. The four of them wrestle the wheelchair up the ramp and into the van.

'Okay, it's early morning,' says Gloria, 'so lets be careful here. We drive to my hometown.' She gives a deep sigh. 'That's where my daddy disappeared.' She leans in, and jabs a finger into Kenny's cheek. 'That bastard, he knows where he is.'

Gina frowns. 'Your hometown? I thought you were from Chicago.' She looks at the others, who nod in agreement.

Gloria smirks. 'I've never said that, girls. And quite frankly, none of you ever asked.' She shrugs. 'I'm not Chicago. I'm near. And it's better for us this way.' She smiles. 'It's a surprise.'

*

8 am

Charlie's team has brought in several suspects for a full interrogation session. It's only when the studded-leather biker Jersey Boy Ross is confronted with some damning evidence from an out-of-state robbery in Ohio that he offers a deal: the names of the restaurant killers, in exchange for leniency on the Ohio job. Charlie replies that he'll do what he can to lessen the sentence.

Jersey Boy gives him the names of the Water Snakes Three.

*

9 am

The black Ford Transit turns off the highway into the Midewin National Park area.

The girls gape at the scenery. Gina slowly shakes her head. 'This where your home is, Glo'? You have a house here?'

Gloria smiles. 'Yes. It's close to where I was born. My great-great-grandfather built his home here. It's very private these days. Back then, it was Native American land.'

Molly says, 'If I lived here, I'd never leave. Especially not for a rapidly growing city like Chicago.'

The van weaves through a deciduous forest. The smell coming from its many varieties of trees is rich and green.

A gated side road appears. Gloria brings the van to a stop and gets out, walking up to the gate and producing a key to unlocks the gate that reads PRIVATE PROPERTY. TRESPASSERS WILL BE SHOT.

She gestures to Gina, who jumps into the driver's seat and edges the van through. 'We ain't gonna get shot, are we babe?' Gina asks.

Gloria gives a head shake as the van enters. She shuts and locks the gate before jumping back aboard.

Gina looks at her with a 'what next?' expression. Gloria waves her to drive forward. 'Drive, baby. It's about a half mile ahead.' She turns to Martha and Molly, who are both wearing anxious expressions, and smiles and winks at them before turning back to Gina. 'Err, try not to get us shot, baby.'

Gina gasps. 'Glo', tell me you're fucking joking.'

Gloria laughs. 'I'm fucking joking, baby. It's all deserted around here.'

Gloria, Martha and Molly all burst into laughter as Gina utters. 'Bastards!'

They follow a winding twisting timber track into a gravel clearing, where a large hunting lodge stands. A sign hangs from its entrance. It reads JONATHAN B HOMESTEAD.

The vans doors open and Gloria steps out, motioning for Gina to follow suit. They walk to the rear doors and Gloria opens them, letting Molly and Martha out.

'Put down that ramp,' Gloria says somewhat excitedly. 'Let's get this bastard to ground.' Molly and Martha slide out the ramp, making a bridge from the van's rear to ground. 'Okay, girls, bring Kenny Bastard out.' Martha begins to slowly wheel the chair out, with them the others assisting.

Martha looks at the lodge, shakes her head and smiles. 'Well, you gonna tell us, Glo'? Who the fuck's Jonathan B?'

Molly adding. 'Whoever he is, this sure is some pile of bricks. I wish I had it. Why, I'd never go out.'

Gina says, 'Yeah, I'd think one of the Mob lived here. It's a fucking gem.'

'Wait till ya see inside, girls,' Gloria says. She points up at the name. 'That there is my daddy's name, girls. This was his place. His retreat. He spent most of his retirement here. Fishing in the nearby rivers and lakes.'

Gina enquires. '"Was"? You said "was", Glo'. You saying it ain't your family's no more?'

Gloria laughs. 'Oh this was a part of our lives that' – she

points at Bailey – 'that bastard there never got his dirty fucking hands on. My brother and I still own it.'

'Your brother?' the women chorused.

'Yeah. I got a brother. I'll explain later. Now ain't the time.' She smiles. 'Gina, you take the van around the back. There's an open barn. Park it under, lock it, bring me back the key.'

Gina goes back to the van, gets in and drives it off.

Gloria claps her hands. 'Alright, let's get Bailey into the lodge and out of sight. Not that I'm expecting anyone to show … but you never know.' She grabs the wheelchair handles and begins to push a silent Kenny up to the entrance. Then, without ceremony, she tips him out of the chair. 'We won't waste our fucking energy on the chair. Drag the bastard inside. Don't think we'll be needing it again. He won't be leaving.' She walks ahead with keys, selects one and opens the door.

She rushes back to help Molly and Martha by taking Kenny's feet. They strain and grunt, finally getting him through the door just as Gina reappears. 'You okay with him, babes?' Gina asks.

'We're good, Gina. Get the door,' nods Gloria. With that, Gina swings the door closed and follows them into the lodge.

Martha's jaw drops as she takes in the room. 'Wow. This sure is a surprise, sugar. Must've cost a small fortune.'

Gloria pulls open the drapes and light floods in, revealing a large Wild West-style space. A floor-to-ceiling granite fireplace dominates the wall, a large oak beam mantel stretching across its width. A huge moose head stares down from above it. Two heavy timber rolled chairs with Indian patterned cushions face the hearth, matched by a sofa that could easily seat four in comfort. In a corner a glass antique cabinet with carved inlay displays a selection of books and photographs. One picture shows a white-haired man holding a trophy-sized fish, smiling proudly for the camera. Oil paintings hang on the wall, all Western-themed.

The floor is covered with Indian carpets, with a sprawling black bear skin laying in front of the fire. Everything was spotless, while still appearing warmly lived in.

Gloria watches her friends' expressions of awe and smiles, clapping her hands. They turn to her, suspicion flickering in their eyes. Gloria points out several doors, saying, 'There are four bedrooms, two on each side.' She spins on her heels and nods over to a pair of swinging saloon doors. 'Through there, the kitchen and breakfast area, which, may I add, holds a fridge and freezer.' She rubs her stomach. 'You'll find both of them full of fresh food.' With a wave she adds, 'So, let's get the coffee and breakfast on the go.' She winks at Martha. 'I've heard that sister Martha is a bit of a chef. I reckon if I gave her first choice of the bedrooms, she'd see to breakfast.'

Martha grins and strides towards the kitchen 'I'm on it. Just show me that stove, gal.'

The others remain transfixed by the magnificence of the lodge. Gloria slips through the swing doors and out into the kitchen area, closely followed by Martha. She points out all her appliances before disappearing, then returning with a chair. Balanced on its seat is a large roll of plastic sheeting. She rolls out the plastic onto the floor before stationing the chair on top. Then she points at Bailey. 'Tie that bastard to the chair,' she says. She produces a pair of handcuffs. Cuff him, hands behind his back.' She walks to a large mahogany chest, opens it and takes out a variety of ropes and tapes, passing them to Gina. 'Once tied up tight, gag him. Costa Nostra style, eh baby?' She winks at Gina.

Gina nods. 'I'll tie him like the pig that he is. This, I enjoy.' They lift the helpless Bailey onto the chair. Molly tapes his ankles to the chairs legs then steps back while Gina works her knots.

'Looks like Gina's full of knots,' Molly smiles. 'You gonna ask if she's out of a fisherman's loins, Glo'?'

Gina pulls a knot tight. 'My family have a long connection with the sea. Mother was born in Genoa. My father's Sicilian.' She stands back arms outstretched, admiring her artistry. 'Voila. A killer tied like a pig, ready to roast.'

Molly giggles. 'Fuck me, if we ain't all killers in here.'

A while later, Molly and Martha are making bacon wraps while Gina's pouring coffee. Molly takes a bite of the warm bread rolls that Martha has filled with bacon, grilled tomatoes and mushrooms. 'Mmmm. I like this bacon. It's got a smoky, nutty taste. Goes nicely with them mushrooms. What a combination.' She breaks off a piece of bread, still soft and fresh.

Martha nods a thank-you to Molly. 'Wait till you taste Martha's oh-la-la peach melba special,' She says. 'Simply to die for.'

'Hope it tastes as good as it sounds, sister,' Gina says. 'You sure know how to make a girl hungry.'

'Better give Glo a shout,' says Molly. 'Where is she anyway?'

'She's with Killer Kenny,' Gina says, jerking her head in Kenny's direction. 'I think he's about to open his peepers.'

'Should I take her some food?' Molly asks.

'Better not.' Gina holds up a hand. 'Leave her for now. I think she's planning his execution.'

Molly looks at Martha, then back to Gina. 'Not here, surely. Not in this beautiful palace?'

Gina smiles. 'I don't think so, girl. But then again, who knows what runs through that brain of hers?'

With that the doors swing open, and Gloria enters. 'Bastard just sits there grinning at me,' she snarls. 'I'm getting nothing on my dad. He just tells me to go fuck myself.'

Gina squeezes Gloria's arm. 'Let me have a go with him. I'll loosen his tongue … or cut the fucker off, Sicilian style. First I'll strip him naked. That'll weaken him. He'll lose all that bravado. With four women watching, he'll wilt. Then—'

Gloria raises a hand. 'You know, go for it, Gina. Find out where he's put my dad's body.'

'Will do, baby. But first, let him think he's holding all the good cards. But first, we eat these fine wraps. Because what I have in mind, I tell you now, you won't wanna eat by the time I'm finished with him.'

Gloria nods 'Yeah, Gina. I like it. We've got as long as it takes.'

'Even if it means …' Gina draws a hand across her throat.

Gloria gives a thumbs-up. 'Yes. Even if it means that, baby. He goes with the cyanide, just like my daddy, and my dog.' She nods as she takes a cup of coffee from Molly, grabs a bacon wrap and bites. 'Oh, this is so good. Give my compliments to the chef.'

'That'll be Martha's creation, the All Bacon Up Yours,' Molly says, making them all laugh.

A little time later, the girls file back into the lounge and take seats with their backs to Kenny. He He mumbles through the tape over his mouth.

Gina goes to him leans in, then rips it off. Kenny winces, snarling, 'You bastards.'

'Did you want to say something?' Gine asks casually.

'Who the fuck are you? One of her fucking playthings?' His bare shift, feeling the plastic sheeting under them. 'What the fuck's with this plastic under my feet? Afraid I'll piss on her precious Indian fucking carpets?'

Gina smiles turns and disappears back into the kitchen. Gloria Molly and Martha stay silent, keeping their backs to him.

Gina returns carrying a small table. She sets it down beside Kenny's chair. On the table are a pair of scissors, a large carving knife, the type of rubber gloves used for washing the dishes, and a deep bowl half full of water. She stands in front of him, running the knife up and down her arm. Then she begins to sing. 'What kind of fool am I, la-da-da, dee-dee.'

Kenny begins to sweat. 'What the fuck's going down here?' he growls. 'You gonna tell me or what?'

Gina stays silent as she slices his T-shirt, jeans and boxer shorts to shreds. Socks last. He's naked, tense, embarrassed. He nervously stammers, 'What the fuck. You a kinda sex freak or something? You … you wanna suck my dick?'

Gina turns to the others, walks over to the girls and smiles, waving the knife. 'So, what's it to be first, girls? Balls or dick?'

'Oh, I'm thinking the balls,' Gloria smiles.

Next Gina looks to Martha. 'Oh it's gotta be the balls Glo',' Martha agrees.

Finally Gina looks to Molly, who winks. 'Oh, it's the balls. Yes, that's my final answer, The balls.'

Gina walks back to Kenny, shaking her head. 'Unanimous decision. We all want your balls, Bailey.' She rubs the knife back along her arm again while Kenny twitches and blinks nervously. She continues to sing, 'What kind of fool am I' and tucks the knife under her arm while she pulls on the rubber gloves.

Kenny begins to struggle, straining against his restraints, making the chair rock.

Gina waves the knife at him. 'You wanna tell me where Jonathan B is, killer?' No? You know, I think you love them nice big balls of yours. So if you don't tell, I'm afraid it's snip snip. I'm going to count to five.' She stares into his face. 'One. Two. Three …'

Kenny spits into her face, then grins.

Gina calmly wipes the spittle off her face. 'Oh I think that's a no-no.' Without a moment's hesitation she lifts his dick and slices off his balls in one swift movement. Kenny faints.

She turns to the girls. 'This is gonna be hard,' she says.

Martha shrugs. 'Oh I shouldn't think so, baby.' She points at him.' Why, that man ain't go the balls.'

They all laugh.

'Wake the bastard up,' Gloria says. 'Continue, girl.'

Gina moves back to Kenny, whose head hangs forward against his chest. She picks up the bowl and slowly pours water over his head. Ice cubes slide out, and she presses them against his neck.

Kenny's eyes flick open. He stirs, looking up at a smiling Gina. 'I'm going to fucking kill you, bitch,' he slurs. 'You no-good fucking whore. You're as good as dead.'

Gina smiles. 'You know, Kenny, I don't think you've got the balls.'

Sniggers come from the girls.

'Soon,' she says, 'I'm taking your dick to go with the balls. So it's one last time, no count. Where the fuck is Jonathan B?' She shows him the knife.

'Okay, okay, bitch,' Kenny snarls 'He's gone. There's no remains. He went through a woodchipper. He's fucking long gone. Fucking dead. He's no more.' He screams, 'You fucking satisfied, bitch? You fucking bitch!'

Gina puts the knife to his throat. 'His remains, Bailey. Don't give me that woodchipper shit, cause I ain't buying it.'

'I've told you,' Kenny says. He nods toward Gloria. 'That fucking dog of hers ate what was left.' A smile curls his lips. 'I fucking watched him lick the fucking marrow out of her daddy's bones.'

He smirks. 'Then I fucked him, and killed the yapping bastard. He sure did wriggle a lot. Then a big yelp, and it was over.'

Gloria's face hardens, full of pure hate. The steps forward and gently pushes Gina aside. 'You're gonna show us all just how he wriggled,' she says. 'Show us. Give us the look my daddy had when you fucking poisoned him. Show us the face your bastard of a brother wore when he helped you. You think you've given yourself an alibi? You lying piece of shit. He's gonna pay too. The evil Baileys, exterminated.'

Kenny grins. 'You wouldn't fucking dare, bitch! My brother's gonna find you all.'

'I wouldn't dare?' Gloria screams. 'You sure about that, you no-good piece of shit?'

Kenny leans forward, eyes glinting. 'Oh, ain't you forgetting that first love of yours? Danny Davies? The hit and run? I stood and watched lover boy die. So sad, I nearly cried.'

Gloria snaps. She pushes a handful of tablets into his mouth. Gina holds his jaws shut, crushing his teeth together. In desperation Kenny tries to spit them out. Gloria screams, 'Come on now, Bailey, let's watch you fucking die!'

Kennys eyes begin to bulge. He coughs and snorts. Blood begins to ooze from his nose. His eyes bleed.

Gina releases her grip. He gasps for air and then slumps forward, his body trembling. His head falls onto his chest. Urine streams down his legs. Then he's still.

Gina goes and hugs Gloria. 'It's over, Glo'. He's finished.'

Gloria shakes her head. 'Cut off his dick. *Then* it's finished.'

Gina turns to Martha and Molly, then pulls out Bailey's penis and cuts it off.

'Get that piece of shit out of the lodge,' Gloria says, bowing her head. In a near whisper, she adds, 'It's done, Daddy.'

*

Sometime later

The girls sit around the lounge. The room is spotless. No sign of Kenny Bailey remains. They sip out of crystal tumblers, a bottle of Glenfiddich at Gloria's feet. She smiles, holding up her glass to catch the rust-coloured light. Then she raises it to her father's picture. 'My daddy's favourite tipple. I toast his memory.' She sips. 'To Daddy.'

The girls all follow suit.

Molly stretches, glancing at the darkening sky.

Martha sighs. 'It's been quite a day. If you all don't mind, I'm ready for my bed.'

'Go ahead, baby,' Gloria winks. 'Pick your cot. It's been a long day.'

CHAPTER 13

Two weeks later

In Charlie Black's office, Tom reports that they've got biker Jersey Boy Ross in a holding cell. He's wanted for an armed liquor store robbery that had gone down in Gary, Indiana. Charlie, tapping his desk, tells Tom that he will see to it and get a statement from him. Charlie's phone buzzes and he takes the call. 'Yeah, let's make it eight then. See you. Bye.'

The door opens Gerry Small walks in, smiling. 'We've fucking got 'em, Charlie.'

Charlie leans back in his chair, lifting a hand to motion Gerry to continue. 'The killers, Charlie. Mario Pascalino. His driver. And we got one Snake that hit 'em. A one loose rattler, who's rattling.'

Gerry leans over the desk, his hands spread wide on the wood, with a smile on his face. 'You know 'em, Charlie. One: Sammy Moore. Two: Sonny Boy James. Three: Marvin Grant. Last of the fucking Waterside Snakes mob.'

'Confession, Gerry?' Charlie asks.

Gerry steps back with his arms folded, and nods. 'Picked up Marvin Grant. Took nigh on four hours, but he crumbled. Tom offered him no death row.'

Charlie nods. 'Yeah, had to be Marvin. He'd be the weakest. So what about Sammy and Sonny?'

'Oh, they're still out there. We got an APB for them. It's just a matter of time before we make a grab,' Gerry says, holding up a hand. 'Sammy's brother Martin was gunned down and burned in that Shades blaze. Marvin says Sammy went to payback.'

Charlie shrugs. 'Least we got something.' He shakes his head. 'We've got no progress with the MacDonald hit. I've spoken with Tom, and we're for putting him into cold. We got nothing, Gerry. A bag full of nothing. I scouted down the avenue.' He shakes his head again. 'That neighbourhood … not a good word to say about him. Only that he was a wife-beater. One bastard of a man. They hated his guts.'

Gerry sighs. 'Somewhere along the line, he made an enemy. You know, I'm happy.' He holds up a hand. 'Yeah, I'm happy to let this one go cold, Charlie.' He nods, turns and makes for the door. Then on opening it he stops and turns to Tom. 'You told him, Tom?'

Tom shakes his head. 'I was just about to.'

Charlie, taken aback, asks, 'Tell me what, guys?'

Gerry scratches his head. 'Tom and I are going for a celebration beer or two later. You in?'

Charlie shrugs. 'I got some business later tonight, but I can do an early.' He smirks. 'You buying?'

Gerry laughs. 'Don't I fucking always?'

*

It's late afternoon, and Charlie's attention is drawn to the TV news channel. A mass funeral cortège is making its way through the streets of West Side Chicago: a line of some twenty-eight vehicles for the funeral of Don Vincent De Generio, along with Mario Pascalino.

Charlie can see members of his team on duty, observing the mourners; the entirety of the mafia crime lords that control every section of every district of Chicago. His people were busy taking photographs of these power players, some of whom have come from as far as LA and the West Coast, going up to Seattle.

In one of the lead vehicles sits Gina Pascalino. She receives a tap on her window coming from Irish mob boss Sean Murphy, who offers his condolences and promises to avenge Mario's death when he moves his Outfit into the vacant De Generio territory.

With a suspicious look, he says, 'You were so lucky not being at Vincent's celebration dinner, Mrs Pascalino.'

'I had just lost my husband. Hardly a thing to celebrate don't you think?'

The Irishman smiles. 'No, I suppose you're right. Maybe you would attend a invitation from me at some future date?'

'Don't think badly of me if I refuse,' Gina says. 'I shall be leaving America, returning to my family in Italy.'

The Irishman bows, turns and returns to his limo. Gina exhales in relief and tells her driver to take her home.

Meanwhile, Martha receives a call from her sister, telling her of the search by the three remaining Snakes, Sammy, Sonny and Marvin. They are coming to her home, asking after her whereabouts, and the warning ends up saving her life. Her sister tells Martha to get the hell out of Chicago as it wouldn't be safe while the three Snakes were still free.

Later news of their arrest, and the life terms they face, would give Martha time to consider her future. Gloria has spoken of her leaving the refuge centre, suggesting Martha could be considered as her replacement.

Molly is thinking of going to Ireland, visiting family she's never met. Gloria has offered her help her. Molly could return to the dwelling she had shared with evil Ryan. But that would only mean reliving those haunting days. No, that isn't to be considered. Better to sell up and go get a fresh start.

CHAPTER 14

It had been a long, harrowing day, and twelve high-ranking Dons were gathered in Castelvetrano, a country restaurant near to the home of Don Vincent De Generio. It sat on the border of Forest Park and Cicero. The Godfather's family had been put to rest in a marble mausoleum at Forest Home Cemetery.

It was one of the New York Five, Don Federico De Nero, who addressed this privately held meeting. He was a Don with a history of murder and atrocities stretching a mile long. A no-nonsense killer with a family history steeped in corruption, he was high on the FBI's most-wanted list. They were hoping, praying, for him to slip up, perhaps catch him on a tax evasion charge like the one that ended Capone. Agents were covering his every move, working around the clock to bring him down. But he De Nero was no fool. He had a few agents in his pocket, their families under death threat.

Don Sebastian Romario a 66-year-old grey-haired administrator out of Atlantic City, gives his thoughts on the murders of the Generio family, as well as calling for a clean sweep of any still-active Snakes. 'Their actions cannot be allowed to go on,' he says. 'Haven't we got enough on our plates with those bastards the FBI forever hounding us, without becoming a laughing stock to the Irish, who are poised to start a street war?' Looking down the line of faces, he shrugs when he reaches De Nero.

Don Al Sandro, his head nodding, adds, 'Even in my home district of Miami I can see where Don Romario is coming from. He's right, of course. I myself have had to quell a few Irish upstarts.' he winks and smiles. 'Of course, they are no more.'

Don Alberto Carlos, head of San Francisco's operations, punches the table. 'So, my friends, where do we start? Who takes over the Chicago nest?'

Don Sonny Boy Alfredo, all the way from LA, speaks with fire in his eyes. 'Whoever we choose must be strong enough to rule Chicago's great metropolis with an iron fist. Who do we have in mind? Not a Boy Scout, I'm hoping.'

Don De Nero slowly shakes his head, smiles and says, 'I have just the man in New York. He's running my upper Manhattan Harlem district. He's a forty-nine-year-old Sicilian who's worked for the great Don's family, the Motisi clan in Palermo. He was born in the heart of conflict, so he knows the score. It'd be my loss, Chicago's gain. His name's Mario Lucio. But you, my friends, must decide.'

Sonny Boy Alfredo, the LA son of the ageing Don, thinks of how this change would surely bring the old street wars back to Chicago. He had recently hosted the Generio hitman who had come to the City of Angels looking for Korky O'Dell. Alfredo hadn't cared much for the man from Chicago, especially his treatment of women. When the man had turned up dead, he'd thought *good riddance*. He wouldn't mind taking on Chicago himself, but the winters there were not to his liking. The warmth of the West Coast, along with Vegas, Hollywood and the glamorous lifestyle, would be too hard to leave behind.

The Don from Seattle, Bruno Columbo, is known for

making wise decisions. At fifty-five, he can read a man's face. He looks at Sonny Boy and knows exactly what he's thinking. He's also heard whispers that the young upstart Roberto Rossi's trying to suck up to De Nero in the hope of making climbing the ladder. Rossi is definitely not to be trusted, and when it comes to running a city of the size of Chicago, he's laughable, a no-no. If he had to choose, then he's inclined to import one of the old family members from the motherland. Perhaps De Nero Would fill the enormous space that had been left by the Generio murders. Perhaps De Nero's suggestion is the right one. One thing is certain: the matter needs to be resolved before it spreads like a virus into every backyard. His vote will go to the New Yorker. It's not really his problem though. He's been in the field too long to know Rossi isn't going to happen.

De Nero rises from his seat and addresses the table. 'Okay, it's time to vote. A name is all that's needed. One thing to remember, your choice must come from the heart, for your choice must close the door and find the reason for these horrific acts. We know about the Shades nightclub and the downfall of the Snakes ... but we don't know who lit the spark that started the fire.'

He shrugs. 'Someone out there does, and we must find this arsonist.' He waves an arm casually. 'So, when you cast your vote, think wisely. Choose someone who could present us with the culprit or culprits, and who can reorganise Chicago by bringing in the drug cartels to make up for the millions of dollars Generio lost by leaving a clear field for the blacks to operate. Surely a mistake. One his family paid for.'

Don Alfredo raises a hand. De Nero nods. 'Something on your mind, Sonny Boy?'

The LA Don shrugs. 'The hitman Pascalino told me in LA the main reason Don Vincent didn't take on the drug cartels was the loss of his granddaughter. Overdose. Killed her. She was a college student.' He raises a palm. 'I'm thinking the Don had a vendetta and took out the supplier, the Waterside Snakes. Sadly for Vincent, he missed a few, and they unknowingly took out the Chicago Outfit's main family.'

De Nero nods. 'This is the first I've heard of the reason for Don Vincent's downfall. I always thought of him as an iron gauntlet. We must send out a reply by finding these assassins and putting an end to any recurring incidents. We've got contacts in the Chicago police department. Get the names. We leave nothing blowing in the wind.'

Columbo speaks with authority. 'I'll organise and see that it's done, Don De Nero. This new man, whoever he may be, I'll offer my assistance, while my eldest son Paulo oversees my Seattle domain.' He shrugs. 'If everyone's okay with that.'

De Nero smiles. 'So, I take it you're not interested in the Chicago empire on a permanent basis, Bruno. If that's your thinking, we'll take your name off the vote. Maybe, and it's just a thought, your well-trained son Paulo should be added in your place. I've heard nothing but excellent reports on his ability.'

Columbo bows to De Nero, the highest ranked of the New York Five. 'Thank you, Godfather, for your kind words. If it's the will of the assembly gathered here today to include Paulo, then so be it. I've no objection.'

De Nero smiles. 'Let's go to dinner, then vote. My vote'll carry the New York Five and will therefore count as a vote of the Five.'

CHAPTER 15

Over in the office of District 17, the homicide squad gathers, waiting for Lieutenant Charlie Black to bring their reports up to date. The results have been disappointing, with very little coming from a terrified community. No one considered clean is venturing out onto the streets, fearing reprisals. Addicted drug users are going crazy, scouring shops and malls for glue as a poor substitute for their desperate need.

Shops and supermarket shelves are emptying, forcing owners to demand supplies from every known manufacturer. Shoplifting has soared to record highs. Midnight cartel mule trains are bringing meth and heroin over the Mexican border, forcing border control units to strengthen by bringing in the National Guard. The police units of Chicago are also calling in reserves of retired officers. Riots have broken out in many major cities. The fire service hasn't seen such chaos since 9/11. The new death drug ISO is believed to be shipped from China.

The vote has finally been taken on the new Don, and the result isn't what anyone expected. The death of Don Vincent De Generio and his newly voted-in replacement causes De Nero to raise an eyebrow, especially after his own suggested appointment gets no interest from the table of twelve. De Nero stands and verifies the result, then shrugs. 'You, my dear brothers, have voted for Don Vincent's brother, Al Ben Lucia Generio. I happened to meet him, as we all did, at his brother's funeral. So it's best we contact him, hear his thoughts on your trusting the great metropolis of North Chicago into his hands. That's assuming, of course, he actually wants the job.'

CHAPTER 16

In the Stagecoach Restaurant west Chicago reception area, The restaurant clock is showing eight ten, when Charlie Black enters the restaurant. A well-dressed waiter approaches carrying a clipboard. He smiles at Charlie and asks.' Have you a reservation, sir?' Charlie nods 'I have indeed, my man. Under Black ... Charles Black.'

The waiter scans his listing. 'Ah, Mister Black. Eight o clock, table for two, corner booth.' He smiles and nods. 'Yes, sir. Mister Black, your partner, the young lady, is waiting. If you'll kindly follow me.'

Charlie follows him through saloon-style swing doors into a large oblong dining room. The lighting glows yellow and orange from styled wall lamps. Old West oil paintings hang under spotlights. Half of the twenty or so tables are already occupied.

The waiter leads Charlie to a private corner booth where a candle's flicker falls across a bright red tablecloth. Out of the shadow, a single glass of wine twirls in delicate fingers. The waiter invites him to sit and produces a menu. 'The wine list, sir.'

Charlie stays standing and waves him away. The waiter shrugs and turns. Charlie follows, catching him by the sleeve.

He whispers something inaudible. The waiter nods and leaves.

Charlie goes back to the booth, fumbling under his jacket, then produces a set of handcuffs. He rattles them at the woman in the shadows. 'You. Gloria Monroe. Alias Gloria Bailey?'

Gloria steps into the light, holds out her wrists and nods. 'Alias Gloria Bailey. Yeah, all the same, lieutenant. Looks like you've found your gal, Charlie Black.'

Charlie waves the waiter back, then sits, taking the glass from her hand and kissing it. 'Happy birthday, sis.'

Gloria pulls her hand away. 'Yeah? So where's the flowers, the cake? Guess you forgot.'

The waiter returns with champagne in a bucket, two flutes and menus. 'Your Dom Perignon, sir.'

'Good man.'

He pops the cork, pours, bows and leaves.

'You're late, brother of mine,' Gloria says.

Charlie shrugs. 'Blame Gerry Small and Tom O'Flynn. They're celebrating. Picked up one of Mario Pascalino's killers. One of three. We've got two more to go. The Waterside gang's finished.'

Gloria watches him top up the flutes. 'Splashing out a bit, aren't we?'

'Why not? We've got a double celebration. Two departments with closure.'

'Three, if you're counting my birthday. See? Forgot already.'

'The plan worked, girl. But you had me worried.'

'Worried? How come?'

'Those headlights you were flicking. That blade you ditched. Lucky for you, overnight rain and a parked hauler wiped your tyre prints. And I cleaned the blade.'

Gloria punches the air. 'I wore gloves, Charlie. You'd have got nothing. We did it. Avenged Daddy. Bailey suffered, I can tell you.'

Charlie's phone beeps. He answers. 'Yeah, Tom. What you got?'

Tom's voice comes through. 'We've got another John Doe. Pulled him out of the East River. Looks like a revenge execution.'

'You need me?'

'Nothing you can do here. Body's going to the morgue. I'll have the full report in the morning.'

'Okay, Tom. Call if you need me.'

He puts the phone away and sighs. 'Your birthday. I remembered.' They clink glasses, sit in silence until the waiter returns.

'You ready to order, sir?'

'Give us a minute. I'll wave you.'

Charlie squeezes her hand. 'By the way, I don't want to hear about you and your girls starting some Murder Incorporated.'

Gloria laughs, makes a gun with her hand. 'Nah, brother. It'd be the Chicago Dolls. But we're retired.'

'Seriously, sis. You do it at your own peril.'

'I won't. Didn't I say we're retired?' She nudges his shoulder. 'So let's order. I'm starving. But I like the sound of Chicago Dolls.'

Charlie nearly chokes. 'No. No way. Just no fucking way.'

His phone rings again. It's Tom. 'We've got a name for the John Doe. Danny Bailey.'